To James, Dan, and Alison
From whom I drew much visionary in

FOREWORD

This is my first book. I have broken the literary rules as you
probably understand them. As you read this book, you will need to
use a digital device to listen to the songs. As you listen, pay attention
to what is happening in your mind. The fantasy I have created is
filled with song. It is a new way to tell a story and I hope you are
involved and even enthralled.
There are twenty-one songs scattered throughout this story; the
songs come from the sixties, seventies and eighties. So this story is
actually a musical, but a very modern kind of musical. I use the
songs as an introspective device, challenging the reader to
understand the purpose of the music in the story. You will, I hope,
come to understand how I have used the songs to manipulate what
you see in the story line. If not, don't worry; just enjoy the story, and
enjoy the music.
But please, as you read, do listen to the music; it is an integral part of
what I have written.

Act One: Morning Mahima.

Standing at the window of his bedroom, Richie Gyndall is looking out into the darkness and the rain. His curtains are drawn; he can see his reflection in the panes of glass. The light in the smallest bedroom in the house is on. He is listening to music, a pen and a note pad held in either hand. His thoughts are tangled up with his emotions. He can feel the wetness of his tears start to form in the confines of his eyes, and he lets a smile widen on his face; words do not escape him. His Grandma told him once that emotions are just the leftovers of the workings of your insides.

She always has a lot to say, Kuvan, my Grandma. Bones or no bones, your insides all produce something. 'But what about my brain?' I would ask. 'Well that's where the fun starts,' she would finish. That was when I was much much younger. Richie would remember thinking that his brains must be formed from the powder produced when bones rub together. His maan would say it was fairy dust, but he was left thinking what to do with it, as he was no magician. Richie looks at his note pad and places the rear end of the pen in his mouth. He draws the curtains wider, turning, and sits on his bed. *If only I could think about what to write, I could profit from all this use of my insides.* He starts to write something:

> My name is Richie, Richie Gyndall. I live in England but am a Hindu of Indian origin. I lead a simple life in Leicester, sharing an end of terrace house in the middle of Blackberry Way. Why would I become rich, as my name suggests? Or, on the other hand, how did I come to have any understanding of these happenings?
> Well, let me not tell you of this straightaway. That is for you to learn from my experience, but, yes, let me help you understand. From the beginning, I knew nothing of my family's hopes for the making of me. Nor much about my

2

ancestry. Not a great deal even of my family tree – after a certain age, that is. What I have learned was through the teachings of my parents, and their parents also. Surprisingly (or not) we share the same house. I, we, and they – so they always tell me – have always been rich!

He rips the page from the pad and throws the paper ball he has made onto the floor, takes off his gown, gets into bed, and turns the main light off from the cord hanging from the ceiling. *The question is, what am I if I am not benevolent?* Yes, again it was her who would offer an answer, but it was more a prompt from her husband at the time. *My Grandpa.* Kuvan remembers another one of her teachings: *Innovatory, Richie, you must be more innovatory.* Richie's smile leaves him as he drifts off into pensive rest. He is asleep. Without warning, it is morning again and Richie is having a waking dream. He can see himself in bed.

Here I am lying in bed. Yes, it's me, the benevolent Richie. Yet again, I am waiting for my alarm to go off in the morning. Anyone might think I am oblivious to what is going on below, but I do know, and I assume, although my assumptions can make me restless of a morning, that all is well. There is no shouting to wake me from my sleep, and only the calls of solitary blackbirds can be heard from my room. They are more of an assertion from outside than a call to wake myself.
Yes, okay, to wake up and make myself get out of bed would be the best thing I can do for your sake. So you too can understand, and see, the world I live in and around. Honestly speaking, though, I don't care to know what you think. I just need to comfort myself a little more; so I doze.

Richie's world escapes from inside his bedroom. He is slowly (though not physically) letting himself drift downstairs. Toward what exists alongside him. All that is written within his family's honourable abode.
Right, so, here inside his household's living room, there is a loving couple. One is his grandpa. He is handed a cup of freshly brewed tea from the tray. The family's best china adorns its remarkable sheen; it is made of silver. As it should be. Richie's Grandpa is not alone in

3

the love he is permeating, because the other half of the couple is Richie's grandma, his wife. She asks her pati, "How many sugars?" Grandpa answers, "That will do!" and, naturally, the couple coalesce for a moment of grace.

Sounds from the active radio can be heard from the kitchen. A man, Richie's father, is situated to the left, as we go back along the path of the sound waves carried past Richie's mother. We pass Kuvan, who is peering through the living room door to see if she can hear her grandson's footsteps. Then we travel onwards toward the front door of the terraced house. As we move outside, we can see what lies around it; this place is Blackberry Way.

Richie's alarm goes off in his bedroom.

These events take place most mornings, and he can genuinely believe that his grandparents are no less in love than they have ever been. *Ha-ha, I know what is happening now; my mother will be calling me shortly.* How, honestly, he can live his life without these regular events, he will never know.

Richie's grandma hears the call she has been waiting for, from the living room door. It comes from the end of the hallway. It is her loving daughter.

"Breakfast is served, maji, and where is that bloody son of mine?" Aarzoo calls out, and Grandma releases her husband's hand.

"Don't worry, Aarzoo. Richie will be fine. You know that he likes to get up a bit later. So that you don't order him about. Anyway, I am famished."

Richie's grandma looks to her loving husband for an answer to her usual morning question. "And so what would you like? Your usual?"

Aarzoo's maji's husband doesn't shift his eyes away from the morning television. He moves his head towards her, and simply nods. This action is enough for her expectation of his acknowledgment, and so she heads for the door. Slowly she straightens her back and goes to get her husband some, not fresh, but tinned, fruit, as fresh fruit isn't to her husband's taste.

Richie's mother stands in the hallway, having moved, and is now looking up from the foot of the stairs.

"He is always trying to dodge out of going to work. He should be ashamed of himself. It is a significant job he has, working for the

4

Partners at the Bank!" she grumbles, explaining her dismay to her maji.

Having listened intently, Richie's grandma heads for the kitchen. You can see the work surfaces and white goods, partially, through the open door. As she moves forward to enter the kitchen, her plumpness is refined by the frame of the doorway. She is clothed in a vibrant black sari with red blooms adorning it – the type she usually wears.

"That's it!" Richie's mother draws breath. "He's never awake."

His grandma says, "Don't be so obsessive, Aarzoo!" She's chuckling to herself. She knows that Richie's punctuality has always been an entanglement that her daughter holds over her son.

Aarzoo walks forwards with controlled persistence, towards the staircase; she is dressed in yellow. She is drawn towards the sounds of Richie's alarm. She is wearing a particular dress which is picked in a different colour every day. At that moment, coughing, more a clearing of the throat noise, comes drifting from the kitchen. The owner of the cough, Richie's father, is out of sight.

We are looking at Richie's bedroom door from the top of the stairs. We are situated on the landing.

Now we see Richie again. He is sitting side-saddle on his bed. With his hands on his hips, he looks at the small space to the side of it. He has already turned off his alarm. It sits on the small chest of drawers in his bedroom, by the side of his bed. He's thinking of all the things he could be doing in the excess of moments throughout the day.

Richie is looking past the two small piles of books, in disarray, on the chest. They all tend towards his favourite type of – typically old – romance. As he looks, he is trying hard to think about what is on his mind.

Richie's mother calls out to him. "Richie!" He looks to the door. He is forming his first fresh knowledge of the day. He feels he has created something safe, deep inside him. Maybe it is from the complexity of the wallpaper's security, which gives him some comfort, and which gathers around him in a hypnotic swirl. These soothing patterns have adorned his walls ever since his father placed them there.

"Richie," Aarzoo's voice calms. "Come on now. Come, do your chores. You need to get the milk."

From the bottom of the stairs, Richie's mother is now walking towards the kitchen. As Richie closes his door quietly, he still in thought and currently out of trouble. The smells from the kitchen are intense. As Aarzoo's maji walks to the living room, Aarzoo is looking back to the stairs in the hallway. "Come on now, boy. Do your chores." His maji smiles to herself.

Richie, waking from his night's drawing, walks down the last few steps of his household staircase. Then, leaving the stairwell, he edges towards the door.

"Don't forget to put this old bottle of milk out now, bachcha!" His mother's reply to Richie's flirty advance.

Within the strictures that his Father has set out. With the chores that he has set out for him to do. Richie, as ever, is not in two minds about trying to get out of the pretence of doing at least something today. He yawns, holding his hand to his gaping mouth, stretching once more. The young man now has his dressing gown covering his half nakedness and his paisley pants. The pants that he wore to bed. Dressed just so, he opens the door to Blackberry Way. Like all the other people that live in his street. They all seem to be doing it at the same time.

Outside now, we are just looking at Richie. He bends down, picking up the bottle of milk that sits on his doorstep.

Slowly we draw away. We can see the milk float at the bottom of Richie's road, now we are looking from the top of the pass. We see people doing their uppermost to keep themselves dry in their doorways. They are all on time and they are all ready to burst into song about the name of their street.

Richie's door nearly bumps him into his front garden, so he takes a step down. Turning, he walks back onto the level of the door and holds it ajar. Shifting, we can see the whole street from its beginning.

Blackberry Way, by The Move: please be respectful and listen. There is much context, and also content hidden within the text.

Verse 1:
Line 1: the whole street sings. [Looking from the top of the street. We start to move down it]

Line 2: the whole street sings. [Reaching Richie's house. We zoom in on him]
Line 3: the whole street sings. [A bird flies from Richie's garden wall]
Line 4: all still singing. [Richie is now in the park looking at a girl; her name is Sherry]
Line 5: all still sing.
Line 6: all still sing.
Line 7: all still sing. [Back at the top of Blackberry Way]
Line 8: all still sing.
Line 9: all still sing.

Chorus:
Line 1: the whole street still sings. [Some people putting out rubbish]
Line 2: the whole street still sings.
Line 3: the whole street still sings.
Line 4: the whole street still sings.

Verse 2:
Line 1: the whole street sings. [We see Richie standing back in the park, by a pond. Flowers are in their beds, and small boats are floating on the pond. He is watching Sherry look out across the water and walks away]
Line 2: all still sing.
Line 3: all still sing.
Line 4: all still sing. [Richie walks up behind Sherry. She is with her boyfriend. He pulls her away by her hand]
Line 5: all still sing. [All eyes are back on Richie. He is standing on his doorstep. He turns towards the front door to his house, still singing, and raises his arms]
Line 6: all still sing.
Line 7: all still sing.
Line 8: all still sing.
Line 9: all still sing.

Chorus:
Line 1: all sing. [Seen from the top of Blackberry Way]
Line 2: all sing.

Line 3: all sing.
Line 4: all sing.

Verse 3:
Line 1: all still sing. [A man leaps out from his door. Closes it behind him in his haste, and then runs out of his property's small garden. Then down his street]
Line 2: all still sing.
Line 3: all still sing.
[One of the people in song, standing on his doorstep, casts his hand into the air, then everyone can be seen from the top of the street. They all throw their hands up in unison]

Line 4: all still sing. [They all throw their hands up again]
Line 5: all still sing. [Richie can be seen clutching the milk. He sings alone]
Line 6: all still sing.
Line 7: all still sing. [Richie watches Sherry leave the park entrance behind her. She and her boyfriend are yards away. He stands at the gate]
Line 8: all still sing.
Line 9: all still sing.

Chorus:
Line 1: everyone is singing. [Looking from the top of Blackberry Way]
Line 2: everyone is singing.
Line 3: everyone is singing.
Line 4: everyone is singing.

Chorus:
Line 1: everyone is singing.
Line 2: everyone is singing.
Line 3: everyone is singing.
Line 4: everyone still sings. [All turn in tandem to walk back inside their houses. Richie is the last to walk from his front garden]

We arrive back inside the house, looking at Richie standing inside, with the front door shut.

"You took your time, bachcha!" Richie's grandpa jokingly greets Richie, approaching the foot of the stairs, and Richie's entrance. Gaurav is now walking past Richie; he is dressed in his dark blue elephant print pyjamas.

Richie is standing behind the closed front door, watching his grandpa's behind advance up the stairs. Richie understands that his grandpa is not for stopping, continuously walking upwards to the top floor.

Richie looks towards his kitchen, from the door. He dismisses the elephant trumpet noise that emanates from the widening gap his grandpa is creating between them. The trumpeting noise stops, just for a moment as Richie's mother calls, and then the owner of the coughing noise, his father, calls too.

"Come on, Richie. Eat your breakfast."

"Yes, and don't be late for work."

Richie can now see himself as the perfect bull elephant on a warning charge as he walks forwards. Then a deep throated, large bull elephant roar comes from upstairs; he feels himself slip into reverse as he imagines his Grandpa Gaurav on the loo. A decision takes hold in his mind as he looks up to the Gods. A noise of breaking wind floats down from above. He will take a bite and then follow his grandpa upstairs to get changed. Richie has a bargaining chip to deflect his maji from making him do more chores, and that is his kindness. He knows turning it on is like sunshine on a rainy day to his mother. "I simply find your curd, maan, the best thing. It's like bread without the crusts," he says. Adjusting his mind to swallowing his food, he puts a spoonful of curd in his mouth, swallows, then takes a bite out of a samosa.

"The British say that crusts put curls in your hair, Richie; now, Maji's curd can make you twice as nice. Remember that, bachcha," Aarzoo tells him. "So if you ever learnt to make it, then you will become a better person, and Richie, don't forget it is cheap to make. When you live on the breadline like our family, then anything that costs less to make and fills your tummy is a wonderful commodity." His bargaining chip hasn't worked.

Speaking with his mouth slightly full, he changes the subject. "What makes Grandma and Grandpa so inseparable, Maan?"

9

"They are like us, Richie. They were always meant to be together."
Richie's father speaks from behind him.

Richie's mother then speaks, turning slightly as she makes another pot of tea. "Yes, that is so, Richie."

"But I thought you and father had your marriage arranged by them; yet they seem so innocent."

Aarzoo has just finished pouring the tea; she turns and cuts Richie off. "Your father and I chose to be together, didn't we...?" Richie cuts her off in return.

"No, I specifically heard Grandma say one day that you two met at our family's get-together with other families that flew over from India in sixty-one."

Richie put down the last of the samosa.

"...Daivey!" Aarzoo finishes.

"It is not necessary to say such things, Richie. I wish you to get out of our sight. For we now have sore eyes," Daivey says.

Richie covers his mouth with his clenched hand, apart from his index finger, and middle finger, which are running across his top lip. He lowers his head, and looks back to his father. "Okay," he says in a higher voice than normal. "Sorry father, I shall go and get changed." He turns and leaves like an elephant that has been frightened away by a gunshot. Upstairs he knocks on the bathroom door. There is no reply, so he walks in. "Grandad!" He shuts the door and goes to his bedroom; muttering can be heard behind him, emanating from the bathroom.

Inside his room he takes off his gown, opens a drawer and starts to change his underwear. Then he sits on the bed and changes his socks. Then he walks to the wardrobe and pulls his fresh suit from inside. *You know? Life puzzles me! One minute we think we know and understand what is written, the next it is all incomprehensibly changed by someone's actions. Ha, what is the truth? Maybe both answers are right.*

"Richie!" A call comes from the hallway.

"Yes, Grandpa Gaurav, thank you!"

Take him, for instance. He came over from India with his wife, meeting a nice family on the plane they were flying on to get to England in, in sixty-one. What an opportunity.

Richie's Grandpa walks to his bedroom door, after looking down the stairwell, where an "Are you still okay?" has lovingly been asked by

Richie's Grandma, talking to her husband from below. *So the story goes. My mother and father met at a disco, a knees-up to celebrate fifteen years of them all being in England.*
It is now nineteen seventy-six. There is music coming from inside a community centre. A car is leaving the car park. As it does it turns onto the road. A group of boys have to stop in their tracks. The expensive car pulls away. The boys run after the car, shouting.
"So, what do you want to do when you grow up?" Daivey asks Aarzoo, who is combing her hair as she yawns.
She yearns to be in love, but anything will do for now. "I am grown up. Tut, you men are all the same."
Richie's Grandpa walks out through the front door of the community centre. "Hey, you two, we've been looking for you, come now." All three walk into the venue.
There are screeches and cheers from the children's two families.
"Look, what do we have here?" Aarzoo's father calls, as he arrives by the side of his wife.
"Yes, that is just like you, Gaurav," Daivey's father, who is also with his wife, calls to his friend.
Both families stand in front of their children.
"So?" Daivey's beautiful mother speaks out.
"Yes, so!" Richie's Grandma follows.
"Have you two…?" Daivey's mother calls.
"Hit it off?" Aarzoo's maji calls.
"Don't be silly, Mother," Aarzoo says, blushing.
Daivey's father winks at his son; his son reaches for the hand of the girl next to him; respectably Aarzoo smiles. As she feels Daivey's hand she runs onto the dance floor with all the other children.
Daivey's father jigs his thumb backward towards the dance floor, and Daivey follows. "He's a good boy, that son of mine. Would never miss a golden opportunity," Daivey's father turns and says to his friends.
"No, he wouldn't, by the looks of things," Gaurav replies, "Perhaps we could arrange a place for them to meet without us. They look so good together. It is Aarzoo's birthday soon, dinner at ours, and then we can keep up to date on how they get on," Richie's grandma rounds off.
"Yes, then we can rotate." Daivey's mother chuckles, clinging to her husband.

Richie is walking towards the kitchen; he is now dressed in his suit for work. His maata janak stands at the living room door, fluffs his hair as he walks by once more. "Grandma, did you and Grandpa arrange Mum and Dad's wedding?" Now he is in the kitchen, and he stretches for something more to eat, over the back of his stool.

"Yes, the wedding…" Kuvan answers.

"Yes, but not us getting together!" Aarzoo follows, drinking tea from a cup. "Us getting together?" Aarzoo is flamboyant in her outburst of speech. "That was your father's doing." She is now blushing while looking at Daivey for reassurance.

Richie is trying not to spill the food; he slowly picks up and puts down the remnants of the samosa.

"I don't want to know," Aarzoo's maan says to her ladakee.

Richie finishes eating, taking a last spoonful of his curd. Then he moves to the sink, where Aarzoo is washing up. Lovingly, he takes the empty bottle of milk from the kitchen windowsill, as she suggested earlier, and turns to leave.

Richie, dressed in his fresh new suit, hears Aarzoo call out to him, "All this must take place after your work activities too, and you still haven't learned to make the curd. You will let yourself down yet. You mark my words."

Without looking back, Richie says, "Aarzoo, there is plenty of time for that. Please, maan, I want more from my life."

His maan is looking out through the window to the backyard. She is looking at her vegetable patch. As she turns her head left, she can see Richie's father standing in the corner of the kitchen. He is drinking from the same best china that was on the silver tray.

"Yes, but Richie, you know the heart of every business is in banking. You should stop salivating over those old books of yours, and pay more attention to what the partners of your bank say. There's much more money to be made out of their business than you realise. Then you can get married." Aarzoo is plunged into despair. "For goodness' sake. You work at a computer, bachcha, forget about paper and words."

"I'll need more than a computer to work out how to marry, maan," Richie says sulkily.

Richie's maan tells her husband, "He's a dreamer, that bachcha."

Richie's father answers, "Just relax. It is just a period he's going through. They'll straighten him up at work – sooner or later." Then, putting his cup of tea down with his left hand, he leaves the lemon yellow and white spotted wall to follow Richie.

Richie closes the front door.

His father, already coming out of the kitchen, tries to shout at him while he might still be in earshot. "Don't forget to behave yourself." But the door is already shut.

As Richie walks out of his property's front yard, he puts down the empty bottle. He stands, then walks out into Blackberry Way, and then turns right, walking along it. At that distance, a manly grunt cannot adequately be heard from inside the house; it falls short around Richie's whereabouts. The thought that his father is following him looms over him, and he looks back half expectantly. Maybe to see his father standing at the front door.

"I need more in my life!" Richie says, submissively.

We are following Richie, as he walks down the street. He looks at all the children playing in the street. They are all on their school holidays. Football is played between the parked cars while some of the kids use painted wickets on a garden wall to play cricket. Someone bowls, and a boy hits the ball. The ball is aimed at Richie. Richie turns, crouches and catches it. He hunkers down, giving it back to one of the girls who are fielding. A young boy on a bicycle with stabilisers rattles over in Richie's direction. "Cheers, Richie," he says.

"It is not your ball, Tindu," the girl replies.

"It's okay, Ileasha, he's only playing," Richie says.

"I'm not playing with her, she's too bossy," Tindu says.

"Come *on*, Ileasha, throw the ball," another, older boy, calls.

"Okay, Mark," Ileasha calls to her friend. "You wait," she says to the young boy, and Ileasha throws the ball. "There you go!"

Rising, Richie smiles and walks on.

So Ileasha likes Mark, who in turn likes Ileasha. Tindu hasn't got a clue who he likes. Ha, it's funny though, Mark and Ileasha will never get what they want from their relationship. This started when Mark kissed Ileasha underneath the light in the playground when everyone else was going back to class at school. It's funny what you hear, and what you understand of what will happen inside the whole fabric of time. All I can tell you is Tindu's family own their own clothes

13

machinery shop, and Ileasha there, her father has a paper and goods shop called 'Stop Once Buy Twice'. Plus a shop that sells airline tickets to the local brethren. He gets cheap tickets from his in-laws who know the family of an Indian Airlines executive. Which means Ileasha will eventually end up getting together with Tindu and they will marry and have their own loving family together. Not that this always happens, but trust me, I know how this one works.

"Hi, Mrs, Patijna. Hi, Charu." Richie waves at the mother and daughter. They are standing in their front garden. Mrs. Patijna is holding a pair of pruning blades, while deciding which stem to trim on her flowers.
"Hi, Richie," they call back. "Just dead heading, Richie," Mrs. Patijna calls; her daughter is simply just smiling at Richie.

So that's Mrs. Patijna and her lovely daughter Charu. Charu is gorgeous, yes that is true. There is a photo of us playing together on holiday on the beach in my living room. I am kissing her, but I do think that is abnormal from what normally happens with her. My mother thinks she is just right for her son, me that is, but I have bad tidings for you all. The Patijna's own a very expensive restaurant and takeaway chain around the city, and we, well we don't own anything. Not that I think it would stop Charu accepting, if I ever asked for her hand in marriage. It's just our family do not have the money, you see. For which I'm glad. Anyway, I'm honestly more interested in being single at the moment. Unless someone else turns up on my radar who is single. Not that I don't like girls. You see, even though she likes me, I know, and can tell, she's not totally into me. Just like my family and their stupidity of wondering why I would like to write for a living. These things do not register as likely to happen. I thought all I needed to do was listen to my heart. Anyway, aside from this, I wish I knew my future more securely. As you heard from my mother earlier, 'The heart of all business is with banking', but I don't think the partners like me too much.

Richie, has walked a few streets, and turned a few corners. He looks at his watch as he walks for the bus. He turns left, out among the slowly busying shops and businesses of the boulevard. He enters the straight road that will take him to the bus stop. A car passes him. To his surprise, it splashes him. Water leaps at him out of one of the puddles at the side of the road at this end of the street. Angrily, he wonders why it is him the vehicle has splashed. Other people walking past him go by without a drop of water upon them.

Two young men, about Richie's age, walking towards the bus stop, look at the stationary Richie. "Fascinating!" one of the men says. "Truly," the other replies.

Richie has positioned himself with his back to the shop fronts, looking himself over. He is illuminated by the bright Indian clothes shops. The light from the new day developmentally envelops Richie within the scene. Openly, he brushes himself down, takes a step back, turns, and looks at himself in the shop window. He can now see his brown, mostly straight, trouser suit. It is darker in places than it was before.

Strangely it is a feeling of relief, not utter frustration, that hits Richie in the chest. Suddenly, Richie is drawn to looking at the bus stop. Time's imagination of missing the bus strikes him, and the splendours of the day envelop Richie in his natural alertness that people are laughing, and to the fact of the arriving bus's noise, which bursts upon him. Funnily, Richie is displeased with being happy over not missing the bus. As a passer-by stares at him, these processes merge into educating Richie that this is just the start of a frustrating day. So much so that Richie tries not to imagine, tries even to forget, the embarrassment he will experience at work when he arrives; one disappointment is certainly enough for him.

"Hold on!" he cries, putting his arm up; swallowing his embarrassment, he runs for the bus.

He stands behind the two men who spoke as they passed him after he was splashed. He waits for the pair to get onto the bus and pay. As they walk onto the bus, to then take the stairs and go to the upper deck. One speaks to the other, yet again.

"Could do with a drop of diesel, that fella. What do you reckon? Ahh, the smell of it!"

"I haven't..." Richie raises his voice towards the two men; the other, who did not speak, is now laughing. He shouts at his friend, "Ah, ha ha ha. Fingered your hole." He is still laughing at his friend. Richie flushes, looks back towards the driver to pay, and then finishes his reply to the insinuation. "I mean! I haven't, I haven't wet myself." The bus driver laughs, "Never mind, mate."

Paying the driver, Richie climbs the stairs to sit down on the bus's top deck, which is generally unpopulated. Walking past the two seated men, Richie says, "Funny colour, black," and the bus starts reassuring its passengers with the knowledge that it is doing the job that it is supposed to be doing, by doing what the driver asks it to do. Pulling out into the road and driving onwards towards the city centre. The first young man to make the comment downstairs then starts as if to speak, suddenly, "We…"
The other cuts him off, "Don't speak for me."
The other finishes, "I mean, I…" The bus changes gear. "… I didn't mean anything by it, pal."
Richie grins and relaxes; he thinks about the ride to work and the next set of troubles he will encounter.

Bus Rider Song, by The Guess Who: please be respectful and listen. There is much context, and also content hidden within the text.

Verse 1:
Line 1: a man at the rear gets up and starts to sing.
Line 2: all join in apart from Richie. [All stand apart from Richie]
Line 3: all join in apart from Richie.
Line 4: all join in apart from Richie.

.

Verse 2:
Line 1: all sit again, and a man on his own near the front, still seated, sings.
Line 2: man on his own sings.
Line 3: man on his own sings.
Line 4: man on his own sings.

[The people from behind Richie get up and sing. Richie gets up too]

Verse 3:
Line 1: all sing and sit down.
Line 2: all still sing. [A man is seen singing in front of Richie, with a bald head. Then everybody can be seen. From the front window of the bus. Leading to inside]
Line 3: all still sing.

Line 4: all still sing.

Chorus:
Line 1: all sing apart from Richie.
Harmonising. [All sing as well as Richie]
Line 2: all sing apart from Richie.
Harmonising. [All sing as well as Richie]
Line 3: all sing apart from Richie.
Harmonising. [All sing as well as Richie]
Line 4: all sing apart from Richie.
Harmonising. [All sing as well as Richie]
Line 5: all sing apart from Richie.
Harmonising. [All sing as well as Richie]
Line 6: all sing apart from Richie.
Harmonising. [All sing as well as Richie]

Everyone sits down again, and by and by most of them get off. As the next bunch leaves the bus, Richie sees a young man walking along the street and into his family friends' 'Stop Once Buy Twice' shop on the high street. The bus pulls away. The bus travels on towards his place of work, and Richie reminisces: *that was Jason. He is the boyfriend of the IT girl, Sherry, who works at the bank. She sits and works at the same desk as I. I find her fascinating, but not him. He is the master of disaster when it comes to me thinking about Sherry. Every time I look at her at work. I see him having a good time behind her back. Mainly trying to date other girls behind her back. Sometimes he's blatant enough to try and chat them up while she sits alone. Hey, don't look at me that way; I've seen him doing it in the cafe that he, Sherry, and his friends all hang out in.* The bus goes over a bump in the road. *Am I not her friend? Well, yes, that is true. All I can say is that I have tried to tell her, but a simple thing like trying to tell someone something of this magnitude is harder than you think. There is another train of thought. Would I not be as bad as him if I did try and explain? Just think about that.*
Richie spies the Leicester Allegiance Bank that he works at, in the distance. He rings the bell, the bus stops, and the wet Richie leaves the top deck. Walking down the stare, he stops at the bottom by the driver. The driver stops the bus, Richie exits. As he exits the driver

17

barks, "See ya 'Dark Sky's Rising,'" and shuts the doors behind him, and then drives away.

Richie is feeling amused, but distinctly exasperated from the drivers comments, and the young man's jests earlier over diesel. He is standing on the curb, the bank is lit with a burst of sunshine. As a car goes by and splashes water onto his shoes. He looks at his shoes, and then looks back to the bank with a face like thunder. The burst of light diminishes, there is a crack of thunder. A new passage of rain forms, so he runs across the road as the traffic dies to get to his place of work.

Act Two: The Seriousness Behind Colleagues And Acquaintances.

The bank's hustles and bustles are hidden from passers-by as the security guard lets Richie in through the front door. Richie has alerted him from outside to his arrival. The security guard is smirking as he lets him in. He beckons him into the tall-ceilinged bank with his left arm, and a slight dip of his torso. He is ushering him towards the rear of the bank's lobby.

The security guard holds one of the double doors open. His black work boots form a continuous line into his black trousers and then we see the prominent mark of a white shirt. He has a Windsor knotted black tie and black jacket, which finishes off at the shoulders with buttoned epaulettes. His smile is hidden, now he stands tall once more; notably, his cap is fixed correctly to his head. Despite its weight, it did not waver an inch, his movement a breach of what gravity wished.

Richie walks into the bank.

The security guard, Sid, goes to the same cinema as Richie. Richie knows this as he saw him last week, inside the building, but what he doesn't know is that Sid watched Richie go to a show. Richie already had enough reason not to look forward to seeing him this morning. Then he got soaked by the passing cars. So Richie tried to be light-hearted with his conversation, but it doesn't work.

"Ah, oh. Hello, Sid."

"Well, what do we have here? It looks like those clouds you are under have gone away in the wind, Richie." This time we can see Sid's smirk fully.

18

"Pardon, what, Sid?" Richie looked back towards him; he has already more or less passed him. He struggles to grasp what Sid has said to him precisely. He is wedged between his nervousness, and his willingness to get to the office.

"Gone before you got there, you should have been, Son."

Richie stops, fully turning towards the man. "I, I don't quite know where you are coming from, excuse me?"

Sid knows that he has Richie bound and tied within his reality, so he adds, "You won't get what you want watching those films, son, either. Ha ha ha ha. You, ha, ha – you are, aren't you, Son – fully gone you are, son. Hahaha."

Richie remembers. "Mind your own business." He leaves the security guard's space. He arrives at the security door, and punches the code into the door lock, automatically walking through the door.

"Gone before you get there, Son, ha ha. You mark my words!"

Richie doesn't stop to listen. He carries on to take the long walk that takes him upstairs to the local bank's administration offices. He is annoyed that Sid always seems to know too much about anyone in particular.

Inside the office, aside from Richie's arrival, all except one of his daily working colleagues are gathering around the kettle. Some are waiting to add sugar to their drinks. One of the office staff adds the sweet granules to her mug and turns to speak to no one in particular; as it is before working hours, some are drinking while chatting. This girl; Richie has his mind fixated upon her and would like to break the silence of this at odd times. Truly he feels his emotions for her would interrupt the end of all time itself, and then again at the beginning of the restart of this world's complexity. Oblivious to Richie's morning's trivia, she hangs her jacket upon an office chair. A workmate sugars the drink she has made her, at the drinks station. Mechanically, not registering Richie's approach to the office door, she heads to pick up the brew herself.

Her name is Sherry; she understands Richie, and Richie feels she is no ordinary girl.

The door to the office opens.

Everybody, apart from Sherry, the love of Richie's life, looks towards Richie's silhouette outlined in the doorway. His profile changes from dark to light in the flick of a switch. In this instant, he knows Sherry is not looking. She never does take note of him at

19

these, his most awkward moments. Nonetheless he feels that Sherry is endearing during his normal working behaviour. Furthermore, as he looks at her, he feels nothing ever will bring them together.

Even though she is Richie's kind of happiness, he feels Sherry would never be attracted to him. Little does Richie know she is becoming aware of her feelings for him.

Richie walks into the office. The straight brown trousers of his suit, and some of his brown jacket, are sodden. His beautiful tie is tucked into his also brown waistcoat. He is pleased with his normality, amongst the distracted emotions he is feeling. He purposely forgets to hang his jacket on his chair, and he strolls toward the radiator. Sherry takes a glance at the abnormal conduct of her friend, who she is secretly shy of as she is shy of the typical office rumours. She notices he can be clumsy around her, but not purposely. As she is stricken with this fear, she does not want to enhance the formality of office practice into something more intense and become embittered with feelings of remorse. She is now looking towards the kettle to hide her feelings. This does not alter the fact that she stands alone. She is thinking of her mother's relationship with her father. She thinks about her Italian father marrying an American black woman who then settled in England. It makes her feel proud that she hasn't made a fool of Richie. She walks around the desks in the opposite direction to all the others. Walking past Richie's chair, Sherry feels secret compassion.

Time pauses all that is around Richie as Sherry walks past him. He raises his arms towards the ceiling and follows them up with his gaze. The light of the day falls upon him for him to be embarrassed – all those still at the drinking station stare. Richie walks past all the milling people to hand, to dry his jacket on the radiator, which sits beyond them. Since his pause, he does not appreciate that he is walking within a brighter light than anyone else, a light formed as the door opened. Even Sherry doesn't notice this as she too is enveloped within a different brightness.

It picks her beauty out from all the disorders Richie has built. She turns her computer on, and having moved back towards the kettle, then switches direction. With the light still fixated upon her, she watches Richie walk to her left-hand side, and then glances to her right. A tangle of different lives looked upon by everyone else within the office. Before meeting her gaze, Richie passes near her, and the lights are close enough to become merged. For a moment, their views become brighter. They then dim and disperse as Sherry walks slightly forwards, towards the drinking station, and reaches out for the kettle, alone.

In his morning's feverish haste, Richie is not willing, yet again, to take in the loving glances Sherry is giving. As Richie doesn't realise that she feels sadness for his situation, he is left with the feeling that she must just feel embarrassed for him.

After their brief moment's meeting outside of the park that day, Richie can't, or rather won't, understand it as a conversation; there were no complete sentences as such. All he can remember, apart from the normal glance she gave him, is an embarrassed 'hello', but outside of work, he knows that it was not much of a recognition. It was more time to say 'see you later', as all he had wanted was for her to see what Jason, her boyfriend, was really like. She had turned away just as he grabbed her hand. Then she had said, "Leave me alone." Jason had laughed out loud at him, but he knew that he was going to tell her that he was cheating on her, and he privately believed she knew too. Richie then remembers walking towards the ice-cream van in the park.

Now that was one of my better days of summer. As I approached the ice-cream van the motor was running and I was looking for change in my pocket. I didn't notice the person buying something. I took a large vanilla ice-cream from the vendor, turned and spotted Sherry licking at her cone as ice-cream melted and ran down the cone. She laughed obliviously and then turned slightly and noticed me.

Laughing, Richie is slightly embarrassed to see his work colleague, and flummoxes a 'Hello' as he coughs. Sherry laughs this time, presumably as they are alone, and again they walk out of the park entrance and giggle at eating ice-cream. They stop; Sherry looks at Richie and laughs once more, turns and leaves him to stand alone.

So that's the lovely Sherry Traverso. She breaks my heart every time I meet her, as most girls do... apart from the office boss, Jacky.

"See you at work, Richie," she calls as she leaves him alone. Another crack of thunder snaps Richie from his daydream. Jacky calls out to Richie, "Was that from your underpants?" The office staff giggle.

Apart from the office boss, Jacky, she would never break a man's heart, or so it is written on the toilet door.

21

We see Geoff putting a pen away and happily reading his handiwork. 'Jacky is a man eater', the graffiti on the office door reads.

The bright yellow wall, behind the radiator, begins to loom as Richie nears. Yet, before he finds out about the painted white industrial radiator, and if it may be on this morning, Geoff speaks. He is castigating Richie slightly.

Richie nears the heater, from behind Geoff.

"Morning, Richie. You are a sight for sore eyes. You were caught napping, eh? You're not just looking like a dark rain cloud this morning; by parting the clouds you've turned into something more substantial."

Richie slows, turning towards Geoff, "So, Geoff, what exactly am I this morning?"

"Well, should I say, as I'm in a cloudy place, or space, Richie, you seem to me to look like a, ha, a massive cumulonimbus. Oh and by the way, Richie, I think you'll find that isn't working today – actually."

Jacky, who sits at a desk near Richie, cuts in to finish the conversation. "Yer. Ha, ha, ha!"

Everybody else chuckles too. Sherry turns with her cup in hand and smiles. The lights dim, and the pair are reignited into the Spotlights. As the two lights seem to merge again, they stretch to one another to become bright. Daylight then resumes.

Sherry says, "Tight-fisted misers want to save more money!"

"Damn it!" Richie calls out to no one in particular, making himself isolated.

Sherry walks towards Richie a touch. Clutching her mug, she looks at it. "You'd think they'd at least try and look after the people that keep this place ticking over."

Richie, standing by chance in front of Sherry, believes that she may have made a mug of coffee, or tea, for him.

Sherry walks away. She leaves Richie alone in his sadness, realising that she actually did not make him a brew. Richie is now looking to himself for comfort. He feels embarrassed. His mistake is bringing more sniggers from the girls in the office to enhance his embarrassment. Geoff is scoffing in Richie's direction.

All those gathered stare at Richie.

Richie leaves his rant to the open space around him, cursing the air, the area made more solitary by Sherry's going. As we see Richie calm himself by looking at the floor, acclimatising, he walks to his chair. To hang the not so much dripping, but wet jacket, on the back of his chair.

Everybody becomes seated in a discordant fashion.

Richie suggests to his table, "Am I deeply down, or are people picking on me for being dark skinned and Indian? I've had people tell me a drop of diesel won't hurt. Tell me my name is 'Dark Sky's Rising', and then I have been told I resemble a dark rain cloud. Let alone all the other stuff that's happened along the way."

Jacky, "At least it doesn't say anything about you on the toilet door."

Geoff taps at his keyboard, then smiles innocently.

"Does God really hate me?" Richie dulls his amusement with a sigh. Slowly the tones of people working arise from all around the office. Time is slowly ticking away through the start of the day. Richie is regularly brushing off his wet trousers while seated at his desk. People are clicking at the keyboards of their computers. Some people are in conversation on their phones, and there is a conversation between a standing couple; there is plenty of desk chatter.

Richie finishes brushing his trousers, and stares for a moment at Sherry.

"Sherry!" He calls. She looks at him with sympathetic eyes.

The office lights go out.

When the lights come back on again, they fall upon Richie and Sherry. The couple is now standing by the radiator. It stands beneath the window; the curtains are drawn. The lights from the office are, again, seemingly only shining on them both. Richie looks at his jacket in his right hand, and then back to Sherry. Sherry, dressed as Scarlett O'Hara, takes a pace forwards to comfort him. Richie puts his jacketed arm around her. Raising his right arm in the air, he pulls it back down with eager excitement. A climatic embrace follows.

Richie is now seated again. His mind is now feeling more snug; it has finished with its playfulness, and maybe the parody hidden within him. Unfortunately for Richie, he now cannot distinguish what is real, from what he has created for himself. He looks to Ganesha for wisdom, the idol on his desk, but can now only see, as he leans towards his computer screen, his grandpa's behind going up the stairs. Sid's words echo in his mind. That he was 'gone before

you got there.' He watches his grandpa's behind; his grandpa
scratches at it. Richie is reluctant to look on.
Only the clock, ticking along, truly marking time, takes Richie's
concentration back to normality.
Everyone ends their staring at him. The noise from the office returns.
Sherry is still looking at him, after he called out to her. "Yes?" she
replies.
Richie looks at his computer. He starts tapping the keyboard and
replies, after shaking his head slightly, "It doesn't matter."
All now look to the office clock. It rotates a couple of hours
forwards. While the rest of the office staff only take a glance at
Intervals, Richie keeps watching it. He takes note of his computer
screen and then looks back to the clock. It is now at eleven o'clock.
"I shouldn't be so playful, but don't you think that there is more to
life than money?" Richie speaks out loud to no one in particular.
"Money!" Jacky repeats. She sits closest to him, within the formation
of desks situated around the office.
"Money!" Geoff echoes from the other side. He sits facing Jacky, but
closer to the boardroom than her.
"Money?" Sherry asks; she is seated on Jacky's side, but nearer
Geoff. As she stands, she holds within her a new light of the ever-
evolving day.

Money, Money, Money, by Abba: please be respectful and listen.
There is much context, and also content hidden within the text.

Verse 1:
Line 1: Sherry sings, while the others tap at their keyboards.
[Coloured disco lights bounce around the room]
Line 2: the whole workforce joins in. [Richie looks down at his
desk]
Line 3: Jacky sings alone.
Line 3: the rest of the workforce join in. [Richie still looks at his
desk]
Line 4: all join again.
Line 5: Sherry sings alone.
Line 6: Sherry still sings. [All, including Richie, look at Sherry]
Line 7: Sherry still sings.

Chorus:
Line 1: Sherry, Geoff, and Jacky sing. [(Office staff dance) Sherry, Jack, and Geoff are now standing behind their desks]
Line 2: Sherry, Geoff, and Jacky sing.
Line 3: Sherry, Geoff, and Jacky sing.
Line 4: Sherry, Geoff, and Jacky sing.
Line 5: Sherry, Geoff, and Jacky sing.
Line 6: Sherry, Geoff, and Jacky sing.
Harmonising. [Office staff]
Line 7: Sherry, Geoff, and Jacky sing.
Line 8: Sherry, Geoff, and Jacky sing.
Line 9: Sherry, Geoff, and Jacky sing.
Line 10: Sherry, Geoff, and Jacky sing.

Verse 2:
Line 1: Sherry, now singing on her own. [All go back to their desks. Richie picking girls up by the hips to pass them by him to dance away from him. They all skip past his seat]
Line 2: Sherry, now singing on her own.
Line 3: Jacky, now singing on her own.
Line 4: Sherry, still singing, has the rest of the office staff (they have been silent) now join in with her.
Line 5: Sherry still sings, with staff. [The rest of the workforce force Sherry to sit down in her chair to face her computer]
Line 6: Jacky sings at her desk [All staff sit down after Sherry]
Line 7: Sherry singing, now sitting, types at her computer.

Chorus:
Line 1: all of the office staff, not including Sherry, sing. [The three Partners walk through the door. Two first, leaving the door to close slightly. Then the youngest of the three brings up the rear. They are singing the chorus too. All dressed in differing pin-striped suits. Sherry stands to attention behind her desk]
Line 2: all of the office staff, not including Sherry, sing.
Line 3: all of the office staff, not including Sherry, sing.
Line 4: all of the office staff, not including Sherry, sing.
Line 5: all of the office staff, not including Sherry, sing.
Line 6: all of the office staff, not including Sherry, sing.
Harmonising.

Line 7: all of the office staff, not including Sherry, sing.
Line 8: all of the office staff, not including Sherry, sing.
Line 9: all of the office staff, not including Sherry, sing.

Chorus:
Line 1: the three Partners sing from the door leading to the Boardroom. [The door is left open]
Line 2: the three Partners sing.
Line 3: the three Partners sing.
Line 4: the three Partners sing.
Line 5: the three Partners sing.
Line 6: the three Partners sing.
Harmonising [all sing]
Line 7: the three Partners sing.
Line 8: the three Partners sing.
Line 9: the three Partners stop singing.
Line 10: Richie sings, finishing the song. [The Partners watch him; they then walk into the boardroom and close the door behind them]

All goes back to how it was before with all the office hustle and bustle.
The door to the boardroom opens as all else fades into darkness. A light, now fresh, shines figuratively upon the character that is already in the doorway. "It's dinner time soon. Think of the money! Don't waste our time," says the youngest of the Partners. He promptly walks back into the boardroom, and all three men shake each other's hands. Within the room itself, the three men are pleased with their response to their workers' relaxation while working.

It is a rainy day in the confines of the grounds of a county manor house. The air is fresh, and fresh with the noise of a rutting buck. The sound is like no other on Earth and can never be mistaken. In these parts the deer were more plentiful once, and farmed for their meat. Now they wander anywhere they like. Eating while destroying what was a habitable space not too long ago. Their sound, it is rather like the deep-throated rumble of a large exit of breath, and is made only by one wild beast, the stag. It is often repeated for lengthy periods of time and can be heard now as the estate animals come into their time to make new life and strengthen their genes. The grunt can be heard right up to the house, and within. Some of the females, the does, bark to call on the males for mating. Breaking the relaxed tranquillity is a puddle-splashing solitary white van which lurches down the driveway of the estate. It is on its way toward the stately home, the centre, the hub of what was working life, of the land that is owned by the lady of the house. The deer walk together on the lawns and Lady Rosetta is sitting in her many bedroomed house, with its many reception rooms and outhouses. It is situated in the countryside between Derbyshire and Leicestershire. The stately home she resides in is made from local sandstone and was built hundreds of years ago. The house owns many hectares of land, and possesses pillars and steps to guide visitors to its raised entrance. The house is in decline. Lady Rosetta is on her laptop, ascertaining what she might need to at least survive here for a few more years. Sixty thousand is the figure at the bottom of the page summary. That has been declined by a local lender, as is legible in red after the amount.

"God damn!" She is regretting that she ever had children. Yes she is depressed, but do not all mothers fall into depression when thinking about what would be best for their family? Least of all when she remembers them individually, but most of all when she remembers they have upped and left the family residence. It is their family home and their inheritance when she finally passes. She feels that she does receive some kind of love from her children, her three boys, now three grown men, but not the amount she feels she gave them as they grew up here. "The world we live in is not the same as it once used to be. I used to be able to sell something valuable to at least keep the house alive. Now we are brassic. Prescot, Prescot, PRESCOT," she calls.

Lady Rosetta is still remarkably fresh in her mind's eye; she is just remembering the old times. Well, no, let's say she's just eccentric in her manner (and her manor) sometimes. "No, I don't suppose you would hear me, my dear servant; you left here ten years ago at least. Those boys of mine are simply not doing justice to their mother, or to keep alive their family honour." She turns to the last painting, hanging on the walls of the large living quarters of the dark damp house. It is of her and her husband. "Honey, they will just have to listen. Yes, I know, Mumsy's boys are better off on their own," She stands behind her chair and looks at the screen of the laptop, "but not left alone so long they relinquish what made them, Roger."

Two men who are sitting in the white van are just pulling up to the front of the house. "Are you sure you're ready, Henry?"

"Yes, let's get at it, Jonesy. I'll have a cup from my flask when we leave," the other replies.

They both get out of the vehicle and walk to the front door. "Christ, who has that many steps to their front door? It sure comes to a monumental moment when people with this kind of money owe money," Jonesy jokes to his partner as he knocks on the door.

Henry looks serious under his three-day-old stubble, "You know what, I don't think we'll find anything here to cover the cost of the bill. This place was obviously a palace, but it hasn't held heat for years, I should say. The electricity bill must be sky-high here; ha, crikey, the numbers."

"Probably too many Microwave ding meals for the rats," Jonesy jokes again.

The door opens and Lady Rosetta is standing at the door. She is wearing a woolly robe, shawl, and excessive woolly hat, all of which are hiding her normally exquisite good looks. Making her not look like the Lady she really is, the subject of invitation to high society balls that she has been used to. Henry and Jonesy both understand that even though she is wearing a woolly exterior she could be, and probably is, wearing expensive clothing underneath her tent-like exterior. Her looks give her that sense of wealth still. The only thing she was missing, they would both say when they climbed back into the van behind them, all she was missing was a duvet draped around her shoulders.

"Yes, boys, can I help you?"

"We're here to take stock of the items in your house that we can take if you do not pay your bill immediately, madam," Henry says.

"Well, I'm afraid, boys, I have not enough funds to pay next month's bills, let alone your bill. You'll have to come in, dears." Lady Rosetta motions the two men inside.

Jonesy walks straight inside, Henry walks in behind him. "The fall of the mighty," says Henry to his friend.

Lady Rosetta frowns. "Can I say, boys, I was wealthy once, well, still am, but my money is tied up in trading and banking."

"Okay, Lady, but can I say: should you not pay your bill we will be seizing all assets, and if you had wanted to keep that large oil painting in this room here, then you perhaps should have traded your banking side of things in a long time ago. This is a lovely gaff, you should of looked after home firstly, ma'am. Come on, Henry, let's have a look around; I don't think we'll find many assets here, though. We might have to look at letting the courts claim back the money through her investments."

"Ha ha, has it got that bad? Well let me tell you, boys. I may have to withdraw some funds from my sons' enterprise." Lady Rosetta blushed.

"Alright, madam," Jonesy walked back from looking into a room from one of the doorways in the hall.

"Let's start high and work backwards. Hopefully it's too far to have to move stuff from up there. Are the stairs safe?" Henry treads carefully up the staircase, and Jonesy follows his colleague.

Lady Rosetta walks toward the hallway phone and picks up the receiver; her phone sits on top of her sole hallway sideboard. She dials the number to her sons' bank. "Yes, extension four five four six, thank you." She waits a moment until the phone starts to ring on the other end of the line.

Inside the Partners Boardroom the phone starts to ring on the youngest Partner's desk. He walks around the desk to pick up the phone.

"Hello, Dobedobe."

"Oh, hello, Mother. How are you? I'm fine, and don't you know 'It's a rich man's world,'" he hesitantly replies.

The other two brothers are trying to stop him making more of a mistake.

"Don't you 'mother' me. I am something more than that. What about my something from a mother to another? Oh, and my line is, 'A man is hard to always know, and hard to find' in my mind 'but others no doubt, can't get him off their minds'," Lady Rosetta coos.

"Sorry, Mumsy, what would you like, mumsy?" the younger partner asks; he turns the internal speaker on.

"What she always wants; money. Now we have to be strong. That money was left to us by our father. It is not our fault she ploughed all hers into that cesspit we used to call home," the older says, while the younger is making a cutting motion with his hand flat across his throat.

Lady Rosetta hears everything that her oldest son has to say.

"Dobedobe, put mumsy's finest offering on."

The youngest partner beckons his older brother to the phone. He walks toward him moaning, "Nooo, not her. You know she can wrap me around her little finger."

"Listen, it wasn't you two who used to cling to her ankles and suck on her tights when they were young," the middle brother bleats, then sucks on his fist.

"Yes, mumsy, what would you like?" the older asks.

"Mumsy doesn't want any more than you're willing to give, of your business, that is. Not at the moment. But I need sixty thousand pounds for starters, to clear debts, and keep assets afloat. Or I'll tell your brothers what happened when you couldn't find what you were looking for and asked…" Lady Rosetta's loudspeaker performance is cut short.

The oldest Partner is fumbling for the off switch to the speaker. "No, that's okay, Mumsy. Sixty thousand," The other two brothers look away, holding themselves in disbelief. "Okay, we will sort it out today, Mumsy." He nods towards his two brothers. "Goodbye, mumsy," and he places the phone back on the receiver. "She will never let us alone."

"Sixty thousand pounds. That's a lot of our money," the middle partner says. "We need plans."

The youngest brother is totally understanding. "Let her play God, we will hold a meeting tomorrow morning and see if we actually need all those staff we have. Come on, they are as much as a commodity than anything else."

Back in the office, Sherry is typing on her keyboard. Turning towards Richie, she responds to his previous opening words before the outburst of the song, "Be as playful as you wish, Richie. Just don't let it take over your life; you never know what might happen."

"Chance would be a fine thing." Richie smiles and buries his head in his work. Geoff is staring.

"Come on now, you heard what the Partners said."

"Yes," Jacky orders. "Back to work."

The boardroom door opens.

The oldest Partner walks into the office. "As you know, we are hitting hard times,"
"Because of that damn woma…" the half conversation, half shout of frustration, comes from the boardroom.
"Yes, hard times. We will be having a meeting tomorrow to try and brainstorm just exactly what we need to do to beat these most modern of times," the oldest Partner finishes. "Okay?"
There are calls of agreement from around the office.

The landscape has changed. There is thick vegetation, vines, and trees in all directions. Jungle animals and insects are calling out. As we move towards a clearing, a large cat can be seen as it roars in the wilderness. Coming out of the foliage there is a grassy mound which, in turn, becomes the base of a wall. We scale the wall, and there is a courtyard with a fountain and palace within. Music comes from the palace. There is music playing throughout the day; the owner of this place loves to keep the ambiance mellow throughout the day and evening. As we move into the palace, you can see a group of musicians playing in an area arranged on the ground floor, within the great hall.
 We move up the stairs, swiftly arriving inside the Sultan's bedroom. We look around at all the plush décor, and the furnishings and ornaments held within. There are all the colours of the Indian empire caressed in soft light, but that is not all, as there are many ornaments of precious metals. A man, the Sultan, we presume, is lying in bed. Also lying on the bed is a bedstead, richly embroidered with silk, and multi-coloured, that covers him. Above the quilt are white silk sheets, and the man in the bed – the Sultan of the region – is wearing a golden silk nightshirt. He has silky black hair that reaches over his ears, to trail behind him. The man has history written into his good looks from the breeding of the family line. His father, his father before, and so on, have had the pick of the most beautiful of women of the region. He himself has had this chance to pick his very own princess. The sultan is a distant relation of the Malli tribe of the Punjab, joining forces with the Oxydraci, who all lived in the north of India, to defeat Alexander the great. He and what is left of his family are devout Muslim people. He has retreated into the mountains where their herbs grow best.

A woman takes a silver tray from the manservant who has come to the door. She turns and places it on a cabinet by the door, and moves towards the bed. The man in bed is Jasmine's husband. She nears the man and speaks to him; he struggles to talk back to her as his head, lightly propped on the pillow, next to her, is constricting his speech. She opens her mouth to speak.

"Husband of mine, sit up. You know you will get better before you get worse." Her English is good but spoken with a local accent. The prince picks himself up by his elbows and pulls himself backward. His wife plumps up the pillows while nestling them behind him. "Thank you, Jasmine," he replies.

His wife moves back towards the tray, with freshly brewed cups of elixir laid upon it. The elixir is freshly picked from the Sultan's herb plantation. The next man, another servant, it seems, is more of a doctor. He is standing next to the Sultan's bed. The Chikitsak moves in to talk to him.

The chikitsak says to his honourable employer, "Madesh, my consummate ruler. You must take every opportunity to get well. You have to get better while you can; this plague, the one that has stricken your whole family, will not last much longer. I fear it will take you first, and then – after your rule has finished – take Jasmine not long after. It has already robbed you of your offspring and the rest of your family. How can we forget your loving children, Kairav and Chanakya? How long you, my ruler, will last, it is not written yet."

Jasmine, has taken a sip of her tea for comfort. She is careful as she is carrying her husband's drink. That is in her right hand. Her blue veil has slipped from her shoulder. The chikitsak moves to one side, to stand at the head of the bed. Jasmine passes her love his cup of tea.

"Please. I am not your ruler for much longer. Nor should I ever have been. But you must realise this. These moments are my time to remember you all, before they are taken away from me. Time is on your side, Chikitsak, not mine, as in my despair I feel I can hardly remember my children. Yet I decree these things. This euphoria that I feel, I liken to passing. It is part of my expectations. More paraphernalia of my conscience and will to survive. Tell me, Ojas, this is it, isn't it? I am gone; I am no longer amenable to your arts."

32

Ojas says, "No, Madesh. There is plenty of time for us to circumvent what may be. Or understand what may not be, but you must remember we are with you until the end of your days."

The tea, the elixir, is now only warm; he drinks incredibly fast for a sick man. He puts the elixir to one side, pulling himself out of bed to sit on its edge in a spurt of exertion. He has cream pleated baggy pantaloons that cut to his waist where the nightshirt pulls up at the sides. Jasmine puts his golden footwear upon his feet and then backs away. She crouches with her arms open wide to him.

"I must not listen to anyone's opinion. I am unable to understand what is already written, as all that is, is written as knowledge of that which I own. So now I can do no more to make my life better. Yet still, I understand what has happened to me. I know what you are all trying to understand about me."

Jasmine says, "No, husband of mine. We do not look for your sympathy. Yet we look at your sorrow, and all our family's sorrow."

Madesh says, "That is where we separate from each other's sympathies. We must be – all of us – free of our sorrows. We now accept our reality. This is the certainty of our allotted time. That takes us to the limit of our realities."

Ojas interjects, "Forget about what is, my master. All of us, our reality is love."

"And that is all I longed to hear, my friend!"

"Jasmine, remember what my father used to say to us, when we first met in the marketplace. That we needed to listen to the old poets, reciting "Agar Firdaus bar ru-ye zamin ast, Hamin ast o hamin ast o hamin ast.", "If there is a paradise on earth, it is this, it is this, it is this.

"Well, Amir was a very influential man. He had a wealth of scripture. I saved you a poem from his archive of literature. It reads, Mun tu shudam tu mun shudi, mun tun shadam tu jaan shudi. Taakas na guyad baad azeen, mun deegaram tu deegari. I have become you, and you me, I am the body, you the soul; So that no one can say hereafter, that you are someone, and me someone else. It is like the saying in our song, Jasmine; Ob-La-Di, Ob-La-Da, Life goes on."

The orchestra in the lobby stops playing, then starts anew. Madesh now stands firm with his legs apart, in line with his shoulders. Jasmine walks back to him. Dipping her head, she has her right index finger held tightly to the middle of her forehead and then releases it. They stand together, and Madesh looks at Jasmine.

Ob-La-Di, Ob-La-Da by The Beatles: please be respectful and listen. There is much context and also content hidden within the text.

Verse 1:
Line 1: the Sultan sings. [The married couple now remember back to when the market was in their courtyard. They are walking about it with their children playing with one another in different directions. The musicians sing along from the lobby]
Line 2: Jasmine sings.
Line 3: the Sultan sings.
Line 4: both the Sultan and his wife sing.

Chorus:
Line 1: all are singing. [The music is coming from the back of the marketplace now. All is portrayed in the depths of the courtyard as sandy colours. (Chikitsak standing by the palace doors, by the band)]
Line 2: all are singing.
Line 3: all are singing.
Line 4: all are singing.

Verse 2:
Line 1: the Sultan sings alone.
Line 2: the Sultan sings alone.
Line 3: the Sultan sings alone.
Line 4: the Sultan sings alone.

Chorus:
Line 1: Jasmine sings. With only backing from all
Line 2: Jasmine sings. With only backing from all
Line 3: Jasmine sings. With only backing from all
Line 4: Jasmine sings. With only backing from all

Verse 3:

Line 1: Madesh and Jasmine sing together.
Line 2: Madesh and Jasmine sing together.
Line 3: Madesh and Jasmine sing together.
Line 4: Madesh and Jasmine sing together.

Verse 4:
Line 1: back in the bedchamber. Madesh sings alone.
Line 2: Madesh sings alone.
Line 3: Jasmine sings alone.
Line 4: both sing together.

Chorus:
Line 1: back in the marketplace, all sing, including Chikitsak, and the instrument players.
Line 2: all sing, including Chikitsak, and the instrument players
Line 3: all sing, including Chikitsak, and the instrument players
Line 4: all sing, including Chikitsak, and the instrument players

Verse 5:
Line 1: all carry on singing.
Line 2: all carry on singing.
Line 3: all carry on singing.
Line 4: all carry on singing.

Verse 6:
Line 1: the children sing along as they hold hands.
Line 2: the children sing along as they hold hands.
Line 3: the children sing along as they hold hands.
Line 4: the children sing along as they hold hands.

Chorus:
Line 1: all sing.
Line 2: all sing.
Line 3: all sing.
Line 4: all sing.

Line 5: the Husband and Wife sing a duet.

Jasmine helps her husband get back into his bed, and the Chikitsak gives his master a sheet of paper from his jacket pocket.

The Sultan asks his chikitsak, "Are you sure this is all that is left of my family?"

The Chikitsak replies, "Yes, master."

The prince looks to his wife and says, "Get my quill and paper!"

On the paper that the chikitsak has passed to his master there is a family tree with the names listed below their photos: Gaurav Malli, Kuvan Malli; below the couple is Aarzoo Malli, now Aarzoo Gyndall. Next to her is Daivey Gyndall, and below them both is Richie Gyndall.

"Chikitsak Ojas, how did we find these people?" Madesh asks.

"It was not hard; we traced the Malli family right back through the ages. To see how far back they were related to your family. It seems they were in your tribe's family clan right from the dawn of time. Aarzoo is no longer a Malli, that is true, but she has washed her child of any of the wrongdoing that your family may have, intended or not, incurred from the Great Alexander, during the great battle for the old lands of your forbearers." Ojas bows his head sagely.

"It is true then, all will be well if I leave my lands to someone so firmly descended from my family roots, but he must not be afflicted with the pain of this ravaging disorder that takes all that I possess." Madesh is intrigued.

"I am sorry, Madesh my master. Are you implying that I have not done enough for your family as it is?" Jasmine returns with the quill and paper. "I have even asked and sought help from a shaman who lives halfway up the mountainside, above where the elixir grows strong and healthy; where the air is thin. He also told me that nothing can be done to save your royal family from the passed-on plague's existence. I am your loyal servant, and I have tried everything I can."

"Ojas, I feel I must be a penitent man and accept that it is time to pass this whole life I have to someone new who has not been dealt the cards I have been dealt. He must be strong enough to be married, to accept the offer I am willing to make to someone who can pass this, all that I own, on to their children, and their children's children. Pass me the paper and quill, my love, and I will write to his grandfather, Gaurav Malli." The sultan reaches out for the implements.

Jasmine passes her loving husband his stationery. "I must go, my love." Ever since the chikitsak spoke about a Shaman, Jasmine was stricken much deeper with grief. Even though she has taken on her husband's religion, the Muslim religion, she has thought more about her past teachings. She is now deep in turmoil and needs to at least go and pray. "I have to check to see if there is another brew of elixir above the fire in the kitchen." Jasmine leaves the bedchamber and makes her way through the palace to the kitchen.
The Sultan begins to write:

> *Dear Gaurav Mallis,*
> *It may have been a long time to forget, or a long time that you have remembered. But I am a distant relation to your family, you being part of my extended family via our ancestors. My children have long gone and passed into non-existence. So it is written. My wife and I will soon pass too. I have much wealth, too much land, and histories that pass unadulterated through the ages. As I am the Sultan of your old homelands, Medesh, I have one wish: to still be with my family and live the life I was meant to. But this is not meant to be. I am one of the many cursed sultans of your family line, though like I say, and repeat, this will not last for ever. Please. I leave your son all of my lands and wealth if he is married. If not he must not hear of these things, until he marries. He must be married as soon as possible, to finalise the conditions above...*

Madesh puts down the paper. "I must rest, my chikitsak, sorry Ojas, I need to..." Ojas's master drops the quill, laying the paper on his lap, as he falls into long needed sleep. Ojas picks the paper and quill from his master's hands and places them on the small side table by the bed. Then he walks to a chair standing in the bedchamber. Turns it softly so it faces his master, and sits restfully. "You must take your time my master, or else all is lost," he whispers.
Jasmine has reached the kitchen. She is stirring a small pot above the fire in the hearth. She puts the lid back onto the pot and turns to one of the women in the kitchen. "What do you know about the shaman that lives high in the mountain pass?"

37

"Not much, my Lady. All I have heard is that he only appears for those who are restless, or needy for life," the woman says.

"Do you think he will appear for me?" Jasmine is eager.

"I am not sure I am qualified to tell you the answer to that question. All I know is that my brother-in-law walked the single track route past the old Litsea Citrata tree that grows at the pass that leads from the top of the herb plantation. On arrival at the shaman's cave he heard meditating coming from inside. When he announced that he was here to unravel the tale he had been told by his wife – she told him about how he, her husband, would not produce children – the chanting stopped and there was nobody inside to answer his questions. They have not had children yet."

"But what does this mean for me?" Jasmine asks.

"Well they say he can only give one prediction, or cure, to each family. If you go to him, take this." The woman turns to a large table taking up half the floor of the kitchen and pulls out a bottle wrapped in a leaf, and gives it to her master's loving wife.

"But it is too late. A prediction has already been made about my family. There cannot be another according to your account of events. I will go and pray at the mosque, pray for forgiveness from the curse of our ancestry." The woman slips the bottle into her mistress's pocket and says, "Take it, just in case. The truth will come to you."

Walking out through the back door of the kitchen Jasmine walks to the mosque built tall and stately on her husband's grounds. She is led by the sight of the tall single tower that looms above the four corner protrusions of the mosque's prayer rooms.

She approaches the front door quietly. Tales her shoes from her feet. Bathes them in the water provided, and dries her feet. Before entering the building she pulls her face covering around her face and clips it to a fastener that is concealed on her headdress. As she enters the mosque words slip from her mouth. "What am I supposed to do?"

The man sitting on a wooden bench behind her, reading the Quran, looks up and says, "There is always something. I can teach some things, but there is nothing I can teach that I do not already know."

"So it is possible that I can teach you, but you cannot teach me. This is what I do not understand to be true: the fact that truth is just. I am to lose my husband to a plague that has ravaged his family for centuries, and I cannot change this," Jasmine tells the Imam.

"There is an answer you are looking for; are you not looking for answers, Jasmine? I am just an Imam who cannot derive my legitimacy from any central spiritual authority. But what I am here to do is serve the community, like I spoke to Ojas the other day. Not all spirituality is taught from above, there is what lies around us, above us, and beneath us. But if you are asking for what is rightfully yours, is it not there for the taking?"

"You spoke to Ojas, he is our Chikistak." Jasmine is full of sorrow.

"Yes, I know his family, and your family, of course, very well," the imam says.

Jasmine lights up with enthusiasm. "That is it; that is my calling. You have answered the question I have asked very well, thank you." She leaves the mosque backwards, bowing her head. Placing her footwear back on her feet, she starts the long trail towards the mountain top and her goal.

The priest shouts after her, "Jasmine, what is right, and what is your right, are two very different things. Please, like I have told you before, don't get them mixed up and so let your future aims become twisted! Please, hold your faith." The Iman is questioning her realisation that her final objective, that of her claim of passage, could ever be different than what was already written. And, if she does not make things perfect, perhaps she could actually make things worse in, not her future, but the certain future, even if it is not her realisation and prediction of a future she has seen.

The path is well worn. Trodden by many over the years, harvesting the crop that grows on the plantation, local people acting as the workhorses cultivating the harvest, the new growth, of the herb that grows plentifully on the lower slopes of the mountains in this region. She feels that she and the sultan supply enough resources to the families of the workers to keep the crop at a steady pace, to be cut and packed for storage most of the year round. Women with back packs are working high in the fields. Plucking only the top leaves of the bushes and dropping them into their baskets. Jasmine feels free for the first time in a long while. She hums a tune her mother taught her in her early youth. It calms her teetering nerves. There is a slight breeze; it rattles the leaves of the tree next to her, and the sound is louder than anything else around her. Suddenly she hears a chanting noise inside her skull. She thinks it is her humming driving her crazy, but no, it is more like a man chanting. "Can you hear that?"

she asks a man carrying a bundle of leaves in a square cloth sack bound with a rope who is passing by.

"The tree? Yes, it is saying hello to all that are able to hear," he replies.

She stops in her tracks, noticing the Litsea Citrata tree that leads to the mountain pass. "No, not the tree; that other, funny echo in the background." Over and over again she hears the same three, maybe four, words. "It is like nothing I have heard before. It sounds like a man chanting."

The man with the sack scowls at the mountain pass. Shifting the load more evenly on his back, he moves away. When he has settled his burden to his satisfaction, he shouts, "The more you listen, the more he has power over you. Some say he is a healer of many illnesses, but others say he tinkers with the spirit world." The man's voice becomes fainter as he moves further away from Jasmine. "If I were you, my Lady, I would leave now before you find you cannot turn back." Jasmine pushes on.

On the rocky plateau there are no plants, grass, or bushes. She has left all the vegetation behind as she passed the tree that marks the path to the Shaman. The breeze is cooler now. She slips on stones occasionally as she makes her way towards the calls of the welcoming spirit world. The smell of smoke and cooking spices fills her nostrils. She looks upwards and sees a cave further up the mountain, away from the path to the left. There is a large boulder at the foot of the climb; she passes around it and starts to climb. The air is thinner here and she can hear herself panting as the wind blows against her exposed skin. It placates her sole for a moment, blowing the chanting away from her, only for it to return as the wind dissipates. She is momentarily overwhelmed by the onslaught of the chanting. She pauses for a fresh breath. Now she is standing below the cave, looking up. It is time to make the last push towards the mouth of the cave. She climbs steadily until she is level with the entrance. A bead of smoke trails along the roof of the cavern, snaking its way into the atmosphere and up the mountainside itself. She takes a deep breath and walks inside. She breathes out through her nose to try and avoid the smoke that swirls around her, disturbed by her movements. She coughs as she takes in some of the obnoxious fumes. There seems to be a fire casting shadows onto the back of the cave and there is a chamber to the right. She finds herself standing before a small, roaring fire. The shaman sits, eating, on the other side. He is smiling at her with a toothless smile. His painted face distracts her from his lack of clothes; he is wearing only a simple dhoti.

"Come, Come. Come." He draws her in with the welcome of an outstretched arm. "Come, sit. Sit, sit."

Jasmine draws up her clothing and sits, crossing her legs in front of the fire.

"What you want, me? Ha ha, he, you never get me, always something else." The shaman smiles his toothless smile.

"No, I do not want you; well, I wish to use your services." She is nervous, so nervous she nearly drops the bottle she takes from her shawl.

"No one wants me, only my services. A man came before from your household, not your family though; you want something else. You must give me what you have first." The Shaman picks up a long pipe from a rock by the fire. In her swiftness to get this over with she hasn't fully looked around. Bones litter the back of the cave, there is a sweet smell in the air, and bats hang in the farthest of the darker walls of the cavern.

Jasmine gets up and walks around the fire, and places the bottle, wrapped in a leaf, beside the man. He turns suddenly; she looks up and the shaman breathes thick smoke from the pipe into her face. She coughs. Gasping for breath, she reels as he breathes more smoke into her face. She coughs again, inhales, and then stands. It is like someone has lined the back of her throat with hot glue. "Good, sit, sit." She staggers back to her place. "Sit, sit," the man says, and she complies.

The way the light of the flames flickers against the rock makes Jasmine feel she can see more than one shaman. Then things became blurry. She laughs. "Ha, all I wanted to do was…"

"Ask, ask," the man says.

"Well, I have come to believe that my husband will pass away, and soon thereafter I shall follow." She tries to make the man understand more. "Ha ha. There is a…"

"Curse, a curse. Yes, I know. The man who came before spoke of such things. Sad situation. Children already dead, no? Sick, sick. First children, then husband, then you, yes?" The shaman pauses.

"That is correct; so nothing can be..." She gets no further; the shaman jumps in. "Done, no. No, Nothing can be done, he, he." He takes another puff on his pipe. "There is more you wish for. I can tell you, maybe?"

She feels great sadness and looks at the ground; drawing her head back she speaks again. "Perhaps there is a way for us to stay together after this sickness takes us all."

The shaman is unwrapping the leaf to open the bottle. He takes a mouthful from it. "He he he." Taking another swig he spits onto the fire and then begins to chant. The flames billow outwards and the fire becomes more intense. Jasmine can see her children playing in the shadows of the cave walls. "Kairav, Chanakya? Is that you?" she asks.

"It is not us. But it may be, mother, ha ha ha ha. We aim to please. Stop it, stop it, she does not wish to understand. She simply asks can you make it in time for her departure." The flames of the fire shoot upwards and there are lots of sparks and popping of wood from the base of the fire itself. The children giggle and say "Maybe we can..." The fire dies down, as the shaman expels more smoke in Jasmine's direction. The fire is now just embers. She is coughing profusely; waving her hand she gets up and clambers along the interior of the passage and out of the cave. The world is spinning and shuddering around her and she nearly falls, just managing to cling to the rock face to stabilise her descent. She makes her way towards the path. Walking once more around the large rock, she stumbles, crying, onto the path itself. As she descends the mountain path, she notices blooms hidden among the rocks to her left. Still crying, she clambers over the outcrop to pick some of the flowers she can see. As she crouches to pick them she speaks; she feels alone. "Anemone Bloom, this world is never satisfied with leaving the living alone." She speaks now to the flowers. "Sorry, for I am not cruel, I will be gentle as I pick you. Only my husband is dying and I wish to garnish him with your grace and beauty." Jasmine picks the white, pink, and purple flowers. Makes her way back to the path and walks the rest of the journey home. It is getting late; she wipes the remaining tears from her travels from her eyes. In the kitchen she orders another brew of elixir and winds her way through the palace to the bedchamber she shares with her husband.

Ojas is still seated in the chair he placed himself in when his master fell asleep. He is trying not to fall asleep himself and keeps waking as his chin hits his chest, making his head rise up and down intermittently. He is nodding in slow motion and then fast, and back to slow.

The door opens. It is Jasmine.

"Ojas, how is my husband? I have been busy walking the mountain, looking for knowledge. I believe it won't be long. Is he still...?"

"Alive, Jasmine? Yes he is." Ojas walks to his master's side and wakes him. "Master, it will soon be more time for medicine. Please, wake."

"Oh, Ojas, how have I survived the night?" the Sultan asks.

"Medesh, it is still day time. You only fell asleep for a few hours. Jasmine is here, back from a walk on the mountainside."

Jasmine walks around the bed and kneels before her husband; moving forward on her knees she places the flowers she has picked from the mountain path in her husband's warm hands. "Please, I found these for you to hold to your heart, and I hope for more now, better things to happen in our futures. I went to see the shaman, but..."

"You did not employ his services, Jasmine, did you?" Ojas says.

"No, Ojas, I saw these before I got there. They distracted me and I came straight home after I picked them." Jasmine looks back at her husband. "I wish you peace in death and hope I have helped you overcome all evil, Madesh." Jasmine starts to cry again. Ojas looks displeased, as if he knows that there was much more that Jasmine isn't telling. He strokes his wispy chin.

"Thank you, my love." Madesh turns to his chikistak. "Tell me, Ojas; I feel I was doing something before I passed out."

"You were writing this letter to your relations in England, my Lord. Here is the letter; you have not finished it yet." The chikistak gives his master his paper and quill.

Madesh reads the letter and then finishes writing: ... *until he marries. As so he must be married as soon as possible, to finalise the conditions above.*

He adds: *Please, you must stick to these rules as I have asked. Yours, Sultan Madesh.*

He signs the bottom of the letter. The Chikistak passes him an envelope. The Sultan folds the letter and places it in the envelope. "Please, deliver this where it needs to go, Ojas."

There is a knock at the door. "Enter," the sultan murmurs. The door opens and a man with a silver tray waits just inside the doorway. Jasmine gets up to take the tray with the elixir, and the chikistak walks to the sideboard. He heats a wax stick and drops a few drops onto the back of the envelope to seal the letter; he turns the letter over and writes an address from another piece of paper that is folded behind the list of names and the section of the Gyndall family tree he holds in his possession.

"It is done, master." Jasmine is offering her husband a cup to drink from the tray. "This letter is your will, Master, and soon it will be winging its way to Blackberry Way, and to the home of your distant cousins."

Act Three: Don't Break My Heart.

Richie walks in through his parents' front door, arriving home from work. As we hear him shut the front door, his grandpa makes himself comfortable; he is watching television in his usual spot.

His mother calls to Richie. "Richie, honey. Come and help me make dinner! I haven't got to press your suit for work this time, have I?"

"No, maji. I must go out quickly. I have not got time; I have something important to do!" he replies and runs upstairs to change.

In the kitchen, Richie's maji is peeling onions. Cold water is running in the sink. As she peels each of them individually, she places them into the light brown mixing bowl filled with water, which has replaced the washing up bowl, which is on the sideboard, cups and plates within. Aarzoo turns and speaks to her husband. He is propped up against the kitchen cabinets beside the fridge; he is in the same place as this morning. "That boy never has enough time to do the things he should. Rather than relaxing, he should be learning the wealth of things married people need to learn."

"Maji," her husband replies. "Leave the boy alone! He is young and needs this time to become fruitful. Look, at least he's out of the house, no?"

"I suppose you are correct, husband of mine." Richie's father smiles; his wife broadens her smile then too, while turning back to the sink to peel her onions. She has a plan to make Richie's plans unstable. Both are smiling beside the sink, and we take a glimpse of Richie leaving the house.

"See ya later, alligators," he calls as the door shuts.

Walking up to town, Richie is wearing a loose, reversible white nylon coat, tailored at the waist. A yellow T-shirt with a logo and Chinos, white motif trainers on his feet. He is carrying a book by its spine; the pages of the well-worn book bristle in the breeze from Richie's pace. All the lights are on in the street; he watches people walk him by, as he heads to the Cinema.

He comes to a junction with lots of shops around it. Mr. Joshi, Iliesha's father, owns his 'Stop Once Buy Twice' shop near here; it is a few doors down after the junction. He can see Mr. Joshi on his phone, propped against the open door of his shop. Approaching Mr. Joshi, Richie notices that he is not interested in what he is doing; he looks directly at Richie. "Hi Mr. Joshi." Richie smiles.

"Ah, Richie," Mr. Joshi says, then speaks in Hindi to his caller, and puts the phone in his pocket. "Richie, call me Rahil, please. It is important to me. Come inside, quickly does it. Ha, you never know what is going to happen on the street."

Walking inside the shop, we see it is as normal as can be for a paper shop that sits on the high street.

Richie looks at all the alcohol sitting on the fridge shelves. "I didn't think you drank, Mr. – Sorry, Rahil."

"I don't, Richie, but these English bastards love a drop of sin, my boy. And hey, it's a big mark-up. The profit on these is amazing. Let me tell you, I can…" Rahil Joshi is cut short by his customer.

"Sorry Mr. – Rahil,"

"Call me Mr. Rahil if you want, Richie, but again that is normally those English nitwits at it when they've had a few. They get their kids to roar at me at times, it's all very funny." Rahil smiles.

"Well anyway, Rahil. I am going somewhere important. So I need to be quick, not super quick, but quick."

A customer and her son walk around the shop. Mr. Joshi walks behind the counter. The boy is wearing a Hulk outfit and looking for chocolate at the chocolate rack. "Hey, Richie, when you say not super quick, not like an Avenger, then." The woman smiles as she gets her card out and asks for twenty cigarettes. Rahil winks at the woman, turns and looks for her usual. "Anyway, Richie, what would you say if I could let you have some cheap tickets to take your family on holiday? You can check out the merch. See if it's up to scratch, then do some sales for me in your spare time."

"We can't afford to do that, Rahil."

Mr. Joshi passes the woman her fags. The woman takes the bar of chocolate from her son and places that on the counter too. Mr. Joshi keys the numbers into the till, and the woman places her card near the payment monitor. "Cheers, Josh," the woman says as her son roars, "Rahhhhhh."

"'Hil, to you, little boy, Rahil, ha ha. See ya, dear." The woman walks back and grabs the boy by the arm and pulls him from the shop.

"Typical." Rahil looks back at them leaving the shop. He walks back to Richie. "Why not, your family must have some money stashed away for a rainy day. Anyway, your father tells me that your mother has been trying to set you up with the Patijna's daughter, Charu, for some time. Ha ha, what a laugh I had with him. He said that your family were saving for a rainy day. Look, if you don't get a second job, Richie, you will never earn enough money to entice Charu's family into letting you have her hand. You know they own a rake of restaurants and takeaways in the city."

"Mr. Joshi."

"Rahil, please."

"Rahil. I'm not interested in Charu."

"Aha, then who are you interested in, my boy? You must have seen some lovely babes on your travels, no?" Rahil raises his eyebrows

"No, I haven't got time for girls, Mr. Rahil." Richie is getting flustered, perhaps there is an underlying purpose to this conversation; something to do with his father's visit.

"You don't like girls? Get out of my shop." Richie looks for help but there is no one here. "No, ha, only joking, Richie."

"When I say I haven't got time, I mean I am working all day and trying to write books Mr. Joshi."

"Now that's what your father said, and I said that's fascinating and we both laughed. How many have you written, Richie, and how are they getting on?" Rahil asks politely.

"Look, Mr. Joshi, Rahil. I haven't written any yet. They are all ideas in my head. That's why I must leave and get to the cinema to watch the latest showing of the film I want to watch. Goodbye, Rahil."
Richie hurries towards the door.
"Your head's in the clouds, Richie; come work for me. Those tickets will still be here. Come earn some real money." Rahil Joshi shouts after Richie, then checks his till for cash.
Right, so that was Rahil Joshi, Mr. Joshi to you and me. He lives on our street. He is a lot younger than my father, what, say ten years or so. He looks up to my father, as I just found out. I think he enjoys my father's wisdom. They are forever chatting when my father has time. I can tell you, though, I do not like what he had to say. Love is a whole new ball game to me. Especially other people's views on where love should be entwined into the relationships I have with certain people. I hate it how some people feel it is their privilege to bestow their wealth of knowledge onto a person. With themselves believing that they understand the person in question's feelings, for example. It's pure, unadulterated self-regard on their part. What do they believe? That I, for instance, can love ninety nine percent of the girls that I meet? Its sacrilegious to someone's soul to believe this, surely. I don't know. I do like Charu, but Sherry simply fascinates me... Huh, oh no, Jason.
Richie sees two young men chatting as he walks to the cinema. Richie notices that it is Sherry's boyfriend chatting to one of his friends, who frequents the cafe Jason and Sherry hang out in. He can hear their conversation; Jason is being his normal cocky self.
"Tonight's the night mate, I'm gonna tell her for sure tonight," Jason half shouts, smiling; he seems to be having fun.
"No, man. You should have told her last time." His friend is quizzical.
"Ha ha, yeah, I know, man. What do you expect? That dork friend of hers from work was following us when I'd just found the perfect place in the P..."
Richie is starting to go into slow motion as he tries to take in what Jason is saying. He is looking straight at Jason as he approaches him on the curb side of the street. Jason turns his head to see who is passing him and opens his mouth to finish his conversation with his friend.

"...ark." Jason finishes what he was saying as Richie walks by. He is watching him as he passes. "There he goes now, man." Richie can hear him talking about him as he moves away from the two men. "Dork," Jason barks in his direction; he grabs his friend's shoulder and walks the opposite way.

The night is fresh and contains all the trials of the evening air. A siren can be heard in the distance; they can always be heard above the evening confusion of the high street.

Down the street Jason is now standing outside of the 'Shop Once Buy Twice' shop. Rahil Joshi is standing in the doorway and is on his mobile phone yet again. He is trying to arrange how much money his vendor is going to charge him for last month's air fare tickets. 'Any little profit is profit,' he says in his native tongue. Jason, holding his phone, looks up and bickers with him, "No need to gibble-gabble, Raj! Can't you see I'm on the phone?"

Mr. Joshi laughs at the conversation he is having with the other caller. He is polite to the young men. Speaking in English, he holds a conversation between the caller and the two men. He is acting as the go between. "Yes, sorry boys, won't be a minute. It's okay, yes, someone outside, nice young men. Yes, from the neighbourhood." He finishes his conversation again in his native tongue, telling the caller that the young men cannot keep themselves to themselves, and laughs again.

"What did you just say, man? Did you just call me a wanker?" Jason felt deeply offended, even more so after his outburst.

Mr. Joshi is staring at the two men in mid-flow of his business call. Jason's friend butts in. "Well, that's just great then, isn't it Jason? As we don't understand a word of what he was saying. We must have got away with it. A, Jay."

Jason puts his hand out and his friend slaps at it; they both laugh. Putting his mobile phone in front of him, Jason finds Sherry's number and dials. He puts the phone on speaker mode. The phone rings, he laughs at his friend, his friend chuckles.

> Jason's Friend: "What, man?"
> Jason: "Just wait and see. This is it, man."
> Jason's friend: "Noooo. No way, man, you can't do this, bro."
> Jason: "Yes I can. Here we go."

Sherry: Oh, hi Jay, how's things?"

Jason: "Oh, I'm fine, hun. I need to ask you a question."

Sherry: "This sounds interesting, go on."

Jason: "Okay, I want to meet you today, I have something to say."

Sherry: "That sounds too intriguing to miss. Is it something important?"

Jason: "Well, yes, ha ha, I suppose you could say that."

Sherry: (nervous) "Okay, how important?"

Jason: "I..." (Jason stops and winks at his friend, smirks) "I suppose that it could be the most important thing I have to tell you. I did try and tell you in the park last week, but I fell short."

Sherry: "Mmm, well, I suppose I'd better get changed then and get ready to meet you. What time?"

Jason: "Oh, about ten o'clock."

Sherry: "Jay, that's late."

Jason: "Yeah, well, I have something to do first, okay?"

Sherry: "If it's what I think it is then I suppose it will have to do. See you later then." (Sherry now excited, she thinks she knows what Jason wants to say to her) "Normal meeting place, right?"

Jason: "Right."

Sherry: "Okay, then, see ya, B-bye."

Jason starts to laugh as soon as Sherry puts the phone down; his friend feels that he couldn't help but laugh, and is now shaking his head.

"She ain't gonna know what hit her, man."

"Awe, come on, man. You can't be so cruel. She's a babe, mate, and I think you've just destroyed her."

"Ha, who knows what she's up to now, man? She could be doing anything."

"She is getting changed to come and meet you to see what you have to say," Mr. Joshi says from behind them.

"Ah, man. It's you again, Raj. What the heck, man? I tell you, you people get everywhere. You don't know what's going on." Jason smirks again.

Mr. Joshi tries to clear up what the young man has to say. "My name is Rahil Joshi, not Raj, and, my boy, I am standing on my own property, paid for by me. And, yes, I do seem to know what is going on. You have just invited your girlfriend to meet her tonight to tell her, most probably, that you love her and want to pop the question. It couldn't be more simple, no?"

"Ah, man, you're at it again. You haven't got a clue. Do you really think I would invite everyone to listen to me telling her something like that?" Jason is in full swing and doesn't care what he is saying. "You prat, I'm going to finish with her, aha ha ha. You stupid idiot." Rahil Joshi loses his temper. "You kind talk to people with no respect. A young man like you should be getting hitched and buying large houses for your families. Making lots of lovely babies. You goddam loser, you're not like me, I can tell you, you don't even know you're doing it, you seminally sticky individual." Mr Joshi looks up, clasping one hand in the other and prays for a second. "Get off of my property, and I don't ever want to see you in my shop, ever again. Go on, clear off."

"This bit of the street don't belong to your property."

"I tell you, if I wanted to make this into a garage then I'd have to pay for the drop curb. Now clear off." Mr. Joshi talks in his native tongue while shutting the door behind him.

"Come on," Jason's friend says, pulling Jason by the arm, "let's go."

Richie eventually reaches the leisure park; he walks straight towards the cinema, the location he loves.

As he nears the cinema, he is pushing against the fresh air around him. Suddenly he is picked out by the lights coming from inside the cinema and the sign above its doors. The darkening mass of what looms above gives way in an instant to the presence of the lobby area. Richie's confidence waivers slightly, his sense of what he was here to do. He grasps the book more firmly. He finds his proprietorial presence is subordinate to what the cinema gives to its members. He is attracted mainly to the theatre generated inside the cinema itself. Richie's future dreams blot out all his memories of the cinema's signage, of what hangs above him. All that is left is absorbed by the light of the cinema. The light that falls in melded tones that he is sure other members must feel as they enter. With the excitement of coming to see the film mounting, those other feelings

begin to fall upon him once again. His heartbeat races with excitement, at what modern cinema offers personally to him.
He walks into the building.
Richie moves towards the counter for a ticket. He hardly notices the posters in the foyer. He gives the girl behind the till the money, his membership card in his hand.
He suddenly realises that last week's tickets are also in his hand. He places them all in his coat pocket, then walks towards the screens, giving the doorman last week's ticket by mistake. The doorman, Bob, takes it without looking and puts it in his inside pocket.
"All alright, Richie. Another showing. Aye, my boy. I bet you're sure glad they reran this little beauty. So how many times will it be today?"
Richie says, "Twice this week."
"Come on then, where're the tickets for this week? You know you can't fool me!"
Richie gives the older man more tickets out of his pocket, and he clips them with his clippers, giving the slips back to Richie.
"Thanks, Bob. You'll go a long way, one day, you mark my words."
"You excite me, Richie boy. You sure you're not talking about yourself? One of these days, you never know!"
Richie passes the man without looking back.
"You'll be gone one day," Bob shouts after him.
Richie has a broad smile. It an inheritance from his father.
Inside the dark auditorium Richie sits down. He opens his book and starts to read. He is determined in his actions; Richie is under no illusions. He will finish reading this book by the time the film ends. When the film starts he is distracted, but only initially, as he remembers the bird that flew from the wall of his front garden, as he put the milk out the other day. The bird reminded him of this situation every time it called, as it often stirred him to waking.
The film rolls along.
A few people, along with Richie, being seated from the start, are now trying to cope with a couple who move into the seating area. Richie turns and marvels at their arrogance. The couple walks back to the rear section. Richie is drawn to the two men. One waits for the other; the two then walk along the back row. Richie watches them sit.

Immersed in his book, Richie comes to a place where the book falls
in step with the film. He relaxes slightly. He lets the movie run
along.

Held deep within the trance the printed text of the book throws him
into, Richie is disturbed when he hears a crash. Richie marks his
place in the book in his mind. The climax is such a moment of
suspense that Richie's assumptions of what life offers run away with
him. He now feels he is the main character. He is dressed in black,
and Sherry is the lead woman, playing herself in Richie's eyes. He is
besotted with the storyline. He can now see himself on screen.

> Richie wolf whistles, getting up from behind a chair.
> Sherry gasps.
> Richie (dressed in black): "What was that for? Have you
> woken up to what an idiot your boyfriend is?"
> Sherry (dressed as the plantation owner's daughter): "Richie,
> You… You shouldn't have been following me the other day
> at the park."
> Richie: "It didn't occur to me that I was interrupting anything.
> That wouldn't have been tasteful, would it? But don't worry!
> His secret is safe with me."
> Sherry: "Come on, Richie, you're a gentleman. Tell me his
> secret."
> Richie: "Now, miss, I don't rightly understand. Come now,
> you are no lady. A true lady would wait for an eternity before
> asking a question like that!"
> Sherry: "Aah..."
> Richie: "Don't think that I hold doubts or secrets about him.
> What if he wants to finish with you? Or is it that I've seen
> him try it on with other girls, right under your nose?" Richie
> watches himself on screen, and mimes to the words in his
> head.

Richie looks back to his book, and, as the film ticks away, he sits
with an unbecoming smirk, dismissing the guilt he felt. Inside the
corners of his mind, he still feels contempt for what he held back
about how he felt. Speaking with Sherry on-screen helps him see that
Sherry's boyfriend is not the person she thinks he is.

Inside the gloomy cinema, the couple who made their way to the back row are making out. Another man, sitting not too far back from Richie, has been putting him off from reading his book. He feels that he can see him without looking at him. The man obliviously crunches through some more of his popcorn.

All Richie ever really wished for was to be the man Scarlett was really in love with, Ashley Wilkes. But that is the point, isn't it? He will never be with the woman, the one that he loves.

Depression descends upon him, and having had enough of the film and the interruptions, his mind is running riot. Richie closes his book and walks along the row and steps into the aisle.

As he walks up the aisle, out of the screen room, his attitude changes. He is now sure-fire happy that he can go home. It is time to please his mother, by doing some chores for her.

As he is leaving the cinema in a rush, Bob shouts at him.

Richie slows and cautiously walks towards the front of the cinema.

"See ya next showing, Nutta boy. You really know how to catch this one!"

Sherry is standing alone, waiting for her boyfriend at their usual meeting place. She appreciates Jason; he presents himself well. She loves his singular personality when he is with her, the feelings she has when he is with her. Wow, yes, that's it. He makes her get out of the house. Out into this bright new world they have created, so her heart tells her that she should try and make the most of all the many options at hand. Make sense of all the opportunities she can find. That's it, isn't it? It isn't that she's in control. The thing is that this world they all... "We all love." She speaks out loud, trying not to alert the people walking by that she is nervous, looking down while gathering her balance; she feels weak at the knees… could change the future by just simply doing something new. Yes, Jason is her first real boyfriend, but that's it, isn't it? What comes natural to anyone is what is supposed to happen. With love comes marriage, then the next stage would be to have children, but first he has to propose. "This could be the biggest mistake of my life," she whispers to the cold night air. Her breath beats in time with her words. "She's full of herself," a woman says to her boyfriend as they walk by. Sherry thinks for a moment while trying to keep warm: *What am I doing. I don't even know if I love him as much as I should. Words defeat me, they really do. This is all I have ever wanted to do. To get married and have children. Now I'm having second thoughts about just leaving and rethinking exactly who is really meant for me. To be with Jason is great, but he's so immature sometimes, I feel... I feel... I feel like I've dressed up too smart, and should high tail it out of here right now. Oh, there he is...*

Jasonfeels in control, though he wishes that he hadn't laughed when the phone call had stopped. But what did she expect? The game of love was long and treacherous, full of large cracks that you could fall into. There were so many girls out there it was impossible to pick the first girl, or second, or third for that matter, that was truly meant for you; surely? Jason starts to panic as he approaches Sherry; she is even waving at him.

Just smile. Don't wave. Keep your hands in your pockets. Don't worry, I'll keep it short and sweet. Tell her straightaway and then just simply walk away. She's just like everyone else. She can't tell you exactly what you think, or understand exactly what you are thinking.

Jason smiles and put his hand up to say Hi; Sherry stops waving, stands quietly.

Damn it, that was the whole point of this exercise, to get her to come to me. This theme of meeting at the same crazy spot all the time freaks me out. Now if she had come running and kissed me, I would have easily been able to turn the tables and make this look right. Okay, okay, right then, here goes...

The couple come face to face.

"Hi, Sherry."

"Oh, hi, Jason. What brings you here?" Sherry tries not to be too obvious, or too flirtatious.

Jason laughs. "Your always so innocent, aren't you, Sherry? You make me laugh."

"Well, at least I can do something right. Not all us girls are trying to be obvious. Maybe I'm just a lonely woman."

Jason relaxes; Sherry always makes him feel this way. Although along with this, he also feels sad for the first time in weeks, then thinks of the clear-cut place to tell her what he has come here to say. "Come on, Sherry, let's walk." Jason walks Sherry towards the fountain. Sherry laughs and they fall arm in arm and into small talk.

There are a few passers-by near the city fountain. In the distance Jason and Sherry can be seen approaching it.

"Do you remember that day when someone put something in the water to make the water into millions of bubbles?" Jason says.

"Yes, that was the first day we were together. The first day I met you." Sherry's spirit lifts.

"No, that wasn't the first day we met. I'd seen you before, but we just hadn't hit it off."

"When you say hit it off, you mean we didn't kiss until later." Sherry looks stern, but makes sure she doesn't become angry.

Jason laughs to one side, away from Sherry. With the slight outburst out of the way, looking back at Sherry, he carries on. "I'm telling you we did, but, hey, that isn't the point, is it? I have brought you here for a reason. And that reason is to tell you something."

Jason and Sherry stop walking. They near enough to the fountain to hear the splashing water. "You haven't come here to ask me anything, have you Jason?" Sherry says apprehensively

"Actually, no, I haven't, Sherry. I've come here to tell you something." Jason looks down at his hands, touching Sherry's. She pulls away and walks nearer the fountain.

"You boys are all the same; you think you can pull the wool over my eye..." Sherry is stopped mid-flow by Jason's abruptness.

"I'm sorry, Sherry, I can't go on with this relationship. It's never been the same since, since, well, girl, it hasn't been the same since that first day, basically."

Sherry sits on the fountain's rim and puts her hands to her face to try to hold back the tears that are threatening. "Well why did you have to wait till now to tell me, why didn't you tell me when you had the chance a couple of weeks ago? It could have been easier to understand." Sherry is stifled with emotion.

"I would have done, Sherry, but that stupid idiot from your work place, Richie, was following us around." Jason laughs. "I can tell you I tried, sorry."

"You can get the hell out of here," Sherry says from out of her hands. "I was with him the day after. Eating ice creams. It was better than any day we ever had together."

"Okay, okay, it's time I should get back." Jason turns to walk away, then turns back feeling like he's done a good job, but could do better. "Well, see ya then, Sherry."

"Good bye, Jason." Sherry doesn't look up, she's too busy weeping. Richie is smiling all the time he passes shops and different businesses in the city centre until he nears the shopping arcade and the fountain on one of the main streets.

Just at that moment, Sherry's boyfriend passes him by; Richie looks at him.

"Alright, Richie," Sherry's boyfriend says.

Richie glances at him. Though embarrassed, he doesn't let it show, and lowers his head towards his forwards trajectory.

We are approaching the fountain and coming to a standstill. Richie now stands by the arcade.

From afar, Richie can see Sherry, wearing a red dress, sitting some distance away. She is seated on the far side of the fountain. Sherry seems sympathetic to Richie's situation, and feelings, but little does Richie know she is on the verge of crying. Sherry's boyfriend has finally said those words he had to tell her when he left her in the park; her boyfriend has so obviously finished their relationship.

A thought that bubbles inside of Richie then rushes upwards. As he peers at Sherry, Richie remembers the smirk he held earlier on in the cinema. Something binds, making his muscles contort, making something grip on the inside of his throat. He totters forward, and then the idea restrains all his momentum. He regains his powers for a moment, and then becomes weak at the knees. He somehow knows he is not ready for this time of personal triumph. He is indeed not the right person for making moves; his inner self holds him to honour. His brain says, *go and talk to Sherry, and quickly*, but his body won't comply. So Richie holds his book to his chest and dreams of singing.

Sherry by Frankie Valli & The Four Seasons: please be respectful and listen. There is much context, and also content hidden within the text.

Line 1: Richie starts singing, and passers-by join in singing, behind him.
Line 2: Richie sings.

Chorus:
Line 1: Richie sings [The passers-by harmonise]

Line 2: Richie sings.
Harmonising
Line 3: Richie sings. [The passers-by harmonise]
Line 4: Richie sings.

Verse 1:
Line 1: Richie sings. [We can see Richie approach Sherry as she has left the park in the bright sunlight. Things are silent, even though he calls her name. She turns to see him, but quickly walks away]
Line 2: [The passers-by harmonise] Richie sings.
Line 3: [The passers-by harmonise] Richie sings.
Line 4: Richie sings.

Chorus:
Line 1: Richie sings [The passers-by harmonise. Richie is now back singing at the fountain]
Line 2: Richie sings.
Harmonizing
Line 3: Richie sings. [Harmonising. Maji is in place of Mother]
Line 4: Richie sings.

Verse 2:
Line 1: Richie sings.
Line 2: Richie sings. [Richie starts walking up towards Sherry. We now look at Sherry]

Line 3: [The passers-by harmonise] Richie sings.
Line 4: [The passers-by harmonise] Richie sings.
Line 5: Richie sings. [Before Richie reaches her, Sherry, already sobbing, bursts out crying and runs away]
Line 6: Richie is still singing. [Richie is left reaching out in Sherry's direction, head down and looking at his book]

Richie walks away out of eyeshot, still singing, ripping up his tickets as he walks. The people singing in his imagination disperse from behind the fountain.
Sherry is walking to the nearest taxi rank. She is cold. Not to her extremities, but the fresh night air is nipping at her from all sides.

She has disciplined herself enough to have stopped crying and is dabbing at her eyes with some tissue. To stop her mascara from running too much and taking over her face. She nears the taxi rank and waits for a taxi.

Jason, Sherry's old boyfriend, is walking home. He kicks at a random item of rubbish that has been thrown to the floor. It was discarded by someone who has chosen his side of the street to dump whatever they held. Jason is reminiscing about all the good times he and Sherry have shared. He can see them playing in the bubbles at the fountain. He knows Sherry would never have seen them as he saw himself with her. Even when it was going well, Sherry was too busy with what went on in the world, and what was going on around her, to notice his depth of attention.

She is a mighty fine girl to him, and always will be, but she has never understood his addiction; that he needs to see her happy. She only noticed him when he felt she didn't feel him fawning over her. He thinks about all the times he waited for her after work. He waited for her as she talked to all the others as they were leaving. Then, and only then, would she walk towards him. He always got to greet her afterwards, as she flowed into her walk home. He was always comforting her but then left feeling unequal.

Sherry is now in the taxi on her way home. She is reminding herself of all the times she waited for Jason to catch her up, like when he waited for her at work. He is always in two minds. She thinks of him looking at ease in her company, and then scowling at all those, including Richie, who were leaving her place of work. She tried to tell him, but he never understood that she needed all of his attention.

Jason is still on his way home. He is now happier with his side of the situation, of not being Sherry's other half, remembering back to seeing her in the park.

Jason greets her and walks her to the gate to enter the park on a sunny day. Perhaps it would be best if Richie didn't follow them, but he's already here; perhaps she would be better off with Richie rather than him: she does work with him.

Sherry, leaning forwards, tells the taxi driver to turn down onto the street where she lives. She, too, remembers the day at the park and remembers two people sailing a boat that day, away from all the others. She was hugging Jason and then turning back the way they had come. To then, finally, see Richie at the entrance once again; he had a book in his hand.

She had shouted, hello, but it had come out louder than she meant it to. Then Jason had laughed. It wasn't fair. He had friends, but would not include her in his relationship with them. He was always leaving her alone and doing what he wanted with them while she sat on her own.

Walking into his home, Richie steps over a letter that the postman has dropped to the floor through the letter box. It lies on the rug. Seeing it, he puts it onto the windowsill, at the bottom of the stairs. Without haste, he wanders up the stairs. He is leaving the household's mismatch of wallpaper, which decorates the hall and stairway. He shuts his bedroom door.

In his bedroom, he is thankful but sad all at the same time about Sherry. His feelings are betraying him. He thinks about what Sid the Security guard said to him. This morning after he was splashed by the passing car. Yes, it is true. Richie agrees with the insinuation. He was 'gone before you got there.' Why didn't he comfort Sherry tonight?

He gets undressed, forgetting about doing the chores for his mother. They are for everybody else now, and so he picks up his book and gets into bed, and starts to read the night away.

Flicking through the pages of the book, Richie can see himself standing outside the cafe Sherry and her boyfriend frequented. Sherry is looking away from Jason; he is holding the hand of another girl, standing beside the counter.

Sherry gets out of her taxi and pays the man through his side window. Her ex-boyfriend is putting the key into his front door. Jason stands, the front door ajar, and turns to look at the night sky. Sherry walks into her home, which she shares with her mother and father. She shuts the door and stands with her hands on her face.

You Win Again by the Bee Gees: please be respectful and listen. There is much context and also content hidden within the text.

Verse 1:
Line 1: Jason sings. [He is standing with his friends secretly looking at Sherry as she sits at a table. She does not want to be with him]
Line 2: Jason sings.

Line 3: Sherry sings. [Sherry takes her hands from her face and sings]
Line 4: Jason and Sherry are singing.
Line 5: both sing.
Line 6: both sing.
Line 7: Richie sings. [Richie remembers too. Though he has no view of them. He is singing in his bed]
Line 8: Richie sings.
Line 9: Richie sings.
Line 10: Richie sings.
Line 11: Sherry and Jason sing.
Line 12: All three sing.

Verse 2:
Line 1: Sherry's dad, walking in from their living quarters, sings. [Sherry's mother is following]
Line 2: Sherry's mother sings.
Line 3: All five sing. [Sherry can see her boyfriend singing. Richie is still in his room]
Line 4: Sherry's dad sings [Comforting Sherry. He walks her past her mother and into the living room]
Line 5: Sherry's dad still sings.
Line 6: Sherry's mother and father sing. [There are new and old family photos spread around the room]
Line 7: Richie sings. [Richie is in bed]
Line 8: All sing.
Line 9: All sing.
Line 10: All sing.
Line 11: Sherry's mother sings.
Line 12: Sherry's mother sings.

Verse 3:
Line 1: Sherry's dad sings.
Line 2: Jason sings.
Line 3: Richie sings. [Richie is in bed]
Line 4: All three sing.
Line 5: Sherry's mother sings.
Line 6: Sherry sings.

Verse 4:
Line 1: Jason sings.
Line 2: Jason sings.
Line 3: Jason sings.
Line 4: Jason sings.

Verse 5:
Line 1: Sherry's dad sings. [Her father is holding her by the shoulders]
Line 2: Sherry's mother and father sing.
Line 3: Sherry's mother and father sing.
Line 4: Sherry's mother and father sing.
Line 5: Sherry's mother and father sing.
Line 6: Sherry's mother and father sing.
Line 7: Sherry's mother and father sing.
Line 8: Sherry's mother and father sing.
Line 9: Sherry's mother and father sing.
Line 10: Sherry joins in with her parents.
Line 11: Sherry sings. [Sherry shakes her father's arms from her]
Line 12: Sherry sings.

Verse 6:
Line 1: Jason sings. [Jason turns and walks into his house]
Line 2: Jason sings.
Line 3: Jason sings.
Line 4: Jason sings.
Line 5: Sherry sings.
Line 6: Richie sings. [Richie is in bed]
Line 7: Sherry sings.
Line 8: Richie sings. [Richie is in bed]
Line 9: Sherry sings.
Line 10: Jason and Sherry sing.
Line 11: Jason and Sherry sing.
Line 12: Richie sings.
Line 13: Richie sings.
Line 14: Richie sings.
Line 15: Sherry's mother and father sing.
Line 16: Sherry's mother and father sing.
Line 17: Sherry's mother and father sing.

Line 18: Sherry's mother and father sing.
Line 19: Sherry's mother and father sing.

Verse 7:
Line 1: Sherry's mother and father sing. [There are new and old family photos spread around the room]
Line 2: Sherry's mother and father sing.
Line 3: Sherry's mother and father sing.
Line 4: Sherry sings.
Line 5: Sherry's mother and father sing.
Line 6: Sherry's mother and father sing.
Line 7: Sherry's mother and father sing.
Line 8: Sherry sings.
Line 9: Sherry's mother and father sing.
Line 10: Sherry's mother and father sing.
Line 11: Sherry sings.
Line 12: Sherry sings. [Richie is in bed]
Line 13: Sherry sings.

We go back down the stairs, away from Richie's bedroom, and zoom out through the Gyndall front door. We can still see the stairs, and closed door of Richie's room. The front and side walls of the house have dissolved, revealing the inside of Richie's home.
Richie's grandpa and his maji's maji are in their living space. We swing around to the right and can see Richie tucked up in bed. His grandpa and grandma look snug, ensconced in the living room. His maji and father are standing in the kitchen.
Everything is perfect as we move away into the stars.

Act Four: Behind Closed Doors.

Lady Rosetta is at home speaking to someone on the phone; it is her accountant. It is early morning and still dark outside. "Yes, hello, Malcolm," she pauses for Malcolm to reply. "Yes, sorry Malcolm. I do know what time it is. Yes, it's still dark outside, but you work for me, and I need your services."
"Just hold on a minute Lady Rosetta. I need to move rooms."
"I appreciate that, young man."
Malcolm ends the call on the premise he will call her back.

Malcolm rises from the double bed he shares with his wife, still holding the phone in his hand. "Oh Malcolm, what is it?" His wife turns towards him, puts her hand out but touches the phone instead of his hand. "Oh, Malcolm, what's going on?"

Malcolm returns her advances by telling her the truth. "I have a customer on the phone, darling. She's a bit potty, but she's loaded, or was. Quite influential when she wants to be."

"Well, darling, as long as you come back to bed everything will be…"

Malcolm doesn't give his wife a chance to finish her advances. "I'm sorry honey, but Lady Rosetta never calls unless it's urgent. And so I doubt that I'll get the chance to get back till a lot later in the day. Can you tell my clients today that I won't be about until tomorrow? Thanks, sweetheart."

"Yes, tomorrow, I'll tell them," Malcolm gets out of bed and walks to the landing. Just as he shuts the door, a call of, "Tomorrow?" comes from his bedroom.

Malcolm calls Lady Rosetta.

"Sorry, Lady Rosetta. How can I help you? I suppose the normal requirements again. Go to the boys and let them sign some money over."

"No, Malcolm, and I'm not that potty today. I don't feel I need taking care of by my faithful sons today. We will be marching in on them like Christian Solders today, Malcolm. I feel it is about time I let them know just who gave them that money they made their little going concern from."

"Yes, madam, about time too."

"I'll meet you at the bank at about seven, Malcolm."

"Okay, sure, Lady Rosetta, I'll see you then."

Lady Rosetta walks out of the front of the house, shutting the door behind her. Walking down the stairs to the front of the house she walks out onto the drive, where an old Range Rover is waiting for her. She had driven it round from the back of the house last night. Getting in, she starts the vehicle, puts her seatbelt on, and drives off through her grounds. She drives out onto the road.

Malcolm, Lady Rosetta's accountant, is making coffee in his kitchen. He finishes pouring the cafetière into the mug. Places a spoon of sugar into the black liquid and stirs it with the spoon. He is still in his pyjamas. The kitchen door opens. He looks at his wife as she walks in.

"Remind me, Lady Rosetta?" she says.

"Oh, Lady Rosetta has been around since the start of time."

"With the business, yes, I remember her now. She hardly ever calls. Pays her bills as quickly as anyone."

"Well," Malcolm says, "that isn't quite right. I pay her bills for her from the account she has with me. She's got a stack of money, but never touches it. She thinks her boys should be looking after her more than they do. But they don't. Her husband died, oh, about twenty years ago. Left her the whole estate. She left herself two million, put the rest away so no one could touch it, and told the boys that they had been given a million each from her husband's trust in the will. What she didn't tell them is that it was actually her who gave them the money. I have papers that the boys signed to release the money into their names from all those years ago. She always said if they don't look after her she would rain down her tyranny against them, ha ha." Malcolm is chuckling to himself. His wife laughs with him.

"Crafty cow," she says.

"Ha, yes, that's Lady Rosetta alright." Malcolm kisses his wife.

The Security Guard of the bank, Sid, lives not too far from his place of work. We see him watching the last of the news, before he gets up, turning the TV off with the remote. He heads towards the kitchen. He picks up his sandwiches, which are in a box in the kitchen, and heads to his front door. From the door he walks up the hall and checks to see if he has his keys on him. He pulls them from his trouser pocket and places them in his blazer. He opens the door, and walks into the morning air. He feels it is going to be a fresher day than the day before, and pats his keys before shutting the door behind him. He walks to the end of the front garden, opens the gate that sits at the end of a slightly overgrown hedge, and walks to work.

We approach a large house, it is a new build, and has a large driveway where three Jaguars sit. All are sporty black models. It is the Partners' house, and it sits on the edge of the city. The front door opens and all three leave the house. The middle first, he is humming, the younger second, he now starts to hum the same tune. The oldest leaves last, turns and locks the door, and then starts to hum in time with his brothers. As they all exit they get into each of their cars respectively. As each shuts their doors one after another they reverse from the drive, and slowly drive down the road that will take them to the bank that they own. They catch up with each other with a burst of speed, and start their travels, forming a convoy to travel the distance to their car park and their working day.

An old, beaten-up Range Rover pulls into a car park in the middle of Leicester. You would think the owner looks similarly shabby as the vehicle. But through the crystal clear windscreen the owner is Lady Rosetta. She is looking her normal beautiful self. She is dressed in a neat blue-grey dress suit, and leather overcoat. She drives around the car park until she finds a space that she can easily drive into. Turning off the ignition she sits quietly for a second, then says, "Now we'll see, boys. I'll wait until I feel it necessary to move." She looks at her watch, just to reassure herself. She knows what time Sid gets to the bank. She feels she has plenty of time, enough to just relax and get her plan in order.

The Partners' cars are waiting at a red light in the city, all three in a row. The light turns green, and the vehicles pull away from the lights one after the other.

Sid is walking to work. He is whistling a tune.

Richie is asleep as his mother, Aarzoo, enters his bedroom and takes his suit from his wardrobe. He wakes as he hears his maji call him from his well-earned rest. "Richie? Richie, I'm just taking your suit to iron it."

"Whaat? No, maan, I have an important meeting today at work."

"Well that's tough, you didn't give me it when you came in, so I need to do it now."

"No, maan, plea…" The door shuts behind Aarzoo.

Richie sits on the side of his bed; yawning, he reaches to turn off his alarm clock: he doesn't realise he hasn't quite done the job correctly. "Ah, what do I do now?" He hesitates. He looks at the pile of books on the side and takes the book he placed there last night from off of the top space. He begins to read.

The book explains the passage of life on a plantation in the southern states of America, of a young woman, Scarlett O'Hara. She is deeply troubled in life with the turmoil of the South's fight, the Confederate Army that left the Union, against The United States Army. There is little food and many mouths to feed, but such is the situation of hard-working people who grow strength into their crops. These are tended to by the people that live on the grounds of the plantation, the black slaves of the South. Scarlett is consumed by her relationships with Rhett Butler and a man called Ashley Wilkes, who will fight for the South. Richie can see the struggle against the Partners of the bank he works at; they are pitted against their employees; typically they are similar to the plantation owners, Scarlett's family, but with one difference. Every time he tries to imagine his office colleagues in the fight against them, the office staff are wearing the uniform of the Confederate Army, and the partners have somehow gotten themselves into the uniforms of The United States Army. He can see them in a pitched battle with only the partners winning. *Maybe they do all hate me, and it is the partners that want to look after me. No, that is wrong, what is wrong with me?* he thinks, then puts the book down by his side. The book doesn't leave his hand as he remembers a scene from last night.

Ashley Wilkes is in the stable with Scarlett. There is music, an orchestra playing dramatic tones:

> Richie as Ashley Wilkes: "Why do you understand what I'm going through, you were in tears last night? Unless you're comprehending our futures together, so what if we're apart? You don't ever see what a state I can get into over you, as I see every time I see you."
> Sherry as Scarlett O'Hara: "State, state, oh Richie, what state do you presume I should be in to understand you when I am not you? Especially when I don't know how you feel. You know I couldn't stand staying there another minute. I couldn't stand it for another moment. That fountain haunts me, Richie, I needed to get away. You know, Richie, you fancy Charu more than you know. Maybe more than me, yet you want to run away. Oh, Richie, I wish you understood your waking emotions more than you do. Tell me what you want more..."
> Ashley and Scarlett fall into a dramatic embrace and look deep into each other's eyes.

Richie is disturbed from his private moments and visions by his father shouting up the stairs. "Richie, Richie. You okay? Richie, your mother has told me to tell you your trousers are ready to put on!"

"Hu, sorry, what?"

"Your trousers, they're ready for you to put them back on."

Richie looks down at himself, still only dressed in his underpants. He shakes his head and tries to wake completely. He rubs his forearm across his forehead; he is still holding the open book.

"Okay, pita jee, I'll just put a clean T-shirt on and I'll be down." Richie stands to fetch a clean white T-shirt.

Daivey is worried his son may have slipped back into restful sleep. "Bachcha, bachcha? Are you still there? Well, I do not care, you do perplex me, you really do. What do you get up to in your spare time? Listen, your mother and I, we think you really need to start growing up and get prepared for living, son." Daivey is worried his son may have slipped back, yet again, into restful sleep.

"Don't worry, pita jee, I'm not complaining about how late this is all going to make me for work. I'll just put the one complaint of mine on hold when I get there." Richie was a little upset still with being woken early, only to be then told he had no clothes to get into.

Richie's pita jee is trying not to be too amused as he sees his bachcha's bedroom door start to open; he walks to the kitchen knowing his in-laws are laughing to themselves in the living room. Richie is halfway down the stairs when his alarm goes off in his bedroom. He turns and runs back up to the top step and into his bedroom. He turns off his alarm, and re-evaluating, picks up his book he is deep into from off of the side. "Richie? Richie, can you hear me. Don't go back to bed, you stupid bachcha. You'll be late." Daivey is acting on impulse; Aarzoo is in fits of giggles as she is pressing the shirt she took from Richie's wardrobe. Richie is stomping down the stairs, looking at his father. Daivey is trying not to smile, but has a soft smug grin. Daivey gives up the silence first. "So, what's that, Richie, work? I thought your mother and my secret would be safe for longer than that."

Richie rubs his face, standing at the bottom set of stairs. "Ah, now I see. You've done this to me to teach me a lesson."

"What we older generation teach are always lessons," Richie's maan calls from the kitchen.

Daivey and Kuvan are standing in the hall by the living room doorway. Kuvan is slightly inside the living room and stands back as Richie squeezes by, then past his father.

His mother is still pressing his shirt and he stands behind the ironing board in the kitchen. We can just see him past his mother's outline as she finishes the last of the pressing.

"You shouldn't take it yet, bachcha," she tells him as he grabs it, and we find ourselves beside the pair, at the end of the ironing board. So Richie places his book on the side, out of the melee that he feels he is stuck fast within.

"Tell me, maji, how did you all know I was getting up early this morning?" Richie asks.

His mother looks up from the ironing board; steam comes out from the iron. "We didn't, bachcha, we didn't." The iron is placed back on Richie's shirt. Richie's pita jee fluffs his hair from behind. Then Richie's maan passes him his shirt. He puts it on, and then his trousers. Tucks his shirt into his trousers, slips his waistcoat on, and puts his slip-on shoes on. Richie's mother now walks past and takes Richie's jacket from the back of the kitchen door, where his ironed trousers and waistcoat had been. She is waiting for him to get dressed. Turning, she walks back to the ironing board.

Sid has reached the back door of the bank. He opens the security door and walks in, right on time. He is instantly aware that the light is on in the passage. That is strange, he thinks, he is sure he turned that off last night. Before he opens the inner security door he listens and stops whistling; the alarm is not signalling to him that it will go off soon, if he does not press the code and reset the alarm itself. He opens the inner door; it opens without him unlocking it. He is left at the entrance with the key offered to the door lock, unused. He walks in, shuts the inner door, takes off his hat and scratches his bald head. "Oh, well, I wish those idiot brothers would tell me when they arrive early." He starts to turn some of the lights on that haven't been turned on and opens the bank properly, before going upstairs to have a cup of tea at the drinking station. Like most mornings he has to fill the kettle.

The partners are walking from the car park to their very own bank, or so they think.

"Maan, I have not got time for this. I did not set my alarm with enough time to do all this," Richie says, still waiting for his jacket to be finished ironing.

68

Richie's mother half looks up with one eye half closed and says, "Just take your curd from the side and eat it like a good bachcha." Richie reaches for the curd and sighs.

The three partners walk into their bank through the back door. They had to unlock it to get in; it locks automatically every time it shuts. Walking through the bank they get to the door that leads upstairs. They punch the code into it and open it. Sid is waiting for them as they do so, on the other side.

The door opens.

"Thanks, lads. I take back all that I said about you." The partners wait for him to walk through and then all file upstairs.

Sid turns as the door shuts on the self-shutting bar at the top. "That's odd," he says. "Oh, well, nothing out of order." He walks to the door to wait for the employees with his cup of tea.

"What are you doing about your relationships with girls, Richie?" Aarzoo asks.

"Ah, now you have reminded me. That nice Mr. Joshi, father, your friend, as he told me. Told me you had been asking him about me. Questioning him about another job. Well I am going to tell you not even a second job will get me to get married to Charu." Richie's mother turns his jacket to steam the arms individually.

"Well it might help," Aarzoo says.

"Yes, no harm in trying. The more money we accrue, the more likely the Patijna's will look on you as the right person to be taking Charu's hand," Daivey says.

"You're not listening to me, Pita jee. I do not want to get married to Charu. I know this, and work this out more and more every day," Richie says.

"Nonsense, Richie, you have been after her ever since you kissed her on the beach that year when you were a child. We can all tell." Aarzoo looks exultant.

"Yes this is true." Richie's grandma walks from the living room with the photo of him kissing Charu in her hands. "If it is not true, why? Who else would you be in love with?" Kuvan is now frowning. "Not some simple woman from off of the street, Richie, we all know you are better than that."

Richie rolls his eyes and says the same words as he always says when he has the same conversation with his family. "I am, am I?" He feels deflated. The conversation becomes more heated this time than ever before. "You ought to be careful of who you hang around with in in the park as well, Richie. We've all heard that you go there too much and read. You could be making more of your life, Richie; any work is good work when it comes to family and friends." All goes quiet, Aarzoo carries on steaming her bachcha's jacket.

Richie's mother has no idea what her mother is going on about or what she is going to say next. She is worried about where this whole conversation is going. Luckily for Aarzoo her Maji walks back into the living room.

The three suited partners walk into the boardroom, and turn the lights on. Sid never comes in here at the best of times. Lady Rosetta is illuminated by the lights above her. "Hello, boys, nice to see you again. What have you got planned today, you're early."

The middle Partner, the first to walk into the boardroom, speaks first. "We have a meeting today, Mumsy."

The younger slaps him on the arm in frustration. "No we haven't, Mumsy. Nothing is going on."

The older Partner squeezes in behind them. "We haven't gotten your money yet, Mumsy, you will have to wait."

Lady Rosetta speaks softly to her oldest son. "This meeting, can anyone from the family join in?"

"Not really, Mumsy, we…" The oldest partner is hesitant. "We need to speak." He pulls his brothers with him over to the other side of the boardroom. They fall into a huddle. There are whispers and stern looks. "What do you want to listen for, Mumsy?"

Lady Rosetta is smiling to herself while looking away from her boys. She looks at her watch and uncrosses her legs. "Well, funny you should say that. It's ten to seven and all will be revealed soon."

"Yes, so the park is out of bounds from now on. Here's your jacket," she says. She is just glad she sided with her mother. Thinking it was a good plan to stop him writing books. "You'll never get what you want from those books, Richie, admit it!"

As Richie puts the jacket on, his grandma walks up behind him with her husband's empty fruit bowl now in her hands.

We now look at maji's maji. "Look at my young bachcha ladaka. You are so handsome, and I can tell that you are in love, bachcha."

Kuvan pulls up the back of his lapel. "Yes, so stay out of the park, as

70

your maji says." Richie thinks she has turned it down. As this is happening, we move behind Richie's grandma, as Richie's mother exclaims, "Maji, I think we have come to an agreement. Richie needs another job to take his mind off everything."
"Agreed!" Kuvan says.
Richie leans to the right and picks something up. It is his book, and, kissing his grandma, he moves quickly to the door. Outside, Richie closes the door, puts the book in his pocket, and then runs for the bus.

There is a knock on the boardroom door. "Ah," Lady Rosetta says, trying to leave her seat to get to the door. The silence is broken as the youngest partner hastily runs to answer the door. There is Malcolm, dressed in his dark, but vibrant, blue suit. "Ah, lads, nice to see you." He walks into the boardroom.
"Who are you?" The middle partner says, as Malcolm walks straight past his brother to sit on the other side of Lady Rosetta at the boardroom table.
"Yes, out with it, man," orders the older partner.
"He's my accountant, boys, and he holds some vital information that you need to see before we have this little meeting of ours this morning. And I know exactly what you are doing with my money."
Malcolm, Lady Rosetta's accountant, pulls out a sheet of paper and a folder from his leather bag.
"But that can't be so," the older says.
"How can it be so?" the middle says.
The younger walks forwards and picks up the sheet of paper the accountant has placed on the table. He reads. "It… It looks like it is so!"

On the top deck of the bus, things are the same as every day, though Richie is panting. We look from the front of the bus to the back. All the people are sitting in the same seats. We now look at Richie alone. He takes his book from his pocket. You can see him do it in one swift motion, right hand to left-hand pocket. All helped by the seat, and the speed of the bus.
He starts reading.
In fast-forward motion, people get up and leave. Richie slowly turns the pages. Looking at him, he is in his perfect moment again. Then,

we look from the front of the bus. We see there is only him, along with another girl. She is sitting behind him, on the opposite side of the bus.

As she gets up to leave, the girl taps Richie on the right shoulder, and says, "I think you missed your stop, Richie."

"Oh, no!" He tells himself off, and follows her off of the bus.

He runs to the bank.

The office is full from all the early arrivals; the staff want to ensure they are in time for the office meeting. Only some have mugs of tea, those that dared, as most are thinking that they need to ensure the meeting is over before making themselves comfortable.

Inside the boardroom Lady Rosetta is talking to her sons.

"So, boys, you get the gist of things. I put this clause into the contract that you didn't read when you signed. To ensure that our family home wouldn't fall into the wrong hands. I'm sure you can see that if you had been the loving children you all started off in life as being, you wouldn't have this problem."

"Yes but, Mumsy..." her older son.

"It's not fair, Mumsy." Her middle son.

"So, yes, we see, Mumsy." Her youngest. At this point there is a knock at the door. The oldest partner walks over and opens it.

Jacky is standing there.

"We're all here, apart from one, sir. I think it would be best to start proceedings. When you are ready, that is."

The partner says, "Okay, Jacky," and shuts the door.

Lady Rosetta hears everything. "So what proceedings are these, my currently employed sons?"

The three partners go into overdrive. "Oh, Mumsy, there's no..." Her older son.

"Yes no need to be..." Her middle.

"Like that, at all." Her youngest.

They speak together, "It's private."

Lady Rosetta gets annoyed. "Private, my arse. Now tell me what's going on, and I might just leave you alone."

"Well, Mumsy," the youngest son says. "We are having a meeting to try and brainstorm how to revise our working ethics to try and claw back the sixty thousand we are having to outlay to you, Mumsy." All three are now facing their mother.

"Okay, then, that was easy, wasn't it? Just tell mumsy-wumsy the truth and all will be fine. Well, come on then, get out there." The three sons of Lady Rosetta smile and walk to the door. Lady Rosetta climbs out of her chair and follows.

Her oldest son notices something is aerie. He is at the rear of the three. "But, Mumsy, what are you doing? You said..."

"I said I might leave you alone," Lady Rosetta replied. "But it's my sixty thousand and your jobs at stake. I want to see how you work together and see what plans you have in place." From behind Lady Rosetta her three sons turn to walk out of the boardroom door, and Lady Rosetta follows. As the door opens, Lady Rosetta is half way across the room. She turns to Malcolm, who has been quietly sitting in the chair on the other side of the boardroom table. "Malcolm, get the new arrangements sorted, and please have the papers ready to be signed when we return. These new arrangements will need to be implemented as soon as possible."

"Yes, ma'am," the accountant replies.

The door shuts behind Lady Rosetta.

Inside the office the three partners are standing just in front of the boardroom door in full view of all their employees. Then Lady Rosetta walks in behind them. The office staff chatter amongst themselves until the oldest partner speaks, "Quiet, please; quiet." The office falls quiet. "Now everyone's here apart from one. Am I correct?"

"Yes, sir." The call rebounds back from the office staff.

"And who may we ask is that?" The youngest asks.

"It's our stock trader analyst, sir. He's sometimes later than most. He writes the company growth chart, and works out what we should be making each month, sir," Jacky says.

Geoff was chomping at the bit to drop his name. "Ri..."

Sherry butted in before Geoff could finish. "I'm sure he'll be here soon, sirs."

Lady Rosetta hurries the proceedings onwards. "Come on now boys, don't dither. Get on with things."

The office staff looked to each other for support. They have never seen the partners not in control of everything that happened in and around the office, or the bank as a whole for that matter.

"Okay, okay," the middle partner says. "Now, what we need is a way to claw back some money. Our stock and readily available funds are not quite as we planned at this time of the accounting year. I'm sure you're well aware the end of the year is coming up in some months, and we are down in profit. As we have been for some time, we have thought about how to fix this problem, and the plan we have come up with is to cut down on our office staff."

There are gasps and much chatter.

"Okay, okay," the middle partner says. "Now this isn't set in stone at this moment, so if you can think of anything, I say again, anything, just let us know and we will talk about the idea to see if it is a good way of making at least some appropriable profit for our company."

"Thank you," the youngest says.

There is a hush then some more chatter as the three partners smile at one another; then Lady Rosetta breaks their silence. "You're going to let them speak first. Come on, boys; let them at least ask you a few questions on who you are thinking of casting aside!"

There are calls of 'yes, please," and 'can we, great,' from the crowd of office staff. The three sons of Lady Rosetta try to calm the situation down. "Now, now, now. Come along. Yes, keep calm. Who wants to go first?"

Still running, Richie nears the bank.

After seeing Sherry that night, he thought long and hard in his bedroom about writing a book. He is sure he's had enough of working at the partners' HQ for conserving money. As he slows down, his brown suit returns to shape around him, then slowly, he hunches over his knees to catch his breath.

The security guard is already opening the door.

"Thanks, Sid," Richie pants, as he lifts his head from looking at his feet.

"No need to thank me, Richie. The bank's ready for opening. I told you that you were gone the other day, pal. You're for it now. Hahaha."

Richie squeezes by the man. Opens the door, after punching in the code —which will lead him upstairs.

Upstairs, Richie instantly sees that the Partners are here early this morning. They are having a meeting with the other office staff. They go quiet for a moment. They seem to be in mid-flow of a conversation with one of the girls.

"Ah, what's your name?" the grey-haired eldest asks.

"Richie, sir!" Jacky replies.

"Richie!" The three partners look at each other, turn, and then reply together.
Richie sees his chance, and promptly replies, "Yes, Richie, sirs, Sorry I am late. It's just that I got splashed by a puddle the other morning."
"Splashed by a puddle?" The youngest Partner repeats after him. "Rather inconsiderate of the puddle, don't you think?"
"Yes." The middle-aged Partner and the oldest of the three speak together. Together now, the trio, synchronising their speech, say, "Don't you think!"
The three Partners then talk to one another in whispers. Richie feels left out in the cold as the rest of the office staff turn to look at him. "Yes, sirs, so now my mother presses my suit for good luck every morning. That is why I am late. Look, I don't have to-" Richie cuts himself off as Sherry glares at him. "So, sorry I'm late sirs, that's all." He walks forwards to join the huddle of employees.
"Yes, so, anyway, let the money rain upon us," the middle Partner finishes as all three Partners turn towards the boardroom and glare at their mother.
"Like Richie's puddle!" Geoff adds.
All the people gathered laugh, "Right, back to work," the oldest son of Lady Rosetta says.
They are all now turning towards their desks. Releasing Richie from his embarrassment, they hold back their giggles; some cover their mouths, intending not to let the Partners hear, although the three masters of money can hear the funny side of Geoff's comment. Lady Rosetta stares at what happens as all the office staff make their way back to their desks, then turns and lets her three boys follow her into the boardroom.
Richie is left standing alone.
Standing to one side, Sherry purses her lips, letting a slight frown run across her forehead. Then she takes a glance towards her desk. She looks past her computer screen, spying the back of her seat, and notices her jacket hanging on it.
The office darkens, leaving Sherry and Richie in one shared light. Richie's mind floats back to the book he is immersed in. The one he was reading on the bus.

Richie's face is sporting a moustache in no way similar to that of the character he saw himself play on the big screen. He looks towards Sherry.

We now see Sherry. She is dressed in Victorian clothing again, as she walks in step with Richie.

Sherry is now standing in front of Richie once again and looks directly at him. He is dressed similarly, in Victorian clothing, in his case a black suit. Sherry looks him straight in the eyes. "What shall I do now? Come on, Richie! What shall I do now? Where do I go from here?" she asks.

"Don't look at me like that, Sherry. I could have told you what was happening and frankly... oh my dear, damn!" Richie's reply is garbled.

Richie was just about to say the line he knew so well from the book and the film. He realises his mistake, and frantically pulls the moustache off his top lip with his left hand.

Richie is sulking now, a hand over his mouth. We know it is because the moustache hurt him, as he pulled, though Richie is more in shock from nearly using the character's words, feeling that if he had, he would never be with Sherry.

Sherry walks away, abandoning Richie with a sultry air, leaving Richie in ravaged guilt.

So now the lights all come back on, with a flicker.

Richie is not in the mood. "What the hell was that all about, Geoff?" Richie calls out. He is shifting the disturbance away from Sherry, as Geoff is returning to his seat.

Sherry holds out her arm. She is back in her daily uniform, and she abruptly stands in in front of Richie, in between him and Geoff, stopping Richie from moving in.

"Now is not the time, Richie," Sherry tells him; she approaches him and puts her arms around Richie's neck. But she simply turns down his collar.

"When is the time?" Richie asks. "Look, I was there at the fountain, I know,"

Richie stops; he's said too much.

"You know nothing about timing, do you, Richie?" Sherry turns back towards her desk.

"But I understand now about that day in the Park when you were with Jason." Richie stops himself from saying anything more. He bites down on his lip.

"It was all your fault," Sherry says, pulling a hanky from her pocket, and then crying into it.

Richie doesn't understand that Sherry didn't mean her insinuation, it is just a reaction. In his mind she is still embracing him, so he can comfort her. Richie sullenly watches Sherry, frustrated, as she walks back to her desk. Jacky, aggrieved, gets up briskly from her desk. Sherry moves around the group of tables, laid out in a circle. Jacky puts her arm around her.

Geoff leans back on his seat and turns his head to speak.

"See what you've done now, boy? You are an inconsiderate person; no feelings whatsoever."

"You'll never know." Richie's sarcasm escapes; he goes to make himself a brew.

When Sherry eventually stops crying, Richie puts sugar into his cup of tea. Now all seems back to normal.

By the time Richie sits down again, and turned his computer on, he feels the first dread of his mixed emotions. Last night's intoxication of relaxation, brought on to calm him from his imaginations. Then, of course, all his feelings being brought together by him seeing Sherry at the fountain. Sherry's lousy luck made him understand that things could be okay. Today's weight of realism casts a shadow upon his mentality, and the rest of this day's working hours leave him with a fuzzy head.

He mulls over his mind all the things that have happened since he saw Sherry at the fountain. He taps at his keyboard. Looking at his screen-saver brings back precisely the feeling he has been yearning for; a feeling, at last, of inspiration. Now is the time to sort things out.

This job isn't right for him. The people are good, but he feels sicker than he's ever felt before. He knows he should never have approached Sherry today, especially while he was not thinking clearly. All the shouting should have been done and dusted last night at the fountain. Why has he not asked Sherry to be with him, then? His silence lets in more noise from around him. Why can't he bring himself to invite Sherry to the cinema? It's simple, really. The book he is reading is his true retro romance and authentic to his love. It won't be on forever. It is only a one-month one-off rerunning of a classic flick. Then dread rises again inside him. To still be somehow playing with Sherry's emotions cuts deep into his heart. His nausea clears. He assimilates everything that's on his mind. He knows what he has to do next. So instead of deciding to ask what could possibly make the money rain on them all, he ascertains once again that this is not the job for him.

Richie is weary about his escalating situation. So, easing his mind, he ponders what questions he should be asking the rest of the employees about the minutes of the meeting from this morning. Suddenly, while he's wondering if he should just throw the towel in on his job, a reel of words starts cascading from the top of his computers screen as he looks at it. 'Don't ask questions, just do,' it says. Then there is another row of falling letters. 'They want one of us out, Richie, and maybe it's you.'

"Do what?" he screams. "What am I supposed to do? Tell me." Everyone turns to look at him. "I'm sorry, Sherry, but I'm just a flake."

"No, Richie," Sherry replies.

"No, Richie, she's fine with me. Okay, you are a flaky personality, but we all live with that, okay." Jacky tries to console her friend.

"Now, look; if you think ..." Sherry leaks these words through her handkerchief while looking at Jacky. Sherry does not take a blind bit of notice of Richie, because she knows more of Jacky's inner workings. Jacky just looks on; she knows nothing of Richie's thoughts.

"No, I don't think, Sherry. I know exactly what to do," Richie says, but Jacky cuts off the words he is trying to summon.

"I think you two ought to cool things right now. Think about what you are doing before you disrupt this whole place; we have to get on here. You must stop this right now." Keyboards and chatter resume around the office.

Richie tries again. "Ah, listen, Jacky, I didn't mean-" but he is stopped by looking into Jacky's dominant eyes.

Geoff butts in. "Yeah, Richie, it's all taken care of now, leave it!" Geoff changes tack, says something about how weird things look on his computer screen. "This is weird. I don't know ..." He holds the thumb of his right hand to his chin and the index finger to his lips. He goes quiet.

All the on-looking office staff go about what they were doing once more. Some who were listening now look back to their screens; some others stand to make brews.

A hush comes over the office, as everyone's accumulated emotions collect around Jacky. Well, that's the way Richie sees it. "Yes, Richie, what's your problem now?" Jacky says. Sherry straightens up after adjusting her shoe.

"I want to give up my job, and this morning? Well, this morning has sealed that feeling within the casket. The casket which holds the brew that has been bubbling away inside of me for a long time. Longer for others, I imagine; I want to write for a living. I'm going to see the Partners, right now."

Richie pushes back his chair and stands up.

Sherry instinctively kicks Geoff.

The office lights dim everywhere, apart from around Geoff; he is in the spotlight now.

Geoff opens his mouth to speak. Standing, he says, "Okay... Okay... So ..."

Don't Rock the Boat by the Ruby Brothers: please be respectful and listen. There is much context, and also content hidden within the text.

Line 1: Geoff sings alone as the music kicks in.
Line 2: all of the office staff stand in time with Geoff, plus Richie. All sing.
Line 3: [Harmonising] all sing.

Line 4: all sing, with Geoff taking the lead.
Line 5: [Harmonising] Geoff sings.
Harmonising

Verse 1:
Line 1: Geoff still leads.
Line 2: Geoff still leads.
Line 3: Geoff still leads.
Line 4: Geoff still leads.

Verse 2:

Line 1: Jacky sings. [She is looking intensely at Richie]
Line 2: Jacky sings.
Line 3: Jacky sings.
Line 4: Jacky sings.

Chorus:
Line 1: all sing. [Different people around the office singing different lines]
Line 2: [Harmonising] all sing.
Line 3: [Harmonising] all sing.
Harmonising

Verse 3:
Line 1: all three Partners sing. [Richie has walked through to see the Partners and the woman that was behind them]
Line 2: all three Partners sing. [Lady Rosetta is seated beside Malcolm]
Line 3: all three Partners sing.
Line 4: all three Partners sing.
Harmonising [The office staff come to the door and lean in singing]

Chorus:
Line 1: all the office staff at the door, the Partners, Geoff, and Richie sing.
Line 2: all sing.
Line 3: all sing.
Line 4: all sing.
Line 5: all sing.
Line 6: [Harmonising] Geoff takes the lead. He is walking out through the middle of the girls standing at the door.
Line 7: [Harmonising]
Line 8: [Harmonising]
Line 9: [Harmonising]

[Richie harmonises]
The song repeats until it is over. All sing as Richie leaves the Partners' office. Richie approaches his seat first, and then all the others return to theirs. Richie sits.

Geoff, the last to his seat, sits, and Sherry kicks him again "Don't be so horrible, Geoff." All this happens as the hustle and bustle of office activities resumes.

Sherry looks at Richie. Richie doesn't know whether Sherry is scowling, or if she is making the start of a smile, or trying to refrain from doing so. Her blue eyes are turning dark, as her head falls to look at her computer screen again.

"That gives me an idea." Geoff sparks into life. "I've got to tell the Partners." He leaves his chair and walks to the boardroom door and knocks.

Lady Rosetta is talking to her boys. "So this document tells you, well, Malcolm, you tell them."

"Yes, madam." Malcolm and Lady Rosetta are sitting on the right of the boardroom table, and her three sons, on the left. "Well, lads, as we see it, Lady Rosetta, your mother, can take this going concern from you, as you have noticed from the pre-terms and conditions to your signing the agreement for the money that was left to you. Or, you can sign this piece of paper giving Lady Rosetta time to look over all you have done and take the majority share in the bank. How much would depend on exactly how you have done." There is a knock at the door. All three sons get up and move behind their chairs. One, the middle son, walks to the door. "Ah, Geoff, what can we do for you? Come in, come in."

"Yes, my boy," says the oldest.

Geoff stands in the office, as the middle partner shuts the door and walks to meet his brothers. "It is Geoff, isn't it? Yes, Geoff, what do you have to say?"

The three sons of Lady Rosetta are pleased that they may have a solution to stop them signing the agreement.

"Well, sirs, it isn't my job to notice, but we have had a slow reduction in people pledging their money into our accounts for some time. It could be time that we looked for new custom."

"Now, there's a good idea," Lady Rosetta says.

"That is true, Geoff; don't listen to our mother, what ideas do you have?"

"Well, advertising costs a lot, but Richie out there has given me an idea. His family are very good friends with a family of restaurant and takeaway owners that work in and around the city. I found this out when visiting there for food one day. What if we offer them an incentive to get them to bank with us? You know how these people are. If they find out that Richie's employers phoned them to make the first contact, it could be a blessing. Who knows who else they could bring to the table?"

"Ha ha, that is a grand idea, Geoff. Who exactly are they, Geoff?" the older Partner asks.

"They are the Patijna family, sirs. They live on Richie's street. Blackberry Way. They own Tiger Takeaways, and Patijna Eat In Indian Dishes, in the city, sirs."

"Thank you, Geoff," the younger son says, looking at his mother. "Will that do, sirs?"

"That will do." The middle Partner speaks, and the older ushers Geoff out of the boardroom.

"So mother, Mumsy," the youngest Partner says.

"Yes, Mumsy?" The older.

"How long do we get before we have to sign this thing and expose our accounts to you?" The middle son asks.

Lady Rosetta stands and says, "I'll give you a month to get as much done as you can. If you do not have the accounts in my hands so I can pass them onto Malcolm here in two weeks, then I'm taking what's rightfully mine at the end of the month, the whole kit and caboodle. And you three are out on your ears; got it?" Malcolm packs his bag and stands; he follows Lady Rosetta out of the boardroom door. "Or, fellas, you just simply sign the papers to put me in charge."

Lady Rosetta speaks to Malcolm as they walk out of the bank. "How do you think they will do?" she says.

"Ha ha, not too well. I think that you will get your fifty-five percent, ma'am. Giving you all you need to control what, by rights, is literally yours in the first place."

"Those bloody sons of mine have me at my wits' ends, Malcolm. Come on." Malcolm opens the door and they walk down the stairs. Back inside the office there are laughs and insinuations. "So, she's their mother," Jacky says in shock. Sherry is already laughing.

In the boardroom the oldest Partner is on the phone to reception downstairs. "Yes my love, I want you to contact the Patijna family straightaway. I want you to leave a message saying that they must contact us as soon as they can. This must be a business call, but I want you to drop the name Richie Gyndall, and that he works for us.

Yes, yes, the owners of Tiger Takeaways. Yes, ha ha, that probably would be easier, yes, phone them there. Thank you."

It's Saturday, and Richie's family are at the local temple. They are in a small room away from the prayer room. They are standing alongside many other talkative people, speaking to the Patijna family about Richie. It's quite the scene:

Richie's mother: "Richie is such a sweet boy."
Richie's grandma: "Yes, sweet!"
Richie's grandpa: "Kuvan!" He stretches his hand out, and holds his wife by the arm.
Richie's father smiles as his wife carries on talking.
Richie's mother: "That bachcha, he works very hard."
Richie's grandma: "No, yes!"
Richie's grandpa: "Kuvan!" A little louder this time.

Richie's Mother looks at her maji. She feels the excitement that the Patijna family brings to her every time they meet.
She looks back at the Patijna family. Their daughter Stands in front, with her younger brother held by his mother's hand, each family standing huddled together like many other families in the temple. The boy is playing up and occasionally picks his nose, wiping it upon himself.

Richie's mother: "Ah-uh," (she is pretending not to notice).
"Yes – Very hard – at the Bank." She looks at her Husband.
"There are Partners, you know!" She looks back at the Patijna family.
The Patijna's daughter smiles and shows off her braces.
The Patijna's daughter: "How-" her question is cut short, so nobody can tell what she was about to say or do.
Mr. Patijna: "He's not working today, I take it!"
Richie's mother: "No, no, no, no, sorry. He is on his way."
Richie's father looks at his watch.
Richie's father: (clearing his throat) "Yes, well, I don't know where he could be. That bachcha!"

Richie's mother looks up at her husband with a slightly gobsmacked look. She is still nervous throughout her conversation. Smiling, she laughs, "Ha – ha, ha."

A young man walks into the space between the two families. He has to squeeze past others in the room.

"Ah, Charu, namaskar." The young man wants to walk away from the burning eyes of Charu's parents, but he turns back and leans towards the pretty young woman. "Aaj raat?"

Mr. Patijna pulls his daughter's attention back to the Gyndall family's conversation. He is not quite sure what the two families want for her. Though, to be frank, she is over protected by the Patijna family. Charu only meets boys at the temple, or when she is at school. So now, missing them bitterly, Charu opens herself up to them at every opportunity. She stands back. She is looking at the Gyndall family with not so broad a smile as she had when she was going to talk to her friend.

While Mrs. Patijna scorns the boy as he walks away, Mrs. Patijna's son follows his sister's friend with his eyes as he disappears into the crowd. The young boy sticks out his tongue and puts his thumb to his nose. Shaking his fingers, he blows a raspberry.

Charu has a kind of love for Richie. That is true. They have known each other for many years, but her time for relationships is not now, she feels. She wishes she had the freedom to be trusted. To enjoy the time she has at the moment, and any other given to her. She pushes at every inconvenience. True. That is why she likes Richie so much. Not idolising him, but seeing the way he can stand guard against life's woes at every given moment of his waking hours with regimental correctness, playing the game of life, like a free spirit.

At that, she notices Richie walking into the Temple, and, without anybody noticing, her maan tries to wake her by prodding her in the behind. Richie, seeing the two families, walks towards them. Richie has just turned twenty. It is Charu's eighteenth birthday today, and Richie does not want to be impolite, or take the pleasure of it being her birthday away from her. Although Richie does not feel he cherishes Charu, he feels pleased for Charu. While he cannot take his eyes from her, he is trying to play down his attraction.

Charu frowns, her head erect but her eyes cast down. She scratches the right-hand side of her forehead – where the hair grows thin. Richie speaks to his mother first.

84

"Hello, maji. I am not late, am I? I know I'm not. I have something important to do later this morning." He looks at the Patijna family. "Hello, Mr. & Mrs. Patijna. Hello, Charu, how are you today? Happy eighteenth birthday." Finishing with his politeness and his hello's, he looks back at his mother. "Mother, I need to pray. Not for any special reason, just to calm myself a bit."

Richie's grandma breaks the silence that Richie was expecting to last a little longer.

"Don't be silly, bachcha. You know you are loved. Now, it is getting late, it is gone nine. Go and say your piece to god, and let your time be your own, bachcha boy!"

Richie's grandpa takes his wife by the arm. He is wearing his typical prayer suit, with a turban and a pastel shirt. Like his wife likes him to wear. A dark blue machine-knitted jumper, dark trousers, and a short leather jacket. His grandpa's beard, which Richie always takes note of when he is seated in the living room chair, seems to grow out from his turban, as do his ears. His beard springs out like the belly of a fat sloth cub – his pastel shirt collar adds to the impression. The beard seems to be heaving under the headgear. As Richie's grandpa moves, it acts as if it has a mind of its own. The last time he shaved it, a few months ago, it took on an alien look that Richie didn't understand. Now, having grown back, it's back to its familiar, feral self.

His voice devoid of emotion, Grandpa tells his wife, "Kuvan, no bachcha boy, Richie! Richie – paripakv aadamee."

"You go!" Richie's father says as Richie is already walking away to the prayer room.

Richie's father turns back to the Patijna family, pleased with himself, and pleased he can make it to the temple, even though he works nights. He asks Mr. Patijna, "How are things – anyway – Tejasvat? Many people have asked for your ladakiyaan hand?" Daivey reaches out and grabs Mrs. Patijna's free hand.

"Daivey, you are a one." She looks at Tejasvat. "Isn't he a one, Tej?" She looks back at Daivey. "Tell him Tej, tell him."

Mr. Patijna says, "And so it is done! You can take her home if you like, Daivey, Oh, boy. Ha, what a laugh that would be." He looks at his wife. "Are you sure you said your prayers, maji? You know he'd work the arse off of you." Tej now looks to Aarzoo and then holds

Aarzoo's hand. "Isn't that right, Aarzoo? Hard bloody worker, your husband."

"Too bloody right!"

"Aarzoo. watch it!"

"Kuvan." Grandpa grabs her arm again.

Richie enters the prayer room and prays in quiet. For longer than he meant, because as he leaves, he notices his family members are not there, along with half the congregation. They have all gone home too.

As he walks through the streets, Richie has time to think about what has been happening in recent months. By the time he gets to Blackberry Way, and home, he sees that most of his family and the Patijnas are all filing in through the front doors to their houses. Three men are talking in the road. Richie can see that they are his pita jee, Mr. Patijna, and Mr. Joshi.

Oh, no. It is my worst nightmare! The men are talking together about me, I can tell. That's all they have on their minds at the best of times: what I get up to, and how I do it. The only thing worse than the blokes talking, I can tell you, is the women talking. At least I have gotten away with that this time. Though, hey, as soon as these men talk to their loving partners then who knows what end of the wet cloth I will receive to wash my sins away. Bloody marvellous, isn't it? When a young man can't even walk into his own home after prayers without being interrupted.

Richie walks towards his home.

"Hi-ya, Richie," Rahil Joshi calls.

Richie's father is talking to Mr. Patijna. Richie puts his head down.

"So, Tej, we told him that…"

Daivey turns to see his son walking towards their front gate.

"Oh, hi there, Richie," Mr. Patijna says. "We were just talking about you. Come here, boy, it's not right that you aren't included in this conversation."

Daivey's shaking his head. "No, Tej, he's very touchy these last few days."

Richie picks his head up and walks towards the three men standing by the kerb. His father is standing in front of him. Mr. Patijna to the left and Rahil to the right. "What can I do for you three? I am in a hurry, though! So can this be quick?"

"See what I told you," Daivie says.

Rahil takes up the story. "Your father here was telling Mr. Patijna, Tej, That you were looking for work, son. Now I overheard and told them that you had yesterday turned me down with my offer of working for me. I was telling them I was distressed about this." Mr. Joshi strokes the top of his head, Mr. Patijna strokes his chin, and Richie's father lowers his head. "So Tej here, well Tej." Rahil Joshi leaves the way open for his friend Tejasvat to finish the conversation.

"So I said, why don't you come and work for..."

Richie butts in. "Not for you at the restaurant? I can't see myself as..."

"Now Richie," his dad says. "Be nice to Mr. Patijna, you haven't even heard his terms and conditions and you're firing on all cylinders, ready to throw your life away yet again. You read too much of people before they let you understand what is really happening."

"Ha, yes, well," Tej says, "Why don't you come and work for my accountant? He will pay you good money to learn the trade, Richie. It is a good job, and it will look good on your CV."

"And if I say no, father?" Richie asks.

"If you say no, you will not leave the house for an age."

"Then I accept, Mr. Patijna, thank you, Tej." Richie shakes Mr. Patijna's hand, turns and leaves for the house.

"That was eas..." Mr. Joshi says, but is interrupted almost immediately. It is Richie.

"A slave I shall become."

"That bloomin' bachcha of mine. I tell you. If I could make him fall in line."

"Mines the same, Daivey old pal, Charu, Well, let me not say. Eeh!" Mr. Joshi fills in his end of the conversation, "Mine, I tell you, she keeps getting me called into school. The cheek of these kids. And I suppose I've got this all to come."

Richie walks through his front door, shouts to his maji. "I'm going upstairs, Aarzoo."

Richie is walking up his stairs:

I can tell you I am not happy with this idea in the slightest. How on earth am I going to make my dreams come true with all this family and friends of the family putting their noses into my business?

His mother wants to shout at him from the kitchen sink; turning, we see her move to the bottom of the stairs to shout, just as Richie shuts his bedroom door.
"I am your maan, and don't forget it!" She can see that his door shuts and curses. "Godforsaken bachcha!"
Richie, standing in his bedroom, throws his yellow reversible coat onto his bed, and stands in front of his bedroom mirror.

Dedicated Follower of Fashion by The Kinks: please be respectful and listen. There is much context, and also content hidden within the text.

Verse 1:
Line 1: Richie's grandpa sings. [Richie stands in front of the long mirror in his bedroom]
Line 2: Richie's grandpa sings. [Richie takes his chequered white, green and yellow fronted jumper off, leaving his blue shirt exposed]
Line 3: Richie's grandpa sings.
Line 4: Richie's grandpa sings. [Richie stands proud in front of the mirror. With his blue shirt tucked into his yellow straight trousers, and with green shoes on]

Verse 2:
Line 1: Richie's grandpa sings. [We flick to London. Richie is looking in all the expensive suit shops in Savile Row]
Line 2: Richie's grandpa sings.
Line 3: Richie's grandpa sings.
Line 4: Richie's grandpa sings.

Verse 3:
Line 1: Richie's grandpa sings. [Harmonising]
Line 2: Richie's grandpa sings. [Richie is now at Speakers Corner, where a Caped Crusader is standing on a box]

Line 3: Richie's grandpa sings. [Richie looks down and pulls his pants outside of his trouser tops. Everyone close to him starts laughing]
Line 4: Richie's grandpa sings.

Verse 4:
Line 1: Richie's grandpa sings. [Harmonising]
Line 2: Richie's grandpa sings
Line 3: Richie's grandpa sings. [Richie is now in a clothes shop coming out of the changing rooms with a white and blue polka-dotted suit and a white and black striped suit on]
Line 4: Richie's grandpa sings.

Verse 5:
Line 1: Richie's grandpa sings. [Richie is walking through London, in front of an open-topped bus. With the polka-dotted suit top on, and the striped bottoms]
Line 2: Richie's grandpa sings. [People quickly join in, and they move to Carnaby Street]
Line 3: Richie's grandpa sings.
Line 4: Richie's grandpa sings.

Verse 6:
Line 1: Richie's grandpa sings. [Harmonising] [Now Richie's enjoying himself at house parties he's been invited to]
Line 2: Richie's grandpa sings.
Line 3: Richie's grandpa sings.
Line 4: Richie's grandpa sings.

Verse 7:
Line 1: Richie's grandpa sings. [Harmonising]
Line 2: Richie's grandpa sings. [Now Richie's seen getting on the train with loads of bags of clothing]
Line 3: Richie's grandpa sings.
Line 4: Richie's grandpa sings.
Line 5: Richie's grandpa sings.

Richie leaves his bedroom. We see his back disappear down the stairs, the front door opens, and then slams. Now Aarzoo, facing the rear of the property, turns from chopping onions into a large brown bowl. The washing up bowl is on the sideboard and the water is running. "See ya later, my Richie." Turning back to the sink, she shakes her head. "Alligators?"

I know I led you towards thinking, at the start of this story, that my name points to a wealthy family. The jokes about my name have been richly at that expense - you can imagine - throughout my childhood; why exactly? Well, that is sitting in the living room of our family's household, a different kind of order. That being, yes, my lovely grandma, and strangely discordant to his lectures, my loving grandpa. I can tell you, I don't know how they became the couple I know and understand so well, but together they are what we idolise from the roots of our family's history. Perhaps they can explain better than I? I'm taking a day off. It is Saturday, and, as you can imagine, I need rest until tonight's activities, I being only twenty. Then I can work out precisely what I believe is the right thing to do in these, my most testing circumstances.

Richie's grandma and grandpa are sitting as close together as they can get. Grandpa is sitting on the chair in front of the television, by the front window. Grandma is sitting on the settee, but as close as she can get to her pati. A picture of them arriving from the aircraft that brought them here sits behind them on a light blue wall.
There is plush, maroon velvet motif wallpaper covering the chimney breast and rear and front walls of the room. The spaces either side of the fireplace are painted a vibrant, bright, rich blue, the back wall is a light blue. There is brown Formica furniture placed at intermediate places around the room. All with a melange of family and friends pictured within them, and upon them. On the fireplace are gold elephants, at either end, a picture of the King and Queen in the middle, and a star-shaped brass clock above. The fire is on, and the room is relaxed. The three-piece suite is royal blue and the carpet red. On the far wall is a picture of a woman making a water offering to Lord Surya.
"You know, I can tell Richie's in love, meree priye," Kuvan says to her pati, taking his attention from the movement of the television for a moment.
"I know, Kuvan. I bet you can remember when we first fell in love."

90

"Yes, but not with whom we may think?" Her mind travels to the rest of her family members around the house. "Tell me! I bet you can't remember the story you told me, meree pati."
Her husband looks in her direction, and then back to the television. His memories are seemingly spilling out over what is actually on the TV, to what is now brought into their reality.
"Back in four BC, Alexander the Great invaded India. He crossed the Indus River. Near my ancestor's homeland. He was on a mission to challenge King Porus to fight for his lands and challenge him over the rule of his lands." Noise from the television depicts the battle.
"He conquered his foe with ease, according to my family's tales of woe. But he travelled far in our lands, looking for spiritual salvation. According to one source, it was because he could not rest. After all, his armies thought the devil was upon them, as they had killed his war beasts, the elephants. He travelled back with the teachings of the Brahmins. He bumped into my family's tribe, and was shot in the chest by one of my relatives." Kuvan's pati turned back to her from glancing at the screen. "But I am glad to be with you, Kuvan."
"But do you remember how we met, priye?" She thinks of the morning she watched Richie hugging the milk bottle on the doorstep. Spying him from the living room window. "Praarthana karana, do tell."
The scene on the television is the market place of a village in India. With the palace out of sight, all that is seen, to the left, is a war memorial. It stands at the start of the built-up area. It is on the left of the open space, where the market place stands. Everything is in black and white. The area is set like a stage would be. With fake barrows, and stalls. All made from flat standing props.
A young girl in a partially see-through pink sari is sitting on the war memorial. A man in tight pants and a thick green, pleated baggy shirt is tiptoeing towards her. Dancing a pirouette by one of the barrows, he takes a Padma flower from a bunch and gives the girl the flower. After she sniffs at it, he grabs her by the hand.
The scenery becomes dark all of a sudden, but the light stays fixed upon the couple holding hands, then the picture freezes.
"You and your family were plantation workers. On one of your days off, you were sitting on the memorial in the village, Kuvan. Like a ridiculously silly girl, you were. I came to tell you that no one was allowed to sit on it without punishment."

91

"Well, you did not tell me that. I thought more of you when you held my hand."

"Me too, Kuvan, but still. It was a ridiculous thing to do; the village guards came with their rifles and tried to take you away. So I pulled you behind me, and we danced through the market place, away from the guards. I was jumping you over barrows in my raised arms, and we ran away together for good. I left my family that day, there in the village, and so did you. Now we have a nice life. Living in England with our family. Who look after us well, Kuvan."

On-screen, the couple, now standing at the right edge of the market place. They run off screen, away from the village guards.

"I'm glad you understand then, my pati. We have all the time in the world."

"Now, Kuvan, you tell me what you remember."

Kuvan Drifts off to the home she once shared with her parents in the same village as her pati in India. "We are standing in my mother's house. I am bundled through the door by you, and we get inside with your cases, Gaurav. My mother is asking: what is wrong?"

Kuvan's Mother: "What is your problem, ladakee?"

Kuvan: "Maan. We have something most urgent to tell you."

Gaurav: "Kuvan is being sought by the local village guard, Aanya. We must get out of here as soon as we can. It is getting dark. If we pack now then we can travel to the airport in the city at the edge of our lands and travel to somewhere new. Maybe England, I am thinking, Aanya."

Aanya's husband walks in from the rear. Kuvan runs off to get her cases.

Kuvan's father: "What did you do to make my daughter a suspect of our guardsmen, Gaurav?"

Kuvan can be heard from her room. She is packing neatly folded clothes into a case, then placing photos on top of them.

Kuvan: "He did nothing, pita jee, he only helped me escape, and now they are after him as well as me."

Kuvan runs back into the kitchen.

Kuvan: "Maji, I need to take things for our life together in England. Please help me pack."

Kuvan and her maan place things into her case. The last thing her maan takes from the side, before taking a silver pot and porcelain cups from it, is a silver tray.

Kuvan's mother: "Here, take this. This is the tray Gaurav here gave to us after we granted that you two could be together. But I won't let you take it until you promise me and your Pita jee, Kuvan, that you will not declare your relationship's sanctification until you two get married when you get to England. Do you two hear me?"

Kuvan: "Yes, maji."

Kuvan's mother checks outside to make sure no one is about. She shuts the door and locks it.

It is now dusk and Kuvan and Gaurav leave the back door of Kuvan's home to get out of the village with their lives intact.

Kuvan's mind travels to the train station. The station is a very busy place, even at this hour. Trains are coming into the open air terminal. It is the hub for catching a ride to places other than the internal jungles of India. A train stops. Before it stops people are getting off of the train. Some people are jumping down from the roof. Kuvan has her and Gaurav's tickets in her hand, which is also being pulled by Gaurav. They are dressed smartly in their best warm clothes for the journey. Carrying coats and cases, Gaurav has two cases in his left hand, they making an upside down V-shape as he does so. Through the steam a whistle can be heard and the train starts to move. Gaurav lets go of Kuvan's hand and puts a case in either hand, then jumps onto the train. He puts them down and then shouts Kuvan. "Come, Kuvan." Kuvan jumps on the train, Gaurav helps her onto it and shuts the door behind her.

Slowly we follow the train as it travels the twists and turns of the ever flowing rails. The train is making its steady and weary way to an airport in the east of India.

Then we catch up with the train, which holds many people above and below its roof top, and we follow a man walking along one of the carriage roofs. He sits, nestling in between the roof-top passengers to sit cross-legged. As he sits he listens to what is around him, and feels the silence from below, but below him inside the carriage all is not silent. Out of the silence the trains whistle blows.

It is later on in the train journey, the sun is rising as it travels on its way to intercept the many other lines that all lead to the city.

It is now daylight. The train has many people on the top of it still, their legs can be seen hanging down the sides of the train, as feet can be seen through the windows of the carriage Kuvan and Gaurav are seated within.

Inside the carriage there are many families. Most have children, some do not, like Kuvan and Gaurav. Gaurav is standing talking to a young man reading a book; it is a book of the Vedas. He walks towards where Kuvan is sitting and sits.

Kuvan speaks to her mangetar. "Gaurav, something must be done for these children. We cannot let them miss out on the teachings they should have. There is precious little time in life, let alone what we can give to one another."

"There is a man behind us, pyaara, I will see if he will tend to their needs." Gaurav is polite, but stern.

Kuvan speaks to the person next to her in Hindi. As she gets up with her mangetar the person shuffles along the seat they share with the couple. "Come, I will be glad to meet him with you." So they walk the aisle of the train until they meet the man reading the book of the Vedas. "My adaamee, suggests that you may be able to help us," Kuvan says.

"In doing what?" answers the man with the book.

"Why, helping us keep these children busy while we travel, and teaching them something at the same time."

"You would like me to teach them some lessons from my book. I can do that, if you collect the children together." The man is polite, cheerful, but serious all the same.

Kuvan and Gaurav walk from seat to seat talking to all the families with children on the train. The hubbub of talk continues, with a crying child at times, and children file out of their seats. A space is cleared and all the parents gather their children to sit in the two rows of seats that are facing each other. Gaurav and Kuvan stand at the end of each seat, and the man with the book of the Vedas crouches in the middle of them.

"Namaste, children," the man says.

"Namaste," the children repeat.

"My name is Nadeem, and I have some teachings from the book of the Vedas, if you wish," he says.

There is lots of chatter between the children; one speaks, a young girl, "Yes please, Mr. Nadeem."

"Ha ha, no, little one, it's Nad…" Kuvan touches Nadeem on the shoulder. He readjusts what he was about to say. "Okay, Mr. Nadeem. Right, who knows the song Allah Tero Naam, Ishvari Tero Naam?" All the children put their hands up. "Right, so then, we all know who Allah is, but who can tell me who Ishvari is." Only one, the little girl who spoke, sticks her hand up. The little boy next to her is whispering in her ear. "So then, who is she, Krpya? Do tell."

"She is the samakaksh of Ishvara."

"Yes that is true: so the Vedas texts tell us. Ishvari is the divine, she is the female correspondent of Ishvara. And Ishvara is," the children just talk amongst themselves. "well, Ishvara is the male divine father principle who came to be all forms of creation, and as these creations, and expressions, are a form of dual consciousness and set into energy, Ishvari is the greatest of all the sources of energy in our whole universe." By now the children have all stopped talking, and are watching Nadeem look at his book while declaiming his teachings to them. "So," Nadeem says. "Who would like to sing Allah Tero Naam, Ishvari Tero Naam?"

All the children put their hands up.

"I think, Kuvan, this is where you come in," Nadeem says.

Kuvan sings. All the children sing with her. Then all the people on the train carriage start to sing. The people on the top of the carriage hear the song, and they start to sing too. The train speeds off towards the city where the airport is situated.

"So that is all I remember, apart from getting off the plane in England, pati." She is looking towards the photo of them getting off the plane. Their friends, and now in-laws, are standing behind them. Kuvan shouts into the kitchen from the living room. "Aarzoo. Aarzoo."

Kuvan's betee walks into the room. "What, maji?"

"We were just talking about love. What do you have to say about that, then?"

"Well, yes, you were talking to Richie about that the other day. Who but Charu is he in love with?"

"Frankenstein's cat." Pati is grinning like another well-known cat.

"Who?"

"Mary Shelly!" Replies Kuvan quickly, not wanting to confuse her daughter. She looks back at her husband. Pleased with his remark, he settles and smiles. Full of love, she does the same. Grandpa picks up his sailing yacht down by the side of his chair.

It is now later that night.

Daivey's patnee beats her husband to the door to wish him goodbye; this Aarzoo's daily routine. It makes Daivey hesitate before he exits the house, for his walk to work on the night-shift.

With Daivey dithering, Aarzoo notices a letter. The one that Richie placed on the windowsill before he went to bed the other day.

"Husband of mine. Did you put a letter on this windowsill?" She picks it up. "It has come from India by the looks of it. It is addressed to this house, but it has my father's name upon it."

"No, Aarzoo, if it were as important as that, I would have said!" Richie's mother's eyes light up with ambition. "Quickly, let's open it!"

"Yes. Quickly, and we shall surprise everyone."

She reads the letter, which is written upon some extremely expensive parchment.

As she reads through her eyes widen, and her mouth opens.

"Quickly, Mother! Father, come quick. We have hit the big time." Richie's father starts to panic with apprehension. "But I've paid all the bills. Aarzoo, Oh my gosh! Don't tell me. They've been conning people at the temple, saying we are worthless, no good time-wasters, and we need the money because, because I can't get enough money to buy my wife a dishwasher. Oh my god, Aarzoo, what have you three been up to?" Richie's dad is holding his forehead. His sizeable black moustache half-covers his gritted teeth. His reflective jacket is kind of skew-whiff. "Oh my gosh! What have you two been up to?" His in-laws walk out of the living room. "Don't tell me you have leprosy, and you need an operation to fix your brains."

"Bloody hell, what are the men at work going to say when I tell them it wasn't my fault. I know what they are going to say. Yes, it bloody was. You fool."

He says, to no one in particular, "How are we going to fix this?"

"With Richie getting married to Charu, my dear!"

"My god, things are bad." Richie's father looks upwards, to nothing more particular than the Deity he cannot see. " That'll confuse the

guys at work!" Looking to his wife, and then his in-laws, puzzled, he asks, "Do we need the money that bad?"
Aarzoo, "Yes, we do, my love. Especially when it's a whole kingdom."
"Christ! We're not ripping off the Royal family as well, are we? I do like the thought, but won't they notice something funny in the family photos?" He envisions a different king and queen in the photo on the fireplace, as he replaces it where it belongs in a moment of offish mindful behaviour. He can see himself reflected in the wrong seat.
The envelope: Aarzoo is holding it at the back of the letter. Kuvan's betee is transfixed upon it too.
Daivey's mother-in-law pipes up, "Do shut up, son of mine. That letter is from our homeland, pati." Richie's grandpa huffs, then irritated, tries to return to the television room, but his wife pulls him back to her. "What does it really say?"
Aarzoo reads. "Well, not a lot – really – just that we are the last of the bloodline of the Sultan in your homeland, Mother, and if our son is married, then that means the bloodline stays open, and, yes, it does say here, he inherits all of the prince's wealth."
"Oh my gosh! We can get a dishwasher after all then, honey. And the guys at work will never be the wiser. But wait a minute. That boy never seems to know what he wants from one minute to the next. Ha, once he knows this!"
"Wait a minute, pati. No, no, it says here, if the boy is not married already? Then, he must not know of his fate, or, Oh, it does not say why, or anything else, I think." She turns the letter in her hand.
"Oh, goodness. That boy will never have anyone. I tell you. I am at my wit's end with him!"
Everyone still stands in the hallway.
Richie's dad opens the front door slightly and then closes it again.
"Well, where do you think you are going, Daivey?" Aarzoo says. "You have someone to talk to, now tell us how you feel."
"I have to get to work, woman. Though, you know? Well, what do you know! All I have to say is this one thing."
"Daivey!"

Another Saturday Night by Sam Cooke: please be respectful and listen. There is much context, and also content hidden within the text.

Line 1: Richie's dad sings.
Line 2: Richie's grandparents join in. [They are bouncing their hands to the beat]
Line 3: Richie's grandparents stop singing. His mother joins his father singing. [Richie's mother shows her husband, her maji, and then her father, the contents of the letter]
Line 4: Richie's mother stops singing. [We see Richie walking the streets, he joins in singing with his father]
Line 5: all sing. [As the image separates into two. We see Richie walking the streets, and the rest of his family in the hallway]
Line 6: all sing. [We see a picture of Richie hanging on the wall of the hall]

Line 7: Richie sings. [He looks at the fountain]
Line 8: Richie sings.
Line 9: Richie sings.
Line 10: Richie sings.
Line 11: Richie sings.

Line 12: all sing, apart from Richie.
Line 13: all sing, apart from Richie.
Line 14: all sing, apart from Richie. [Richie's maji shows the letter to everyone again]
Line 15: all sing, apart from Richie. [Maji's maji goes and gets the picture of the girl the rest of his family wants him to marry, Charu]
Line 16: all sing, apart from Richie.

Line 17: Richie's grandma sings alone.
Line 18: Richie's grandma sings alone.
Line 19: Richie's grandma sings alone.
Line 20: Richie's grandma sings with Richie's grandpa joining in.
Line 21: Richie's grandma sings alone. [Grandma shows everyone the photo that she is holding of the family with the girl they want Richie to marry. They are happy]

Line 22: Richie sings with the rest of his family backing. [He still walking around the city]
Line 23: Richie sings with the rest of his family backing.

Line 24: Richie sings with the rest of his family backing.
Line 25: Richie sings with the rest of his family backing. [He looks at a girl on her own as he walks, she is with a couple of the same age]
Line 26: Richie sings.

Line 27: Richie's father sings.
Line 28: Richie's maji sings.
Line 29: Richie's grandma sings.
Line 30: Richie's grandpa sings.
Line 31: all sing apart from Richie.

Line 32: Richie is back singing. [He is leaving a chip shop with an open bag of chips, and a wooden fork]
Line 33: Richie sings.
Line 34: Richie sings.
Line 35: Richie sings.
Line 36: Richie sings.

Line 37: Richie sings. [Richie is sitting on the fountain, where Sherry was seated]
Line 38: Richie sings.
Line 39: Richie sings.
Line 40: Richie sings.
Line 41: Richie sings.

Line 42: Richie sings. [Richie walks back into the cinema and sings with cinema staff]
Line 43: Richie sings.
Line 44: Richie sings.
Line 45: Richie sings.
Line 46: Richie sings.

Line 47: all sing. [Richie sings (One more time) then all join in again The screen splits in two]
Line 48: all sing.
Line 49: all sing.
Line 50: all sing.
Line 51: all sing.

Richie's mother is standing at the top of Blackberry Way, waiting for Mrs. Patijna. She is not her usual self, obviously, after reading the letter last night. She sees Mrs. Patijna, who is dragging her young son up the street, along the middle of the road. Piya and her son then get to the other side, and join Aarzoo. Piya Patijna greets Aarzoo like every Sunday morning, by bowing and hugging and saying hello in Hindu. They walk together to the Temple. Mrs. Patijna finally subdues her child's antics.

On the way, Mrs. Patijna asks Aarzoo, "So, how are things with your husband? I feel he is not quite his normal self recently."

"No, Daivey is a good man," Aarzoo says.

"Ah, yes, but are you getting yoopee?" Mrs. Patijna smiles at her friend as she is walking while now less strenuously dragging her son along for the ride. All this, after asking her essential question of the day. "No, Mrs. Patijna. Mr. Gyndall is yoopee every day. He is always up after work. We have a strict timetable."

"Ahh, but are you getting it bahut oopar?" Mrs. Patijna reiterates.

"Bahut oopar? Very? What do you mean, Mrs. Patijna? Daivey is a bahut hee sammaanit aadamee." She looks forwards after these words; she tries hard not to smile even as a light expression crosses the broadening of her mouth. "Very notable!"

Mrs. Patijna looks at her friend, perusing and examining her neighbour at length.

So now, Mrs. Patijna, with a kind of frustration deep in her throat, although smiling, remarks, "Bahut oopar! Are you getting it up, Aarzoo?"

They both now look forwards as they walk in harmony once again. Mrs. Patijna, carefully after her initial outburst, politely puts a softened question to her friend.

"Tej is a very caring man these days. Especially after the bachcha is born, you know how things can become, when there are no children about."

They both smile and giggle. Mrs. Patijna's bachcha looks out into the road.

"Look, Piya. Daivey gets up every morning."

They start laughing together as they walk, but Aarzoo, keeping her wits about her, glances at the floor.

Mrs. Patijna's son looks at them for inspiration.

"Ha, ha, he he, bahut!" Aarzoo explains without looking.
They cannot help but laugh again while Mrs. Patijna's son tries to
cross the road but is suddenly pulled back by Mrs. Patijna's hand.
Aarzoo carries on. The two friends, although not in sequence, do not
quite get their English perfectly correct. The two women are
thinking about what their husbands' thoughts towards them are. They
look at each other with love in their hearts – engulfed by each other's
circumstances – but they are worlds apart.
"Ha, ha, ha, ha." they both laugh in delight.
After their laughter, they synchronise their walking tempos.
Walking towards the temple, Aarzoo hesitates to explain something
to her friend, "Pat. I must explain something to you today."
"I'm all ears, Aarzoo, as always when you talk." They seem to suck
themselves into the temple building instantly.
Inside, not wanting to displease,head straight for the prayer room.
They are full of pleasure for themselves and everyone else. To be
able to make their peace with all the living, all that is living
alongside themselves. With the spirit world, to be able to be in tune
with what is, and not question what may be. With the child, although
it is not his day.
In the prayer room, there are many couples milling around, or
offering a prayer. Mrs. Patijna and Aarzoo dip their heads to the
priests that stand to the sides of the prayer room and move towards
the Deities, placed around the room. They move between them,
again dipping their heads, and now pressing their foreheads with
their right index finger. Then they bring their hands out backward,
towards each Deity. They get to their knees, and, instead of praying,
they speak. Mrs. Patijna's son just follows. He is already absorbed by
all of his interests. He is full of attraction and fascination with the
couple's Sunday antics.

Aarzoo: "So we received a letter last night."
Mrs. Patijna: "From who?"
Aarzoo: "It doesn't matter."
Moving on to the next Deity, performing the next ritual, they
speak again.
Aarzoo: "Richie wants to get married, with Charu." Mrs.
Gyndall takes a look at Pat, her friend.
Mrs. Patijna: "Charu?"

101

Aarzoo: "Yes, Charu!"

Mrs. Patijna: "Well, wouldn't you know." Mrs. Patijna is smiling, her pride sealed in her eyes; they are now closed. She believes her friend sincerely answered her question, of how understanding was her relationship with Daivey.

Aarzoo: "She'll make us all rich, Pat!"

They slowly move onto the next Deity, performing their Sunday rituals again. This time as they look at each other, Mrs. Patijna smiles at Aarzoo.

Mrs. Patijna: "That means you'll look after everything."

Aarzoo: "You know the bonds we live in are older than our ways, Pat."

Mrs. Patijna: "We'll talk about this after we leave."

The priest, standing beside the Deity, watches them as they move around, and coughs a dry, grumpy cough. Slight contempt is written upon his face; his demeanour is now as if to pardon himself from the couple's antics.

Getting to their knees, the women carry on talking among themselves. They are wrapped in each of their separate worships. This conceals the exact awakenings they have just arrived at between them. The only sounds are the prayers of the people scattered within the space of the prayer room.

The prayers from the congregation go quiet as they stand. They perform the ritual that they have done every week, on Sunday, of their lives, while living in the vicinity of this temple, they both so love. They keep contempt from every pore of their bodies, even though it has over-spilt slightly. Not wanting to leave anything behind, for their gods to be extinguished, they momentarily consider what could be more religious than marriage.

As they rise, the priest standing in front of them bows, putting his hands together as he stands.

They miss out the last few Deities, missing them out of their prayers, and their meander. They are moving past and through the worshippers – those within the prayer room. Piya and Aarzoo walk out through the gateway. To what end is life's living peace and harmony? Dragging Pat's son with them, they seem to step into light itself.

They are in a hurry today, Aarzoo having to catch up with Piya. "Let me tell you. Richie loves your Charu." Piya is humming to herself as Aarzoo looks at her; she slows down, falls behind her friend. "Piya, I'm telling you. It's the truth. But Richie. Our Family. My Family, they have a secret. We are related to some very wealthy people. And now all they have is going to be left to us. That means we have to get Richie married before he makes a grave mistake and we lose all."
"Richie, ha ha, sorry, I shouldn't laugh. You're telling me that Richie has been made heir to your wealthy family from India. Just tell me how much they are worth? I can't believe it Aarzoo, you must be spitting venom in Richie's direction."
"Piya," Aarzoo falls back a little once more. "Piya," Aarzoo says as she pulls level, "Richie is still my son. And there is no estimated wealth of our relation, but we know that he owns a very large area of land."
"This all sounds good, Aarzoo, you just keep up." The two walk off towards Blackberry Way.
They are back at Blackberry Way.
They chat at the corner of the street.
Aarzoo speaks first. "Is there anything else I can get you, Mrs. Patijna? We're not going to be hanging Richie out to dry here. Marriage is going to be good for him. To be that age and either not to be attracted to the opposite sex, or not be married. It is not forgivable."
They both break into more giggles, "Pat!" Aarzoo clears the air.

Mrs. Patijna: "Well, yes, you could get your husband, and we can meet at our house, and then tell Charu. I'm sure she'll be very receptive to the idea, she loves Richie."
Aarzoo walks up to her front door, past the point of no return, to open the front door, and go into her home.
Aarzoo: "Daivey? Daivey!"
Daivey walks out of their living room. He holds a plate with some of Aarzoo's home cooking upon it. All this while chewing on that what is in his mouth.
Aarzoo: "Daivey? I was just about to ask where you are!"
Mr. Gyndall: "Why, what is it, Aarzoo?" He finishes what's in his mouth and then speaks freely, "Mmmm, and by the way, these are delicious."

Aarzoo: "Okay, but we haven't got time for that. We must go to the Patijna's household and speak to Charu!"

Daivey: "Chm." He is clearing his throat as if not sure of the rush. "So soon? We haven't told Richie yet."

Aarzoo: "Just come on, husband of mine. We haven't got time for that, and remember we're not allowed to tell him anything. You know what my father's family has stipulated in the letter."

Daivey: "Yes, I know, but bakavaas. I'm not so sure we should worry about that."

Aarzoo: "Keep your mouth shut, and follow, man."

Mrs. Gyndall turns in her hallway and leaves the house. The door does not completely shut behind her.

Mrs. Gyndall waits for her husband in the street, on the opposite side. Daivey catches up with her. They walk down to the front garden of the Patijna's.

The front door opens, and Mrs. Patijna's friendly smile greets them. She opens the door fully to welcome them inside. Her husband, Tej, is standing in the hallway, with Charu, pretty and polite. She is standing behind him. We do not quite see her Sunday best as she is obscured slightly by her father.

We see things from Mr. Patijna's view of the situation. Mrs. Patijna bows to her family friends.

"So, Mr. Patijna has said he likes my idea. That you shall proceed with the taking of our daughter's hand in Richie's, but he insists that he pays for our two family's meal. And Richie has to acknowledge her respects, firstly."

Aarzoo tries to speak, but her husband touches her shoulder to indicate he will talk first.

"Yes, I know how this ordeal starts, but Charu surely must acknowledge that she wants to have Richie as her husband."

We can see the facial features now of Mr. Gyndall. He stands away from the front door enough for the light to dim slightly as what is left bounces off the Patijna's vibrant mix of green wallpapered hallway walls.

"We have your daughter's best interests at heart, and Richie's, of course; you must remember though, he must know nothing about his inheritance from our in-law the Sultan." Aarzoo turns to look at her

husband, and we can see that the two are not quite in sync with each other. Along with their views on Richie's welcoming of the idea, there are the undertakings of this mammoth occasion. Daivey is shaking his head. "I thought no one is to know about all of this." "What more do you have to say, husband of mine! If Richie is to marry Charu, then they must know of the inheritance."
There must be movement, and it is from further inside the hallway. Even though we cannot see it, the Gyndall family look towards Pat, drawing towards the movement.
Charu is standing in front of her father and recites the words she remembers to think of every night before she goes to sleep. Those that she has always had on her mind. All ready to say at this poignant moment of her life.
"Thank you, Mr. and Mrs. Gyndall," she says. "I owe you everything. Marriage will be the happiest and best days of my life." "Thank you, Charu."
Charu places her hands onto her shoulders, looks down, and then, bringing her head back to speak, says, "Paradise isn't instantly adorable, but Paradise is not yet at my door." We see her face and her smile; she is readying to sing.

Halfway to Paradise by Billy Fury: please be respectful and listen. There is much context and also content hidden within the text.

Verse 1:
Line 1: Charu sings alone.
Line 2: Charu sings alone.
Line 3: Charu sings alone. [Charu dances into the living room of the Patijna's household]
Line 4: Charu sings alone.

Verse 2:
Line 1: Charu sings alone. [She now picks up a picture of Richie in his school uniform]
Line 2: Charu sings alone.
Line 3: Charu sings alone.
Line 4: Charu sings alone.

Verse 3:

Line 1: Charu sings alone. [Coming back into the hallway the two couples sing (Heaven)]
Line 2: Charu sings alone.
Line 3: Charu sings alone. [The two couples sing (treasure)]
Line 4: Charu sings alone.

Verse 4:
Line 1: Charu sings alone. [Charu dances back into the living room and stands in front of the picture of her mother and father on their wedding day, and swaps portraits. Putting hers next to Richie's. She now holds her mother and father's portraits close to her chest]
Line 2: Charu sings alone.
Line 3: Charu sings alone.
Line 4: Charu sings alone. [She ambles, still singing, back into the hallway]

Line 1: Charu sings alone. [Still walking. She repositions herself]
Line 2: Charu sings alone.

"Will Richie have his job still, at the Bank?" she asks, as all that fills her smile is her braces.

Richie is woken again early this morning. He is disturbed from his thoughts, and visions, by his father shouting up the stairs. "Richie, Richie. You okay, Richie? Your mother has told me to tell you your trousers are ready to put on!"
"Huh, what, sorry, oh no, not again?"
"Your trousers, they're ready for you to put on."
Richie looks down at himself; he still in his bed. He wipes his eyes and manages to wake completely. He holds his forehead with his left palm. "Okay, pita jee, I'll just put…" His father is smiling, Richie thinks for a second: *you've guessed it, I have been here before. This world I live in is very perplexing, beyond my wildest dreams. Now not only do I start afresh new day, I have to put up with these bloody idiots doing their Groundhog Day routine on me. At least it's Monday.* The blackbird calls to his window; he imagines the start of the film all over again. "Okay, okay, father, I'll just put on something clean:" *a T-shirt or something,* "and I'll be down." Richie

stands up and grabs something to put on. He reaches for his dressing gown at the back of his door.

"Bachcha, bachcha? Are you still there? Well, I do not care; you frustrate me, bachcha, you really do. What do you get up to in your spare time? Listen, your mother and I think you really need to start growing up and get prepared for life, son," Daivey says.

"Don't worry, father, I'm not complaining about how late this is all going to make me. I'll just put the two complaints of mine on hold until I get there." Richie is very upset.

You know, not everyone has a household like mine. It is the living breathing resemblance of an egg timer. The only difference is with an egg timer you have to turn it on its head to start all over again. With this one all you have to do is think you have the right to be normal.

Richie is halfway down the stairs; hesitating, he turns and runs back up to the top step and into his bedroom. He turns off his alarm just as it is starting. "Richie, Richie, don't go back to bed, you stupid, bachcha. You'll be late." Daivey is acting like last week for a purpose, to teach his son a valuable lesson. Aarzoo is in fits of giggles as she presses the shirt Richie left for her to wash at the weekend. Richie is stomping down the stairs looking at his father; Daivey is trying not to smile, but again he has a soft smug, more dryly granted, grin on his face this time. Daivey makes way for his son, and Richie realises he must talk first or his pita jee will. Or his faith tells him he will say the same words as last time he was woken early. He tries to be tactful, and mentions his work place. "Father, work are asking about ideas to claw some money back. So I am told. Have you got any ideas?" It doesn't work.

"That's enough of work talk. Anyway, you do enough for your employers at that stupid bank," he says. Today is a different day altogether. It is a day when you realise you need to get married, and married you will be to Charu." Daivey means business, and will not be happy until his son is compliant. He walks towards the kitchen where his grandma is holding the picture of Charu.

Richie follows his father's movement and spies the picture "Ah, now I see. You've done this to me to teach me a lesson and this time you mean business. Well, I'm not asking for Charu's hand."

"What we older generation teach, are always lessons, bachcha, and that's all the deity will teach me too. That's how it is done, and it is not as if we haven't already done so for you, bachcha," Richie's maan calls from the kitchen.

Daivey and Kuvan are standing in the hall. Kuvan walks back inside the living room and stands back as Richie squeezes by, past his father.

Aarzoo is now pressing his jacket; his shirt is hanging on the ironing board by its hanger. So too his waistcoat and trousers. Richie stands behind the ironing board in the kitchen. We can just see him past his mother's outline as she finishes the last of the pressing.

"You shouldn't take it yet, bachcha." She is pleased but tearful at the same time; he grabs the shirt, and we find ourselves beside the pair, at the end of the ironing board.

"I do not know why you are upset, mother."

"Maan or maji, Richie."

"Yes, that is all the same. Come now, my family." Richie turns and sees the rest of his three family members behind him. Kuvan is smiling; the other two, Daivey and Gaurav have stern faces. "Am I not English like you and mother, pita jee? Surely I have the right to pick who I want for myself through life's changes."

"It is not the way the world changes, Richie, it is the way you handle these days that seem to be the same but are not. We must pick ourselves up and carry on. And if something is set to challenge you then you take these days head on and do what you must to get the job done. Now, no more silly talk that you will not get married."

Richie's pita jee fluffs his hair from the front. Then Richie turns and his maan passes him his jacket on a hanger. He puts it back, hanging it where the shirt had been before. Richie puts his shirt on, and then his trousers. He tucks his shirt into his trousers and put his slip-on shoes on. Richie's mother now passes him his jacket, yet again. She is waiting for him to kiss her before he leaves the kitchen. Richie puts his jacket on, kisses Aarzoo, then heads for the front door. "See ya all." He walks through the door. Turning, she walks back to the ironing board.

"I feel so cruel. I don't know how to contain myself," Aarzoo says, turning to place some more ironing she has beside her and stack it on the kitchen work top.

"Ladakee," Kuvan says.

"I shouldn't worry, Aarzoo, this will be the greatest thing Richie has ever done," Gaurav says, then turns and walks back into the living room.

"Aarzoo, my precious patni. What would you be doing if he didn't accept? You would be in more of a rage with yourself, yet now you are only sympathetic to your son's needs," Daivey explains.

"He accepted, he accepted?" Aarzoo says, in shock.

"Yes, dear, he accepted." Kuvan is holding her daughter from the side, to comfort her.

"Of course he accepted, he only complained the once, and then took it like a man should." There are screams of excitement, and much laughter.

Richie is walking to the bus stop.

Well, would you believe it? They have done what I have not asked them to do. I do not believe them in the slightest. They are so impulsive. I can tell you, all I am going to do is ignore what has happened this morning, and forget all they have said. They probably are just baiting me with what could happen, and not what really is happening. Which is nothing, yet, as we don't have enough income to fuel the happy thoughts my family have of marrying me off to Charu, in the first place.

Richie approaches the bus stop.

Ah, that's it. My family are just telling me that this will happen when I have taken the job as an accountant with the Patijna's.

The bus pulls up and all the waiting people get on the bus. As Richie sits on the top deck all goes in fast motion, with Richie in slow motion, looking around as the bus follows its journey to his work place. He gets off of the bus, waits for the traffic to calm, and then walks across the road.

All I know is that if nothing is said for the next two weeks, then all is forgotten.

From the roof of the bank we see Richie walk into the bank.

All is going well for Richie and the rest of the employees at the Partners' bank. Every productive day has crept along, seemingly, at Richie's new rate of routine. Though, as he looks back, he understands. Time waits for no one person in the same way. He thinks of people standing and drinking with their coffee in hand. Or a cup of tea at the kettle. It's enough to relax him from the pressures of work. He is thinking of their daily routines for a reason. To detract himself from the heavy workload he has been given, ever since he talked about leaving. Richie doesn't leave his seat as the daylight drifts away, and later the office lights are turned on. All the office staff will go home, and then come back to work; this all goes along at normal speed, except for Richie, it seems. He plods slowly through the swiftness of his computer's actions, resting when he can, as the rest of his workmates, and he himself, occasionally, go about their routines. Nearly two weeks pass by.

He is snapped out of his mind's delve into the workings of the Bank. Geoff breaks the silence.

This Friday morning is ticking along. Luckily for Richie, he feels settled, as the weekend has finally arrived. The day is going well until Geoff breaks into his reverie.

"Richie, Sherry!" Geoff says Sherry's name with more spite than haste. "What are your projections for this month?"

Sherry says, "Don't pick on him, Geoff. He's been helping me with my work all week until today. I've just got the hang of things. It's not his fault he's behind."

Jacky, already smiling, keeps her thoughts to herself as she clicks at her keyboard.

"Sorry, Sherry. My offset is in your mailbox; well done for keeping up with all this extra workload. Along with keeping the office software glitches from happening things must be very hard for you, so don't listen to Geoff. Geoff, if you'd bothered to look, you have this in your mail box too." Richie looks from Geoff to Sherry. "Don't let him wind you up, Sherry. You know what he's like. He floats from one area of our lives to the other." The office staff all look towards Richie. "Without a care. He thinks he knows better, but what does he know?"

The rest of the office starts to applaud Richie, apart from one.

"So, what's the big idea, Richie?" Richie looks to his left. He sits at the point of the circle nearest the door. The door that brought them all into this place of subjugation, and of the flirtatious exercise of money: of other people's money.

"What, Jacky? Have I put too much into the projections of next month's expenditure? I mean, what we had coming in last month – that was not enough. We need more coming in from your end of the pie to make this work, and I can tell you I gave you the right areas to place your money. And if you are not going to let me leave, you're going to have to read it and weep, 'cause I'm telling you that what we made last month was a pittance compared to what I'd predicted." Richie stands up. "That goes for all of you. God damn, why is it always me that gets into trouble?" He sits and loses himself in his work on screen.

Inside the boardroom, the three partners are sitting at their desks, all in separate locations around the room. Suddenly the internal phone rings on the oldest Partner's desk.

Picking it up, he answers, "Yes, hello Sonia, what can I do for you?"

Sonia: "It's an external line, sir. It is the Patijna family, A Tejasvat. He is returning the call that I made, as you asked."

Oldest Partner: "That's great, Sonia, patch him through." (he smiles, putting the phone in speaker mode) "The start of something grand maybe upon us, brothers."

Middle Partner: "Fantastic."

Youngest Partner: "Understandably good news."

Tejesvat Patijna: "Hello, hello, is this the Leicester Allegiance?"

Oldest Partner: "Yes, Mr. Patijna, or should I call you Tejasvat?"

Tejasvat: "No, No, No, call me Tej."

Oldest Partner: "That's very informal of you Mr. Patijna, Tej. So, Tej, shall we get straight down to business?"

Tej: "That is what I am calling about, sir."

Oldest Partner: "As far as my brothers and I are concerned, we know you own a chain of restaurants and takeaway services in and around the city. But what we are offering is a wealth of financial services for you to tap into."

Middle Partner: "Well done."

Youngest Partner: "Good show."

Tej: "Okay, but maybe I can help you too."

Oldest Partner: "I am sure, and that is a nice way of starting business, Tej. Well, as you are aware we have localised banking for you, and of course all of your friends who work for you, and also those in and around your business. Ha ha, and maybe your business competitors. We can make your business more competitive than anyone else's, Tej, of course. I am sure you are aware that Richie Gyndall works here for us, he is a marvellous boy; he knows your family very well, I hear?"

Tej: "Yes, yes, that is all very well, and sounds very understanding. You will have to send me your business banking information after you hear what I have to say about your remarkable working colleague. It is true then, that you are simply looking for more business investment, huh?"

Oldest Partner: "Yes, we need as much investment as we can get our hands on."

Middle partner: "Good job."

Youngest Partner: "Bally right and all."

Tej: "And you own the bank yourselves?"

Oldest Partner: He clears his throat before answering. "Why do you ask, Tej? Are you interested in keeping the local banking business alive and thriving?"

Middle Partner: "Of course he does."

Younger Partner: "Of course, good man."

Tej: "Yes, yes. We do as a family unit, but we do not know if we trust the Gyndall family at this moment in time. Richie is a very lucky man, you know."

Oldest Partner: "Well, Tej, he's more of a boy than a man, but yes, he is very lucky to be working for us, yes."

Tej: "Ha ha, yes that is true, that is why we must talk. There is much more to Richie Gyndall than you know; if you think he is simply a once a week PAYE earner you are very wrong. This goes no further; he must not know of the consequence when he marries my daughter."

Oldest Partner: "Don't tell us."

Middle Partner: "No, he won't, Tej."

Younger Partner: "He gets half the business, and will bank with us respectively?"

Tej: "No, no, you are not listening, let me tell you. He is going to be left a lot of money, a bequest of royal wealth, so it seems; the Gyndall family received a letter from their in-laws to tell them all about it. He must not know that if he marries, and the Gyndall family and ours have come together to make this happen, he will become more wealthy than anyone of us can imagine."

Oldest Partner: "Why are you telling me this, Tejasvat?" He holds his index finger up beside his head, ready to demonstrate something.

Tej: "Well, as you know, and I've been thinking about this, so don't interrupt until I say so. Royal lands and estates can have their money tied up with employee contracts, and all the other excesses that come with keeping their lands in tip-top condition. The money that he will receive may be hard to get hold of. But if we can arrange a loan with your bank, so that I can realise my idea of creating the largest chain of curry restaurants in Leicester, or even the country, then I would be very grateful. Do you see where I am coming from, sir?"

Oldest Partner: (lowers his hand, pointing to the boardroom table. His two brothers start to clap) "Is that so, Tej?"

Tej: "And I'm sure Richie and my daughter wouldn't be shy and want to change their minds, and I would not feel I needed to redirect them, that is, from doing all their banking in England with your local Leicestershire bank, sir."

Oldest Partner: "Well, tell us, Tej, how much land will Richie Gyndall possess when he receives his inheritance?"

Tej: "That is not the problem, sir, the problem is with my business getting their hands on the money we need. Without the Gyndall family's knowledge, that is, and without Richie finding out about the inheritance, sir. Then hopefully you three will be able to highlight to Richie the importance of him getting married to our daughter at any cost."

Oldest Partner: "You have our email address, Tej, and we have your number. I will get a girl onto sorting out business with you right away. Then I will deal with this Richie Gyndall of ours. Firstly, Tej, will you send us a photo of your daughter? I have a plan. Then we will have a chat with young Richie for you and us all. Thanks for all your wisdom,

Tejasvat, and thank you very much." The oldest Partner presses the button on the phone to disconnect the call. All three partners clap.

The oldest Partner calls Jacky. "Can you get in here straightaway, Jacky?"
"Yes, sir," Jacky says, and looks at Richie. "Keep the noise down, Richie, and hopefully everything will be okay." Jacky gets up to go to the boardroom to meet with the partners.
Richie says, "It's always my fault."
Jacky knocks on the boardroom door.
"Come In, Jacky." She hears the three brothers shout together.
She stands just inside the door with her feet shoulder's width apart, and her hands crossed behind her back. "Yes, sirs, what can I do for you?"
"You must tell us what rumours are circulating about Richie," the youngest Partner says.
"Well, sir, nothing, but I can tell that he has a liking for Sherry Traverso, sir."
The middle partner chimes in. "Well, you will receive an email from us for a Mr. Patijna. We want you to talk to him and give him as much of our services as you can; meanwhile keep a very close eye on young Richie, please, Jacky."
"Got it, sir. Got it." Jacky turns and leaves the boardroom.
"Right, Mr, Patijna has sent us the photo of his daughter," the oldest partner says.
"I will go and speak to Geoff. He's the one who set this up," the youngest says.
Richie talks with Jacky as she shuts the boardroom door behind her. "They haven't let you go, have they, Jacky?"
"No, Richie, quite the opposite. I've been told to keep my eye on you." Jacky sniggers as she sits down.
"You all should have let me leave. I heard what was said in the meeting a few weeks ago, and it would have been my greatest pleasure to fill that space. Now the person who will walk in front of the firing line may be any one of us."
Richie's voice trails away just before he berates every one of his workmates in this room about how he feels about them not letting

him leave to do what he has always wanted to do. Jacky's smile chides him into being pulled away from his feelings.

Luckily for Richie, suddenly breaking the peace (the momentum of the argument having settled swiftly) the youngest partner walks in from the boardroom, and speaks to Geoff. As Richie sits looking at his computer screen, a stream of words falls from the top to the bottom of it, 'You could be for it now, Richie,' it says.

Richie cannot contain his surprise. "Not you again." He stops, maybe understanding just where this came from. Then more words fall. 'She's such a bitch, isn't she?'

The youngest partner looks up from Geoff's ear and says, "Your time will come." to Richie.

Geoff looks at Richie, and then at Sherry, and Richie sits more correctly at his desk. He is defusing the situation now by cowering behind his computer screen, and then scratching his leg. He is agitated to his maximum with nervousness over his thoughts on how his family can wind him up so greatly about marrying, and with this, he is still not able to understand why they pick on him so much. Just like everybody here in the office. Then there are more words, 'What will be will be." Richie looks at Sherry but she is deadpan in her appearance. Perhaps, he thinks, it is not her after all?

From the edge of Richie's vision, Geoff disappears. Richie still hides behind his computer screen, and spies Geoff walking towards the Partners' office door.

Richie smirks anonymously. "You are done for now, Richie," Sherry says.

Above his computer screen, Richie watches Geoff, he of strange behaviour, walk back out of the Partner's office to get to his computer. Sherry and Richie look at each other, trying to relax. Standing behind his chair, Richie notices Geoff tap at a few keys. With Geoff's mouse's last click, attention moves away from everyone else's nervousness for Sherry and Richie's future; Geoff notes this by staring at Richie and smiling. The rest of the office are all sitting in their workspaces, for now.

Richie, looking at his keypad, notices out of the corners of his eyes and ears, that the office printer has come to life. Geoff walks over to it, picks up whatever he has printed, and promptly walks back into the Partner's office.

"Keep your head, Richie," says Sherry, who has captivated Richie's life so much and so often. "It's probably someone to replace me. I'm the one that overthinks out of this lot about all our situations. And this is to keep them from replacing every last damn one of you!" Sherry brings her hanky out of her dress suit jacket to meet her nose. She is holding back tears that she felt should have come when Geoff first opened his mouth. She looks down at her knees.

Moments later, Geoff comes back into the office from the Partner's office.

Geoff says, "Sherry. Please come in to see the Partners."

Sherry, looking firstly to Richie, who has his head diverted from her deep into his computer screen, stands and walks towards Geoff. Richie takes a quick look, sees the back of Sherry as she meets Geoff. He is gobsmacked by the situation, even before Sherry walks into the Partners' office.

We are inside the Partner's office.

"Ah, dear Sherry," one Partner says. "Yes, dear Sherry," the older Partner says. "Oh, yes. Dear Sherry," the middle Partner echoes. Geoff moves into the vicinity of the middle Partner's desk, situated by the door at the foot of the boardroom table.

The other two Partners' desks are situated in front of the window. Their desks flank the boardroom table.

The middle Partner shuts the door behind them all.

At the far end of the room, beyond the boardroom table, the wall holds a broad picture of the three Partners. They are standing in a half-hexagon shape, their arms crossed. The three would-be millionaires are looking out upon the living versions of themselves. The older, and wiser, Partner interrupts the silence that envelops them. The older Partner says, "So what do you know about Richie, my love?" The embodiment of the three Partners' working stipulations is there in his speech, trying to empower her into thoughts of her relationship with Richie. He is not quite hitting the mark of the rational that Sherry needs at this moment. What she holds close, is not within the reality of all of their lives yet.

"Nothing Sir!" she says, feeling for her hip to see where the hanky has gone, even though she does not have pockets there. "Nothing at all."

"No, Sherry." The older Partner looks upon her. "No!" the other two Partners repeat.

Geoff reaches out to Sherry, "Don't worry, Sherry. Our intention is not to find out about what you two have been up to together. Not in the physical sense. We know that there's more to your friendship than that. It's more what you might know, my dear!"

Geoff now looks with darker eyes towards the three Partners, who are standing together. He already sounds like them.

Sherry, trying to hide her thoughts of what a brown nose Geoff has concealed beneath his skin tones, says, "All I know is, he hides his love of situations behind closed doors."

"So, you think he might actually agree to this, erm, arrangement?" the middle Partner asks, and he and his two work colleagues start talking about 'The empowerment of the boy'. Together they all look at Sherry and Geoff. Holding power, they loom over Geoff from their differing points of placement. They seem to be physically distancing themselves from Geoff. It seemed he has done their dirty work. They are somehow depicting themselves as if they stand within the painting, with the three standing guard over their power.

"What about marriage, and his own wealth?" the older Partner asks her.

"Well, he knows how wealthy he could be. From the way he speaks about going it alone to write. But I'm not sure I know anything about marriage."

"So, he obviously wants to make money," the middle Partner adds.

"Well, girl, we shall see about that side of things. Call Richie in, and we shall discuss the matter. Now no mentioning the phone call we had from the Patijna family, girl," the younger Partner commands.

Sherry goes to the door, confused.

Richie, sitting behind his desk, hears the door to the Partner's office open.

"Richie. I'm sorry. But will you come here?"

She is confused as she knows of the Patijna family.

Richie, full of self-doubt, gets off of his chair and walks to the door. He moves around Jacky to the entrance of the boardroom. He is more nervous than confused as he has never been in here in his life. He is too flummoxed by the whole situation to understand, or wonder what is bothering Sherry.

As Richie nears the door, Sherry looks back at him. She is glancing around looking for clarity in the office space. She is in full view of everybody else in the room; she is in a mild form of shock.

Richie is astonished as Sherry opens her mouth.

"They want to know about your relationship with someone, I think." Sherry finishes the last sentence of her appraisal of the situation with dignity. With her self-doubt, she still understands that no one can understand the trappings of her mind. As all she knows is that she wants him more than before.

Jacky sneezes.

Richie walks into the room already stoked from the argument earlier, and opens his mouth at once. Taking in his surroundings, he says, "Look. I've had it up to here. You lot cannot tell me anything about love," as he opens himself up to those within the room. Sherry stands behind him, shutting the door. The three Partners grin at him, their feelings showing. In some way, they absorb his reactions, seemingly growing on their own two feet, then looking in on, and at, Richie.

"Look, boy, Richie, is it? Look at my desk."

Richie looks towards the middle Partner's desk at the head of the room. There, sitting there, taped to another photo, is a picture.

Sherry, not noticing it before, is shocked; it is Charu.

Sherry reaches for the right pocket this time. She finds her hanky, and applies it to her nose.

"I… I, I don't know if I quite understand. What are you implying?" Richie reaches for the side of his face with his palm and rubs his cheek.

"Look, boy. We are not implying anything. You must understand that you don't need to know, but what you must do is take this in hand."

Richie thinks for a moment. He knows that his family has this long-lasting relationship with the Patijna family and that they have asked him to realise he must marry Charu. But bringing this into his working domain; it is not the done thing. They would never… Then he realises that the Patijna family are in the restaurant game. Then the penny drops.

"It's all about money, isn't it? My family have phoned you, haven't they? I knew there was something funny about prayers the other day."

The older partner answers. "No, Richie, not your family, but the Patijna's, yes. They want us to make you aware of the fact that you could make this all much more than a charitable case of investment!

You could be not just working in this bank, but taking it on as a joint venture. You could become part of the chain, my boy."
"But they have asked me to be their accounting junior. No? And, well, I know I love Charu." Richie takes a longing look at Sherry. At the start of his conversation, she looked at her feet to avoid her woes. "But pardon me, this is all a bit sooner than I thought!"
The older Partner interrupts Richie's get-out clause speech, and tells him something. His superior lets him understand with wonderment and the endearment in the looks and gestures that the trio of Partners makes toward him.
"Look, Richie! They have told us that you need to get hitched, and both of your families know the honourable rights to that." The phone rings in the background; it is an internal ring tone. "It's just a fact, two people coming together! Now, look, what the heck?" The youngest Partner, midway through his speech, picks up the phone and answers it. Sherry takes a glance at Richie without him knowing. "Yes. Yes, yes, alright, but no? Tell them we are talking to him right now." He listens intently. "Cooking, yes, hold on!" Putting the phone to his shoulder, he tries to speak to Richie. "What's this about food, boy?" Sherry cries some more.
The other two partners, fixated on Richie, look at the younger Partner, and then back at Richie. They are looking for clarification. Richie just shrugs his shoulders. So, the younger Partner goes back to the conversation he was having with his receptionist. "Sorry, I remember, restaurants, no Sonia, we don't want any food delivered, dear."
"Yes. But yes!" The younger Partner says.
He had been looking towards the window, his chin hovering over the phone, but now looks back towards Richie. "Yes, we are. Tell them he doesn't want anything. Yes, and we are sticking to their side of the conversation. No. Oh, the letter, no." He looks back, more now towards the window than before. "No, we won't! No."
Putting the phone down, the younger Partner moves over towards the other two Partners. There are murmurs. All three then turn their backs and whisper together. Richie, Sherry, and Geoff are experiencing three different emotions.
Turning to face them, all three Partners speak as one yet again. "Our …" The older Partner carries on alone, "The … situation. We're only asking a bit more of you, man. As a man!" The other two look at

their colleague. He stands in the middle of the three. "You never know what tomorrow may bring!"

Richie is annoyed. He has heard some confusing things during the phone call. The problem was the younger Partner's lack of clarity; his speech was not of his usual professional standards.

"What's this about a letter?"

"Yes, about the letter, boy," The older one says. "You must be appropriate and to the point, man."

"Man up, man," says the middle Partner.

"Your love of Charu is paramount!" The younger Partner takes a turn.

All three then murmur again to one another.

Then they all speak towards Richie as One. "We're telling you, Richie. You are a little bit us; we're a little bit you!"

A Little Bit Me, a Little Bit You by The Monkees: please be respectful and listen. There is much context, and also content hidden within the text.

Line 1: all three Partners harmonise. Taking the lead when they feel it is necessary.

Line 2: all three Partners harmonise. [We see each of the Partners as they sing]

Line 3: all three Partners harmonise.

Line 4: all three Partners harmonise.

Line 5: all three Partners harmonise. [At this point, Geoff reaches for his pocket and passes Sherry another hanky. Sherry, giving Geoff her old hanky back to him, repetitively pats her eyes. Geoff holds the hanky up by his fingertips and passes it to Richie. Richie puts it in his pocket.]

Chorus:
Line 1: all three Partners harmonise. Taking the lead when they feel it is necessary. [At the start of each verse, Geoff goes to the door to

check if anyone is listening. Jacky is knocking on the door on the other side]

Line 2: all three Partners harmonise. [We see each of the Partners as they sing]

Line 3: all three Partners harmonise.

Line 4: all three Partners harmonise.

Line 5: all three Partners harmonise.

Line 6: all three Partners harmonise.

Line 7: all three Partners harmonise.

Line 6: all three Partners harmonise. [We see each of the Partners as they sing]

Line 7: all three Partners harmonise.

Line 8: all three Partners harmonise.

Line 9: all three Partners harmonise.

Line 10: all three Partners harmonise.

Chorus:
Line 1: all three Partners harmonise. Taking the lead when they feel it is necessary. [The Partners pick up the taped-on photo of Charu, and show it to Richie]

Line 2: all three Partners harmonise. [We see each of the Partners as they sing]

Line 3: all three Partners harmonise.

Line 4: all three Partners harmonise.

Line 5: all three Partners harmonise.

Line 6: all three Partners harmonise.

Line 7: all three Partners harmonise.

Line 11: all three Partners harmonise. [We see each of the Partners as they sing]

Chorus:
Line 1: all three Partners harmonise. Taking the lead when they feel it is necessary.

Line 2: all three Partners harmonise. [We see each of the Partners as they sing]
Line 3: all three Partners harmonise.
Line 4: all three Partners harmonise.
Line 5: all three Partners harmonise.
Line 6: all three Partners harmonise.
Line 7: all three Partners harmonise.
Line 8: all three Partners harmonise.

End Chorus:
Line 1: all three Partners harmonise. Taking the lead when they feel it is necessary.
Line 2: all three Partners harmonise. [We see each of the Partners as they sing]
Line 3: all three Partners harmonise.
Line 4: all three Partners harmonise.
Line 5: all three Partners harmonise.
Line 6: all three Partners harmonise.

"And so, Richie, you must remember that the time is now!" the older Partner finishes.
Richie says, "Yes, but like the enjoyment I get from life. I'm like to live for the moment! I don't want to think about tomorrow."
The three Partners all look at one another. Geoff grins at Richie.
"Ah, but Richie, you never know what's around the corner." They are all in agreement, Geoff nods at the Partners, gesturing that, "Yes, the time is now." They all nod their heads; they are now looking at Richie. Sherry turns to leave. Richie somehow restrains himself from making some loving gesture, and simply follows her. Geoff, smirking, follows too.
From inside the office, Geoff shuts the door but finds he cannot; someone is holding the door. He is confused; we see him back away. "We're a little bit righter!" The older Partner shouts from the open door. The other two Partners move to his side, and shout, "You must do it, now is the time, remember. Now back to work."

The security guard in the lobby of the Bank, without waiting to be asked, opens one of the double doors to let the employees out.

Geoff tries to squeeze out past the rest, but is told, "You iniquitous sod. You won't get past me!"

Richie sarcastically assaults Geoff with Geoff's last comment before all three of them left the Partners' office.

"Ah, but Geoff, you never know what's around the corner."

Geoff growls, "Shut your mouth, wise arse!"

Sherry, and then Richie, leave first as they are in front of the rest of the queue. Geoff has to wait at the rear.

Sherry and Richie stand on the pavement. Sherry, looks across to the other side. She turns to meet his gaze. He is all set to leave her behind.

Richie takes a glance at Sherry, looks down at the pavement, and then back to Sherry.

"I didn't know you cared," Sherry politely says to him.

"About what? My family and their values?"

"No, stupid. About me." She looks back to the other side of the street. "I always thought more of you, Richie."

She is looking back towards Richie. But all the other employees are filing out of the Bank. As they scatter in differing directions, she struggles to see Richie.

Geoff, the last to leave, walks to her left and pulls Sherry away.

"He's got more than himself to think about now. Come on. We're on a night out tonight. Don't forget."

The three of them move away in opposite directions. Sherry turns back towards Richie for one last, loving look. Her gaze doesn't fully express her feelings, so she calls out.

"See you, Richie. Be good to her, won't you!"

As she walks away, Richie can hear people chattering and bows his head. He puts the back of his wrist to his bowed forehead. He can see Geoff and Sherry walking away in his mind. They are silhouetted dark shapes against the red sunset. The sun hangs over the end of the street.

Strangely, to Richie, it is Geoff that takes the reins at that moment.

"Go home and let them show you some way to get her back." he sniggers. Leaning back between himself and Sherry, he then half shouts, "After all, tomorrow never comes!"

Richie is confused; he doesn't understand what Geoff is trying to imply.

Geoff, not entirely understanding his reasons, drops the final words he has to say. These words are designed to open up Richie's unlimited imagination. So Richie's destiny seems to be set in motion. "Come on, Sherry, he'll never make it tonight!"

Richie is unsure at that moment that all would happen that was supposed to happen.

As Richie walks in through the front door of his family home, he is somehow glad. It seems no one is going to stop him from leaving for his room. Then …

"Richie, come here, honey." A voice sounds from the living room. These are the words he has not been waiting to hear. So, dragging his feet, he tiredly walks towards the door.

Upon entering, Richie understands the situation he is in and stops just inside the doorway of the living room. He doesn't want to make much of an entrance.

He understands the situation clearly as he sees the other four of his family in front of him. He stands stiffly, like a soldier.

Looking from the living room window, we see Richie's grandma walk towards him. From out of the family huddle his grandpa moves to stand in front of his chair.

Richie can see his grandma is holding the photo of Charu.

"Don't worry, bachcha," she says and then is surprised, as her husband opens his mouth. Instead of her darling Richie. "Ha. That's for thinking about Frankenstein's cat." Gaurav then sits.

"Frankenstein's cat? I have no idea what you are talking about!" Richie says.

Richie's grandma opens her heart to him as Richie looks from her position to be full of tears. So she tells him, from a distance, "You would never know how Frankenstein's cat looks. Unless you were standing at the angle that I am!" She scowls, and peers backward towards the other members of her family. All this happens while she clutches the photo of Charu to her chest. She is not wholly at odds with herself.

> Daivey: "Now, Richie. There is no need for language like that."
> His mother-in-law sits in her favourite seat. That would be the sofa, on the nearest cushion to her husband. She is now staring at the photo of Charu.

"We have this thing already sewn up, my bachcha. Whether you want it or not."

Richie: "I know. The Partners at the bank have been advising me to take the offer up all afternoon, and I realise it must be profitable for us all." He speaks calmly.

Aarzoo: "No, the Partners haven't spoilt it have they?" She looks to her husband for inspiration.

Richie: "Well, how else would anyone perceive the situation? The one you have created with the letter of the law. The Patijna family has contacts on the high street. With several restaurants and takeaways. I suppose Charu has me tied up. I'll be doing all the paperwork for them in my spare time."

Richie's Grandma, the only one not staring at Richie, now looks at him.

"What else is there?"

The other three chime in in one monotone voice. "Richie?"

"Now, it's for the best." Kuvan quietens, then looks to the others for inspiration.

Richie flaps his arms and leans slightly back, straightens up. He holds his arms slightly back and out straight. He speaks in a lonesome voice. "Just what do you want me to do?" Grandpa is in a mood to respond. He tells him, "Leave your suit on, bachcha. We've got a dinner party to go to."

Kuvan whispers to the photo. "Ah, Richie?"

Sitting in the restaurant are both families. They sit either side of the restaurant's large function room table. Charu is at one end, and Richie stands at the other with his arms still out straight. It as if he has never moved from his front room.

There are two photos, one of Charu and one of Richie, situated in the middle of the table. The waiters are serving piping hot food for everyone to eat. Some people are eating. Some are waiting, with food on their plates. Maybe for something spectacular to happen.

Tej, Charu's Father, opens the conversation. "Tell us, Richie, what is on your mind."

Richie, with his arms still straight, is staring into space. He opens his mouth to say something. Suddenly he is struck with Charu's beauty. Richie looks down at his chest.

Richie's heart is filled with sadness over not only the situation the couple have been manipulated into but also with feelings of sorrow over what the two families have tried to make out of them. Richie is left with the misery of someone who understands that this should not be happening at all. He feels oddly proud as his mind takes the paths any normal person take in these, to him, impassioned and tense times.

Charu, he realises, is in the same situation. She is like the partner of someone else he can trust. Richie is left feeling that he is not at the point or place he ought to be with Charu, as with other girls he knows. Grumpily he thinks that finding his soulmate is his job. He leans on the table and looks at the floor.

His relationship with Charu is more like sister and brother to Richie, or maybe a cousin. They are too close for romantic love to be a reality. Sure, Charu is a girl of unchangeable beauty. More to the point, however, he understands that females need more than friendship to get to know and understand them correctly. He needs that one specific individual. Richie knows the one that he yearns for. Maybe, in the end, they simply existed to be with one another. Even though there is love between him and Charu, is Charu the one? Richie's mind refocuses – or is this all a mistake? Richie glances at his mother and father.

Daivey and Aarzoo suddenly appear to be dressed as the lead characters from Richie's book. Daivey is seated, slightly away from the table. He is beside Aarzoo. Aarzoo has been eating onion bhajis and is scraping the plate with her fingers.

Richie realises his imagination is taking over. He looks at Charu, and sees Sherry looking at him while leaning forward, whispering in Charu's ear. Richie is rooted in the efforts of thinking about why this is happening, half reaching for his suit pocket.

His father speaks to his wife. "Don't eat too much, Aarzoo. These bhajis are just the starters. There's more coming in from the kitchen; and don't scrape your fingers."

Muffled sounds come from Richie's mother.

Daivey repeats himself. "Stop being such a stuffer. You'll end up as bad as maji!"

Richie sees his grandma stare at his father. His father and mother are now dressed as before, and they chat, as Aarzoo's mother watches her daughter closely.

126

Aarzoo says, "What, Daivey? You know I didn't want to."
Daivey replies. "Yes, but Aarzoo, nor did I."
They both giggle.
Richie looks away and then back at the pair. His mother and father
are now dressed in their wedding day outfits. Aarzoo and Daivey
smirk and giggle at each other. They are joyous at the times and
joyous at the occasion; they are immediately disturbed.
"Christ, is that what you two were like on your honeymoon?" says
Richie.
"Listen to Richie. You are soon to be wed, the same as us, so don't
belittle the situation," Aarzoo replies.
"Yes, I'm sorry, Son. Marriage is just the way it is." Daivey sticks up
for his wife. Daivey looks back at Aarzoo. It is just the same as the
day of their wedding. He can remember being nervous, waiting for
Aarzoo.
Richie's Mother and Father's matchmaking was not something
Richie would have ever wanted. Or so he now thought. His family
should have understood their true selves, and their very own
realities.
Richie's family were not properly aware of Richie's needs; did his
grandparents ever love his parents? He looked at his grandparents;
they were undeniably stern-faced.
It is the day of Richie's mother and father's wedding. Aarzoo is
standing at the edge of the ceremonial path to the floral arch on a
circular stairway altar where the marriage will be sanctified; a fire
pit is in the centre. Richie's father walks towards her. He stands
halfway down the stair as Aarzoo greets him. They walk together up
the final flights of stairs to see the priest. He waits until they join
him. The priest greets them both. Then the priest places his hand on
theirs to welcome them into matrimony by tying their hands
together. Daivey picks up Aarzoo and carries her down the circular
stairs that create the altar they were married within. They don't look
like young people; they look the age they are now.

If this is what is waiting for me for the rest of my life, then so be it.
Look at my grandparents. They haven't changed a bit. This whole
marriage sacrament makes me wonder, were my mother and father
ever in love? Well, yes, I suppose they must have been. Though

looking at them, they still don't look like they know what they want. Well, luckily, they had me.

Richie shakes his head and immediately notices Charu, looking at him with serious doubts that he is the right man for her. All at the table are looking at Richie; his mother and father are now dressed, at their son's engagement dinner, in fitting attire. The waiter is still serving food.

Yes, I know that we live with our family names. It's listed as our own in the official papers of my birth. They inherited it too, just like me, and Charu has done the same for the rest of her family when she was born. We live with this tag: conception and time have fitted this to us; so why tie someone else in to confuse it? Cripes, the Paddington Bear books I read as a child explained that Paddington only ever had one label attached to him. What would Paddington have done if his family had put another upon him? 'Oh, and by the way. You can only borrow him. So up yours.'

Richie can see what would happen if he did marry Charu as he looks at his mother and father, wondering why they would arrange such a farce.
Richie pulls himself out of the dizziness he was imprisoned in. "I'm sorry, I apologise to you all. I'm not sure if I know what true love is."
To Richie, his name is his own, to be developed throughout his own life. To better all that went before with real authority. For the love that he's gained through his genes.
It is his and Charu's fellow family members that have made these moves on him. Obviously, they are the carriers of the previous labels. Though there is something more special about his grandparents, he is sure of that. His family is now surely too authoritarian to be loving him and Charu correctly, as they ought to in the real world.
Aarzoo is looking at Daivey, remembering him walking to meet her at their marriage ceremony.
Remembering how pretty she was, she will also never forget the kiss Daivey gave her after the service had finished.
"Maji," Richie asks, "what is the name of the game of life?"

Richie finally awakens to how dangerous this situation is, and his grandma's next speech strikes deep into his self-perception.

"It is self-awareness, bachcha, and I'm afraid you get what you are given and shall have in this world." She looks at the rest of the two families. "Take it as you will."

Richie's grandpa raises his arm to comfort her.

What Richie doesn't know is that she has thought hard about what she just argued. With her last look at Charu, Kuvan realised Richie had more than his own life to lead. Kuvan was feeling this way as her emotions overflowed, back at the house. Even when she'd taken up the photo of Charu, showed it to the rest of her family, in the hallway, when the letter from the Sultan arrived, she just wished Richie would admit his emotions.

Suddenly she feels she can't even look at Richie. Trying hard, she slowly risks a glimpse of her one and only grandchild. He doesn't notice, and she is thankful for that.

"Ah, bachcha."

While gently looking at Charu, all Richie can see in his mind is his outburst towards Sherry, back in the office. The words of Rhett spin in his head. The words of the blockade runner and socialite of the film; Richie is overwhelmed by him. In his day-to-day life story, Rhett somehow is life's glue, holding it together. But Scarlett loves Ashley; is he more like Scarlett than he thinks? The noise from the fan spinning above the table distracts him. Every turn reminds him that he should shout at himself. Then he hears the end of the line. Music begins to play inside Richie's mind.

He says, "I suppose, Charu, this is it? But put simply, I don't really care for the thrills and the spills!" Richie knows that he will think about these simple words for a long time as something in him tells him that he spoke them with spite. Moreover, his heart is divided over his feelings, but that isn't the problem. The problem is the despotism; the power over his decision taken by those around him. His grandma recoils. "All I want is what's right!" His grandpa is putting his hand to her shoulder. Everyone at the table looks to him, and then back to Richie.

Richie registers just what his grandma has said, and his heart sinks. They are renewing themselves through Charu. Then he is struck by the familiar scenario. They all saw life the same way. They were gathered here to honour the hero that he was not.

He despises himself for being trapped in the deep water he finds inside himself. He is deep within the situation that the two families have imposed upon him. With his wantonness enveloping his mind, he is at odds with himself, trying and refute their case, although his emotions, controlled into wanting a relationship, are running riot. Richie remembers when he had no energy to summon from out of the pit of his stomach, to ask Sherry on a date when she was seated at the fountain. He can also see himself with a moustache like his father's. He can see himself ripping it from his face. In the office, in the bank. As he stands there he feels himself grow his father's moustache; he is scared, trying in a panic to stop the growth. He looks down and around as it grows. *Damn, is this a symbol of recognition?* The easy way is staring him in the face. It is Charu. He wants to tell them all that he doesn't want to live like his mother and father, ending up in an arranged marriage; but recognition always has an opposing force. Is he fated to end up like his mother and father?

Other girls, he's noticed, simply don't fall for him. When he looks at what life will hold for him in his future, he can see how the girls he will meet and has met, act differently toward him. Simply put, he feels they loved him for sure, but didn't understand him, or understand his true feelings. He thinks for a sliver of time, trying hard not to forget the spite he felt earlier. His mind is correcting his thoughts. He has always thought that arranged marriage should never happen; it's too crude. For other reasons than those, his mother and father can see that he has always thought, yes, thought that he would forever be gone before they got there if they planned this.

He laughs inside himself.

Sid sure was getting his comment deliberated over, as all I can think of is his comment 'Gone before you get there', but what did that mean? Yes, Richie had thought that there was no way on the living earth anyone, especially his family, could make him do something that he didn't want to do. So this coming together was never going to happen. He could just be mistaken over how he feels about Charu. Richie looks at the two sides of his untimely fate. He has never before been faced with the pressure of an arranged marriage, but now it has happened in his home-world. Time has never risen against it, never being one to war against nature. Perhaps that is what he needs. He thinks about how he feels: that he wants to be like Ashley

Wilkes. He is free from fixture and facts, but ready to fight for what he thinks best. Even if it was slavery. Didn't Richie's fellow workers fight for him when he wanted to quit the bank? So were not all workers fighting for slavery in their own way? This couldn't be right, what he was thinking. Maybe that is what he needs. A war. A Civil War, like in Margaret's book, no, more like a family civil war, or a cultural change. Ashley fought for the South. So that should make things more encouraging, make him want to be with Charu. What does he want? He can't break his train of thought. He is stuck in between his love for his reality, and the way things are. He can see the three Partners at the bank meeting, him standing there with wet clothes. They are wearing United States uniform with Confederate hats. Lady Rosetta is flogging them as they shout at him in tandem. He is still wearing his father's moustache and they are repeating the words, 'What do you want' at him. Things have simply been this way for eternity. He feels restrained from his thoughts for a moment. Richie thinks no one can change what he is feeling now. Conditioning doesn't come into it.

Richie knows his mind is fit. Rhett Butler never married until later, when she gave in to the thought that she would never be with Ashley Wilkes; then Rhett took it out on Scarlett when he found out that she loved Ashley. How would Charu feel, if only she knew? So, where does his life lie? All he wants to do is close the door and walk away. Would Sherry end up looking like Rhett if he got married to Charu? He can't tell what his mind is going to release. Then he sees Sherry standing behind Charu; she is holding Charu's head either side of her face. Sherry is fighting Richie's request to stop; Charu is laughing. He simply thinks that he will be able to falsify the fact that some people have arranged marriages. To get away from being put slam dunk into another one, he supposes. He especially understands this when he looks at the way he has been managed into this position. No, his mind reminds him. These are the facts.

He takes a deep breath in. Now is the time to break the mould.

"I have one thing to say, and this one thing, it is the only thing I am going to say to you before we fall apart. I have the utmost respect for you all, and I do not wish to break the spell cast upon me from when I was born into this world. What I cannot say, though, is that I can love as much as Charu can. She has never changed. All my life, she has been there, and nothing will ever change the interwoven moments we have had together. What you are saying is that we must be more than friends. I accept what you ask with fondness in my heart, but I find it hard to understand anybody with Charu's abilities to take on other people's warmth. That she is able to focus that upon those that are at her beck and call, is astounding to me. As such, I am astounded by this whole situation. So – so I take this opportunity to welcome her as a person that I love."

Richie can't believe what he has just said.

He flings his arms out wide and begins to sing.

One Fine Day by The Chiffons: please be respectful and listen. There is much context and also content hidden within the text.

Line 1: Richie sings, with his family harmonising.
Line 2: Richie, still singing, now has the Patijna family harmonising with him.
Line 3: all harmonise with Richie.
Line 4: Charu sings with all harmonising.
Line 5: Charu sings alone.
Line 6: Charu and Richie are silent. The rest sing. [Richie is looking dangerous. The side of Charu's mouth twitches and she looks away from Richie]
Line 7: Charu sings.
Line 8: Charu sings.
Line 9: Charu sings.
Line 10: Charu sings.
Line 11: Richie and Charu sing.
Line 12: Richie and Charu sing. [Charu is looking at Richie]
Line 13: Richie and Charu sing. [The whole room harmonise while looking like they are talking to each other, and all are in shock]
Line 14: Richie sings alone.

As the room becomes quiet, Richie waits for Charu to move. She doesn't. So he places his hands, this time, fully in his pocket. He feels something in his right pocket and looks down. He is pulling something to the top of his pocket. He spots what is there, somehow also fixing Charu with a serious look, a look of recognition. His face taut, he leans forward on the table.

From the other side of the table, everyone is drawn to Charu's appearance. Richie feels his extended memories fall around him, and notices the moth drawn to the light in the middle of the table.

"Are you doing this because of your honesty, or is it just because I think of you as honest? To do this, I must trust in you more."

In the instant it takes Charu to say these words, Richie falls in love again but wishes his passion was being delivered to the doorstep of someone completely different. He stands tall once more.

Circumscribing Richie away from the party is the ever gentle squeeze of his imagination. He can see what his actual path is, but reality speaks in so many different directions. What way is the right one to choose? He feels as if he has made up his whole life from his imagination. It was okay to serialise his authentic visions of what he thought were the truths of his mind's parodies of everyday life from what he was actually doing. He needs to make the correct decision at least once in his life. There is the hanky in his pocket. It reminds his heart. He knows there is more outside of this situation of what he thinks of as compelled kinship. So that's it, he thinks. He could make this a war, make them into ordinary people, and not just the family members he thought they were at the time.

"Sorry? Everyone, sorry."

One of the waiters cuts into the conversation. He is serving food to the Patijna's son, who is seated in between his mother and father.

"Don't say sorry. Eat up. Please, the more, the merrier."

Richie moves to leave but turns as he gets to the door.

"But that's just it. I am not it." Richie is at the door.

"Richie!" Richie's grandpa, already standing as Richie spoke the word 'sorry', beckons Richie to stop what he is doing. "If you walk out of that door, things will never be the same between us, Richie. I am the head of this family, bachcha. So, we don't want a war of words, do we? I am telling you. We know this is the best thing for you!"

"But Grandpa, I do not want to have my heart corrupted. This face that I carry is more of kindness and thought for all that is going on around us."

Richie opens the door, runs through it, out of the restaurant, and down the street.

Richie's grandma reaches to her husband and pulls him down towards his seat. "There will be no war if we just all calm down. Be civil now, Gaurav. Richie has always had his own mind. Let him tell us what he needs. His total understanding, we now know, is written in our hearts."

Aarzoo looks distraught. "But what about the money!"

Richie is standing with his back to his bedroom door. He is still dressed in his work suit, flustered from the half walk, half run, that he has made to travel here. Turning, Richie hangs his jacket on the back of his bedroom door. He lies on his bed, turning on his radio. Lying in bed, Richie can see himself leaving the restaurant and looking at Charu through the window as he walked away. He is leaving her unattended. Through the window of his mind, he imagines what Sherry is doing. Richie has a tear in his eye. He can imagine Sherry and the rest of his workmates. They are all chatting and laughing as they're about to leave a bar on their night out. Richie, having already pulled the hanky from his jacket pocket, holds it to his face, breathes a deep breath, and holds it to his heart. He remembers back to the film he is engrossed in watching at the cinema. Richie is on the doorstep of Sherry's home; Sherry will walk down the stairs after her father greets Scarlett:

> Richie as Scarlett: "How is Sherry today, can I see her soon?"
> Sherry's father: "Sherry is on her way, you'd better be quick in making your mind up what to do, Richie."
> Sherry's father leaves.
> Sherry walks down the stairs dressed as Ashley.
> Richie as Scarlett: "Sherry, Sherry, let me come to the Kingstone Pub with you?"
> Sherry as Ashley: "Richie, all I can remember is leaving work today."
> Richie as Scarlett: "Oh, Sherry, I have something for you."
> Richie and Sherry walk to a window of the house. "I know it was you who kept sending me those messages on my screen at work."
> Sherry as Ashley: "Why, Richie, you have got to come up with something more special to say to a girl who knows what she's done. It could have been any one of us."
> Richie ties a Union Jack sash around her waist.

Richie as Scarlett: "Yes that is true, but I have done what is best, I have gone to war with my family. They don't know you yet, but they will grow fond of you, I am sure."
Sherry as Ashley: "This war of yours may never end, Richie, if you don't stop being so stupid and own up to who you are!"

Richie is now looking up at his ceiling. The radio DJ is talking about something, Richie does not listen. Suddenly all focus is on the radio, and somehow, Richie disappears into the speaker.

Hungry Heart by Bruce Springsteen: please be respectful and listen. There is much context and also content hidden within the text.

Verse 1:
Line 1: Richie sings. [We see Charu enjoying her meal with the Gyndalls and the others of her family]
Line 2: Richie sings.
Line 3: Richie sings.
Line 4: Richie sings.

Chorus:
Line 1: Richie sings. [We see Richie lying in bed. He is thinking of, and the words speak of, the Kingstone bar]
Line 2: Richie sings.
Line 3: Richie sings.
Line 4: Richie sings.

Verse 2:
Line 1: with Richie still singing. [We can see Sherry and all the people out from work walk into the Kingstone pub]
Line 2: Richie sings.
Line 3: Richie sings.
Line 4: Richie sings.

Chorus:
Line 1: Richie sings. [Richie is seen back inside his Bedroom]

135

Line 2: Richie sings.
Line 3: Richie sings.
Line 4: Richie sings.

Verse 3:
Line 1: Richie sings.
Line 2: Richie sings.
Line 3: Richie sings.
Line 4: Richie sings.

Chorus:
Line 1: Richie sings.
Line 2: Richie sings.
Line 3: Richie sings.
Line 4: Richie sings.

From outside of the restaurant, we see Charu sitting in her seat. She is seated at the table inside the restaurant. She is smiling as her thoughts for her situation have changed. Everyone thinks they understand what emotions Charu is going through. Charu's mother, distracted from the conversation she is having, is not eating her dinner; she is staring at her daughter. She is worried about her daughter's heightened emotional state. Charu's mother thought that all was going well. Until Richie upped and left, she was not too displeased with her daughter's reactions. Then Charu stands, dropping her knife and fork onto her plate.
Mrs. Patijna asks, "Are you all right, child?"
Charu replies, "No, I am not. I have had enough! You lot have pushed me and contorted me until I don't know what I am doing all of my life long. You have ruined me, and my life, once and for all. This is the last time you get to control me, and all of my understandings. Now it is my turn to take control of my life for a change. I am doing what I want to do from now on. That's it. I am taking back my consciousness! I am phoning my friend." Charu takes her phone from her pocket and presses the dial button. "I'm at my family's restaurant. As if you didn't know. Please phone me back as quickly as you can."

Charu says, "I cannot believe you tried to arrange a marriage between me and someone I loved and thought of as a friend. There was no need to do such a thing."

Piya and Tejasvat look at each other and then at their daughter, "It wasn't our fault, dearest."

"Fault isn't something I bring to this meal, your arrogance dilutes your honesty, and now it is my turn to arrange something with the person I like the most. Making it clear it is done with arrogance is my first insight. I should have done this a long time ago. You all took me as a foolish, and now you are all made to look the fools."

With the room now darker than the light that is shining upon her, Charu sits down and leans over her plate. Her head bowed, she has her eyes shut, as the light upon her reflects off her black hair. Her phone rings and she answers it. The rest of the restaurant is quiet.

"Yes. My family's restaurant." She is fully concentrating, controlling her emotions. "The one on the high street. Yes, that's it. The one with the tiger on."

Charu puts the phone back into her pocket, lifts her head, and then speaks to the table.

"My friend from the temple is here." He walks into the room.

Disco lights flash over all of the other members of the two families as they chat amongst themselves. They are deep in dismay at the situation. Though no one says a word about the broken relationship, it seems. They all settle down as white light shines upon them. They are highlighting their delirium.

A fresh light illuminates the boy from the temple. The other is focused on Charu. The boy from the temple steps out of his light, and then, in the dark, moves into Charu's light.

"We are both going places tonight." Charu now talks to her friend. "You can walk me around the City." The boy pulls Charu, light and all, towards the other spotlight. It is where he left it, at the other end of the table.

Once they are both connected, standing in the combined light, Charu and her new friend turn to leave.

Charu turns back, her friend pulling at her hand, and puts her thumb to her nose. She waves her fingers while blowing a raspberry, and then both disappear.

As the overhead lights come back to the room, Charu's brother is laughing at the rest of the two families seated at the table.

137

Act Five: Beeyar, Vain, aur Sprit. (Beer, Wine, and Spirits)

Richie knows where all the people he works with are going tonight as there's a band at the Kingstone pub up in the quiet part of the city. Richie is still dressed in his work suit, walking along the pavement towards the pub. With nothing more on his mind than the book he is reading, Richie is relaxed. He is nearing a full building. It is bigger than anything Richie has passed by in the last few moments. He stands for a moment, hearing music, and looks towards the source of the noise, noticing it is coming from within the building. He looks at the sign; it reads The Kingstone.

You can understand that I have a love for what powers this world, and love for our right to be able to do what we want, when we want. Though to understand that we must abide by what we are taught, it is the same for you as it is me, no, but what about our lust, lust for self-preservation? That I understand now is more creative, and combines the two trains of thought. Our self-awareness, and that what we have learned. Self-preservation carries on even when we think we are alone in our wellbeing's magnitude. We ourselves must have to overcome the obstacles that are placed in front of us as we alone travel through the hurdles of life. What we…

A man stumbles out through the door of the pub; the music becomes louder, then quiets as the door shuts behind him. He staggers up the road.

What we let people see isn't always what we would like the person to see of ourselves, nor do we what we understand that is written bellow our shell-like exterior. But what lives and breathes beneath our skin can only be exempted by ourselves, so then, that is what is providing us with new desires to make us change what belongs in our lives. To those of you out there that do not understand, you haven't made those decisions yet. Believe me when I say they will come. Ha ha, if this all goes to plan it will prove something to you, then I will tell you later exactly how our future can be held by us all.

Richie walks inside the pub.

There is lots of noise and chatter, normality for everyone in the pub, but it takes Richie's ears a little while to get used to the influx, which has made him pin his ears back as the door shuts behind him.

He is looking across the bar area. He can see all of the people he knows from work; they are all in different areas of the pub. There are many pods of people at intervals around them.

The whole floor space is brought alive, bustling with nightlife.

The band has stopped playing since Richie walked into the bar.

Then, as Richie pays for his drink, he turns to look at where the band is situated. A guitarist plays a few notes. A man enters from the left-hand side of the stage – he looks like the bar manager to Richie – and speaks.

"Ladies, ladies, please. If you will, ladies, please take advantage and make your proposition to the man of your choice. We are going to do something to bust this place right apart tonight – it an unpleasant surprise to belittle the Partners at our local bank. Now gentlemen, yes, please, please, ladies, of course! No money must change hands, for legal reasons. What we are going to do is let the Partners pay for the rest of the evening."

All the ladies in the vicinity of Geoff scream.

Behind the bar, one of the barmaids, pulling a pint, speaks to her boss, and the boss of the other working bar staff.

"You should've known. How couldn't you have let your husband do this in the first place? There was no way those bloody misers should have gotten away with this!"

Her boss replies, "Ha, how dare you criticise the Partners! Mind you. I thought that. So if it's for the benefits of their employees' at tonight's party, then it is okay with me! So I'm gonna bill them for the previous round also."

"She can!" says the barmaid and looks front.

Jacky, picking up some drinks for a group of women she is standing beside, opens her mouth at the bar, saying, "Oh my. Oh, my. Where're the ladies. I think I'm going to lose consciousness!" The barmaid smirks.

> First Barmaid: "Jacky, is it? Yer, don't faint, Luv. You'll spill your drinks!"
> The Barmaid's Boss: "That's Okies with me!"

139

Bar Manager (shouting from the stage): "Gentlemen, come on, let them make some bids," We can now see from where the band is situated. "Come on, give some of that honey! Don't be bashful, you lovely people!"

Geoff, standing with a group of women, shouts. "I'll take Miss Happy Features here."
He is looking at the girl to his left. She moves from his left, putting her left arm up in approval.
The Bar Manager says, "Come on now, we need more activity from you girls. Come on, let's give it another try."
"Forty pounds," One of the girl's shouts, standing near Jacky. "For Miss Fanny, Jacky!"
Jacky is flummoxed and looks at the floor, and then seemingly dumbfounded as she stares into space. "Well, that's the most romantic thing I've ever heard!" she says.
"Damn," says the girl. "No money must change hands?"
Jacky's hopes of a relationship finish, as her fancy girl who bid for her snaps her hand back away from the stage back towards her.
Jacky blushes while looking in shock at the girl. The other girls shout at the pair, "Maybe later?"
Away from the confusion, little does anyone comprehend that Richie has secretly walked towards the stage area.
He is shouting out above the low murmur that the pub has achieved at this point. Richie says, "But I've just brought a drink, it's not fair."
The Bar Manager says, "Sorry, Richie, mate. It looks like you were a little late. Doesn't it, everyone?" Some cheers and then jeers come from the crowd.
Sherry moves towards Richie. "Oh, Richie! You should have put that on our tab. Geoff has the kitty. If you ask me, the Partners are not going to get away with this. They can pay for all our drinks tonight."
"That's it! The drinks are on the house?" the barmaid shouts.
Sherry beams with delight, "That's it, Richie. You've done it! You can have me for free from now on and forever."

Gentleman Bar Manager: "That's it, Richie everyone." The man on stage shouts in the microphone that the drinks are on the Partners' tab. "Right, Richie looks like he's the first to get hitched to a lady. For the account of Sherry Traverso."

Geoff: "Who?"

"Sherry Traverso!" Richie laughs, Sherry looks embarrassed and slightly disappointed with Geoff.

The Bar Manager: "Miss Traverso is not pining tonight, Geoff. She was in mourning over something else. So I'm told." Sherry is looking at Geoff.

Geoff seems serious, and then feels for the girl to his left. Proud he has made acquaintances, he adds, "So, I'm sure you other girls will be more than happy to oblige your other halves." All the girls around Geoff walk away. The last to leave, the girl he had his eyes for lets him know that he should, "Just get the beverages, lonesome?"

Richie: "Did you hear what he said! He said, Miss Sherry Traverso! Does that mean?" Richie realises Sherry's sudden understanding of their first moment together.

Sherry: "Yes, like he just said, and like she just said; lonesome, but you are not now. Ha, it looks like you've done two great things tonight, Richie. Oh, I'm spellbound. Richie, I'm so glad you're here."

Gentleman Bar Manager (looking directly at Sherry): "She doesn't even consider it, Richie! Do you understand? Tonight is all for you."

Sherry looks shocked, but privately feels an abundance of feelings for the situation. She laughs, "I'm not in mourning at all," and so she tells everybody, "Yes, this is me, and Richie will take what he's given!" The crowd starts jumping up and down.

Everybody slowly draws breath after the outburst, and then turn towards Sherry. She, wearing a black dress, walks to the front of the stage, pulling Richie with her. She is getting accustomed to the crowd, and her joy of the situation, over Richie adorning her with his presence. Richie is shocked. He asks Sherry, "But how could you know about what has happened to me tonight?"

"Don't be silly, Richie. I don't know anything. It's that I've just decided. I can't take this anymore. I quit this slave-labour side of town."

Richie says, "Look, Sherry, if you need to get me alone and question me about why I didn't comfort you at the fountain, well, the thing is Sherry, it wouldn't have been the right thing. Or the right time, like now. I know I haven't always loved you the way I feel you deserved, Sherry, but it sure has felt like love."

"My God, it was you at the fountain. Oh, Richie, you should have come to me. You know I knew there was something wrong with my last boyfriend! Richie darling, I've always had my eye on you. To this date, I haven't taken my eyes from what you have been doing. I love you, Richie, and always have. Tonight I only just came to this conclusion. Come with me, Richie, and we'll go and work for somebody else that looks after their employees with a lot more care."

"That sounds great, Sherry, I hate working for the Partners. We could even start our own business, but tell me something. Was it you or Jacky that placed those words on my computer screen? I thought it was you to start with, but Jacky stands up for us all."

"Ha ha," Sherry laughs outside of the conversation, then brings it back on track. "Yes, Richie, it was me. Who else would do that, and be like this?" Sherry gives Richie a big hug.

The crowd parts.

Sherry walks through the parting crowd. Jacky is fanned by the ladies around her with beer mats pulled off a table. She looks to have regained her cool. She smiles at the woman who paid for her.

A man walks from the back of the stage. "Choose your loved ones for The Happening."

Richie bows to Sherry. "We've kind of shocked the Partners tonight. Haven't we, Sherry!"

"It's a little bit like the Happening, isn't it Richie?" Sherry replies.

"The Happening, Sherry?" Richie asks.

Everybody now splits into couples. Some are men and women, and one pairing is just women.

It is Jacky and her new friend.

The Happening by The Supremes: please be respectful and listen. There is much context and also content hidden within the text.

Line: Sherry sings, with harmonising from all. [All dance hand in hand, and dance through the middle of paired people. There is much dancing from both sides, including Sherry and Richie. With Sherry always holding her own]
Line: Sherry sings, with harmonising from all.
Line: Sherry sings, with harmonising from all.
Line: Jacky sings, with harmonising from all.

Line: Sherry sings, with harmonising from all.
Line: Sherry sings, with harmonising from all.
Line: Sherry sings, with harmonising from all.
Line: Jacky sings, with harmonising from all.
Line: Jacky sings, with harmonising from all.
Line: Sherry sings, with harmonising from all.
Line: Jacky and Sherry sing, with harmonising from all. [Jacky and Sherry are holding hands and dancing through the middle of the two pairs of people]
Line: Jacky and Sherry sing, with harmonising from all.
Line: Jacky and Sherry sing, with harmonising from all.
Line: Sherry sings, with harmonising from all.
Line: Sherry sings, with harmonising from all.
Line: Sherry sings, with harmonising from all.
Line: Sherry sings, with harmonising from all.
Line: Sherry sings, with harmonising from all.
Line: Sherry sings, with harmonising from all. [Sherry dances back up to the rear of the line with Jacky]
Line: Sherry sings, with harmonising from all.
Line: Sherry sings, with harmonising from all.
Line: Sherry sings, with harmonising from all.
Line: Sherry sings, with harmonising from all. [Jacky is seen kissing the woman that bid for her. Then Sherry congratulates them both]
Line: Sherry sings, with harmonising from all.
Line: Sherry sings, with harmonising from all.
Line: Sherry sings, with harmonising from all.
Line: Sherry sings, with harmonising from all.
Line: Sherry sings, with harmonising from all.
Line: Sherry sings, with harmonising from all.
Line: Sherry sings, with harmonising from all.
Line: Sherry sings, with harmonising from all.
Line: Sherry sings, with harmonising from all.
Line: Sherry sings, with harmonising from all.
Line: Sherry sings, with harmonising from all. [Sherry stayed in shot at all times. She is seen singing the last few lines to Richie in front of the band, and gesturing to the pairs of people]
Line: Sherry sings, with harmonising from all.

As they embrace each other, Richie speaks to Sherry. "That is the first time anyone has fully approved of me." Then speaking to the whole pub, he says, "Come on, everyone!" he waves towards the door. "Come with us."

Richie pulls Sherry along through the pub. She asks, "Why, where are we going?"

"Ha ha, we have a date at a very special screening, Sherry."

Everyone leaves apart from the regulars. One is seen sitting at the bar. He is watching everyone leave. The band packs up and goes too. The regular at the bar finishes his pint of beer. Places the glass on the bar, and orders another drink. The barmaid obliges.

Outside the pub, there is a taxi rank across the street. Everyone in Richie's party gets into taxis. The band are the last to get into a cab. They are all, apart from the drummer, carrying their instruments.

As Richie's taxi pulls away, he gets out into the middle of the road. He is beckoning everyone to follow.

Inside Richie and Sherry's taxi Sherry gives Richie a light kiss on his left cheek.

So, I spoke earlier about exactly what the future holds for us all. Well, I'm sitting here next to the lovely Sherry, and I never thought this would happen!

Richie looks at Sherry, Sherry smiles at him: *I love you, Richie Gyndall.*

So, again, let me tell you, even as we breath the past, the future is told to us, whether we like it or not. We can even listen to what it tells us by simply imagining what we are missing. It not only looks like nothing was different than before, when we look back on life, but those electrical sparks of our will to make right what is wrong are still there. It only takes a nano-second to forget, then all we hold dear can be lost in a moment of realisation of our past fears. Am I telling you that our futures are already written? Perhaps I am, then. So maybe it's time you should just listen to what I should have said a long time ago! If I had asked Sherry here to be with me at the fountain there would have been a lot less suffering for sure, but would all have turned out so well?

Richie: "Will you marry me, Sherry?"

Sherry: "You're asking me to get married to you?"

Richie: "Yes, we will give our jobs up and seek exactly what is meant for us, honey."

Sherry: "Then if that means I don't have to dwell on the fact that you and I took on what those dickhead Partners had planned for us, then yes, Richie. And more than that, I would prefer to be free from the chains of the partners' restrictions, and to fight for our futures together. So, yes again, yes, Richie, I love you."

As I thought. This one's got more fight in her than me, I think?

Richie: "Great."

The convoy of taxis pull up outside the cinema. The one Richie frequents so often. Bob is standing inside at the front of the cinema. He is situated just inside the lobby, waiting at the front door instead of collecting his tickets – he is directing people as they walk in.

The film Richie watches passionately is advertised on the threshold of the Cinema.

Richie walks inside, with most of the others following. Richie grabs Bob.

"Hiya, Bob. Give me your clippers, Bob." Bob unquestioningly does as Richie asks.

Richie is now holding Sherry's hand. He calls the rest of the people that have come into the cinema, included the band. "Come on, guys. Come on in!"

With Richie taking the lead, they all follow.

Richie starts to click the clippers, and a beat appears from the rhythm he is making. All glance at a man as a guitar begins. The musician starts to play, as all move through the lobby. People are jumping around with popcorn. Throwing packets of crisps and sweets and taking drinks as they all start to sing. Two people run into the toilet and lever one of the mirrors off of the wall. They leave with it.

Everyone moves into the room showing the film Richie has been watching.

Dancing on the Ceiling by Lionel Richie: please be respectful and listen. There is much context, and also content hidden within the text.

Verse 1:
Line: Richie sings. [As they all move into the cinema]
Line: Richie sings.
Line: Richie sings.
Line: Richie sings.
Line: Richie sings.

Chorus:
Line: Richie sings. [One of the couples that have stolen the mirror climbs onto the other's shoulders, and puts the mirror in front of the projector hole. The scene from the film, the one where Rhett buys Scarlett, is projected onto the ceiling]
Line: Richie sings.
Line: Richie sings.
Line: Richie sings.

Verse 2:
Line: Richie sings. [Richie is standing in front of the screen, with Sherry]
Line: Richie sings.
Line: Richie sings.
Line: Richie sings.

Chorus:
Line: Richie sings. [The couple is still sitting on the other's shoulders]
Line: Richie sings.
Line: Richie sings.
Line: Richie sings.

Chorus:
Line: Richie sings.
Line: Richie sings.
Line: Richie sings.
Line: Richie sings.

Verse 3:
Line: Richie sings. [Richie moves back into the cinema walkways, with everyone else, Sherry following]
Line: Richie sings.
Line: Richie sings.
Line: Richie sings.
Line: Richie sings.
Line: Richie sings.
Line: Richie sings.
Line: Richie sings.
Line: Richie sings.

Chorus:
Line: Richie sings.
Line: Richie sings.
Line: Richie sings.
Line: Richie sings. [Sherry and Richie move outside the cinema, to kneel in front of Bob, who blesses them. Both bowing their heads, Richie passes Bob his clippers back]

Chorus:
Line: Richie sings. [There is lots of dancing inside and outside of the cinema]
Line: Richie sings.
Line: Richie sings.
Line: Richie sings.

Verse 4:
Line: Richie sings.
Line: Richie sings.
Line: Richie sings.
Line: Richie sings.
Line: Richie sings.
Line: Richie sings.

Chorus:
Line: Richie sings. [All are dancing on the roof of the building. It is daylight, as if they have been celebrating for days]

Line: Richie sings.
Line: Richie sings.
Line: Richie sings.

Chorus:
Line: Richie sings. [Getting back into a taxi, Richie and Sherry move away, as Charu is walking with her friend from the temple]
Line: Richie sings.
Line: Richie sings.

Deep within the security of the palace walls, somewhere in the north of India, the dying Sultan of the innocent kingdom lies stretched out in front of his wife. He is lying in the four-posted bed of his bedchamber, looking grey and withdrawn. By his side sits his lovely wife, Jasmine. She holds his hand while he seems to her to want to rescue her from the bitterness, and the sadness of what has taken his body. His loyal Chikitsak and a manservant are also in the room. The Chikitsak is standing by the bed, behind the Sultan's pretty wife, and his manservant, standing beside the Chikitsak, is pouring tea from a pot. The cup is sitting on an extraordinary silver tray. The Sultan is likely to pass soon. His life is leaving him finally within the next few moments. All by his side can tell.

> Sultan: "Ojas. My only real friend. What has this world done to deserve this? But I fear this falls upon the afterlife's deaf ears. I will get there sooner than later. Time's epitome of our last moments,"
> Jasmine: "No, my maananeey pati. We are here." The manservant is walking, carrying a cup of tea with one hand, towards his loyal master.
> Sultan: "Moments shall live forever in me. But I am ashamed. Your delicate ears are not for me for much longer, Jasmine. I fear that it shall not be long before I am taken. Though fear not, my loving patnee. You shall see me take you all. You hide within the love that I carry into the land of our god. I will then be standing tall, with all of my knowledge of our lives written by him. Your delicate self does not deserve to see me take only part of you all, but that is already written to happen, just like when our children

148

disappeared from about us. What you must all understand is that I do not fear to leave you. My fear is manifesting from the idea that there may be no one who will take my reins of my kingdom after I am gone. Ojas, you must go to England and tell the boy Richie exactly what is here for him. None of his family must have the chance to take what is rightfully his away. Like so many are to do to me, I feel. As of now, the rules have changed as I am to die sooner than I thought. You must see that the new Sultan marries the woman he truly is made for, unlike you, my true love, whom I picked from many, and so who could not resist. I cannot order him to be forced into what he doesn't desire, even if he does what they ask. Chikitsak, you must take funds and provide what you must to see this done!"

Chikitsak: "Theek hai dost! Okay, friend, I shall take from what you all have given me, and make this trip for you. But I am afraid too. I must be here to attend to your needs while you surrender to leaving us all too soon!"

Sultan: "Pass the notepaper and quill, Jasmine. So I can write to the new Sultan myself."

The Sultan slowly pulls himself to the rear of his bed, and his wife, having put the writing implements onto his lap, props him up from behind.

Oh! You Pretty Things by David Bowie: please be respectful and listen. There is much context and also content hidden within the text.

Verse 1:
Line 1: the Sultan's wife Jasmine sings.
Line 2: the Sultan's wife Jasmine sings.
Line 3: the Sultan's wife Jasmine sings.
Line 4: their aids sing.
Line 5: the Sultan sings.
Line 6: the Sultan sings.
Line 7: all three sing together.
Line 8: all three sing together.

Verse 2:
Line 1: the Sultan sings.

Line 2: the Sultan sings.
Line 3: all three sing.
Line 4: all three sing.
Line 5: all three sing.
Line 6: all three sing.
Line 7: all three sing.
Line 8: all three sing.
Line 9: all three sing.

Chorus:
Line 1: all sing. [The band starts to play]
Line 2: all sing.
Line 3: all sing.
Line 4: all sing.
Line 5: all sing.
Line 6: all sing.
Line 7: all sing.
Line 8: all sing.

Verse 3:
Line 1: the Sultan sings. [He sees himself in the market place with his family]
Line 2: the Sultan sings.
Line 3: the Sultan sings. [Sultan looks to Jasmine]
Line 4: the Sultan sings.
Line 5: the Sultan sings.
Line 6: the Sultan sings.
Line 7: Jasmine sings with tears.
Line 8: the Sultan sings.
Line 9: the Sultan sings.

Chorus:
Line 1: all sing.
Line 2: all sing.
Line 3: all sing.
Line 4: all sing.
Line 5: all sing.
Line 6: all sing.
Line 7: all sing.

Line 8: all sing.

Jasmine looks at her loving husband. He is tucked away in the depths of the throw on his bed. "Be well!" she says, now looking down and crying.

"The Homo Superior!" the Sultan says. He is scratching at the parchment, trying to keep his writing under control. Signing the letter at the bottom of the paper, the Sultan is drained.

He suddenly leans back, grey and drawn. The mood in the room is turning sombre. It is like the taciturn appearance of the Sultan. He is spent, his family's magical energy has dissipated and somehow is beyond the rules of doctoring.

"Now is my time, lovely Jasmine. Burn my shell, do as I ask. Or I will not escape these lands for an eternity." The Sultan speaks softly.

"I will do as you ask, Madesh, please, please, do not leave yet," Jasmine turns to the Chikitsak. "We must be able to do something more…"

The sultan breathes his last breath.

"No, my master," The Chikitsak calls to give his master with all his last strength, but it is too late, Madesh is gone. "Master, no!"

Jasmine turns back in disarray, "Madesh my husband, no, hear me, you were the only one for me, no!" Jasmine is crying, Ojas is kneeling while resting his head and his hands on his master's bed. Both begin to cry more tears of sadness.

It is late evening, and unusually it is quiet now in the palace, the musicians have stopped playing; there is a knock at the bedchamber door. Jasmine, the only person in the room, lifts her head from the side of the Sultan's bed, and calls, "Enter." The bedchamber door opens and a manservant walks into the room. "There are two people here to see you, Jasmine."

Jasmine stands and the Imam from the mosque, and also the shaman, walk into the room. They are both dressed in white.

"He has passed, he has passed, yes, yes?" the shaman asks. The manservant brings in the shaman's lamp and places it beside the head of his master's bed. Leaving, he comes back with a copper bowl elaborately stylised and full of warm water. He puts it to one side. He opens the door and two women enter. They place rice balls around the body and place flowers at their master's feet.

"If you mean my husband, yes he has passed, shaman," Jasmine answers. "Will you protect him from the spirits, shaman, until he is buried? Please, I can ask of you no more than you can provide. Is this a possibility, or will those who cursed me take his spirit before he can pass on his soul? Priest, as Madesh was a practising Muslim, who will wash the body? Madesh has no family, only those in England."

"I will take care of all Madesh's needs, Jasmine; you will have to send me his closest servants. I have the cloth to shroud him in. It is all we can do in his time of need. This is not the norm, but it has happened before in these most extreme times." The priest is staring at Madesh.

"You must leave; no one must enter from now on. Bring flowers made into a leopard's form, and I will place it next to him. This all must be done before the funeral takes place." There is a roar from the jungle as the shaman goes quiet. "He he he, it is happening just like I envisaged. Stay alert, Jasmine, your time will come." The shaman starts his mantra.

The Imam says, "I know you are from a long line of Hindus, Jasmine, but you too are a practising Muslim, as were the wishes of Madesh himself. No cremation must take place."

Jasmine is crying once more. "I know priest, but the shaman is here as part of a way to celebrate Madesh's life, leaving him in our lands; he will not interfere with the ceremony."

All others in the room leave. Jasmine shuts the door behind her. Ojas is situated a few meters away, his hands are together; his fingertips touch his mouth.

Bringing his hands away from his mouth, he asks, "Is all taken care of, Jasmine?"

"All that is done cannot be changed. Madesh is safe while the Imam and the shaman are guarding him. I must gather the women of the palace, and we must fashion flowers for him to capture his spirit, so that they will depart from the cremation when they are cremated."

Jasmine tells the Chikitsak, "Stand guard over the door, Ojas, I must do what the shaman asks."

"If it is his will, then let it be so," Ojas replies.

The ever present placid mood of the palace has changed since the Sultan has passed. It is now sombre, the band have stopped playing

152

but still sit at their place inside the great hall of the palace. As a mark of respect for their music-loving master.

It is now morning, there is much activity.

The shaman's mantra can be heard around the palace.

Outside in the palace grounds to the rear of the building, five women and Jasmine are placing flowers onto a representation of a leopard that sits in front of them. Jasmine and the women are singing a prayer of peace. Men, to their rear, are making the last uprights to support a pyre that will suspend Jasmine's husband's flower copy of the leopard. Jasmine places the last of the flowers onto the animal.

"Come, we must take this upstairs and place it next to your master, my husband, and then I must get changed for the funeral." She speaks with ease, for a person who has lost a loved one. Maybe because she was ready herself to be taken, as she knows that it won't be long until the curse takes her too. The men building the fire are already dressed in white. The women pick up their creation and carry it inside the house. Outside the bedchamber, Jasmine knocks on the door. The shaman is inside with the priest. The priest is reading from the Quran and the shaman is sitting cross-legged behind him in the middle of the room, chanting. Both stop what they are doing, and the priest calls out.

"Come in, come in." The body of the Sultan is now on a colourful stretcher. He is ready to be carried down to the grounds of the mosque for the Salat al-Janazah prayer. Jasmine lets the women through the door, carrying the shape of the leopard made out of flowers. "Place it next to the body. Now, now. Now, now, yes," the shaman cries.

Jasmine rushes to her husband's body, "First I must kiss him goodbye." She kisses him on the cheek, moves back and the women place the leopard next to him on another stretcher. The shaman starts another mantra.

All leave the bedchamber.

It is later on in the day, Jasmine is bathing in a sunken bath while her female servants look on. From the rear we see her finalise the last of her bathing by rinsing off the suds from her arms with a cloth. She stands and walks out of the bath towards the girls in front of her. The women dry her. They open a white gown for her, and she climbs into the dress. She turns and walks towards us and the door to the bathroom, the women following. She walks out of the bathroom and towards the bedchamber; three servants and the Chikitsak are standing at the door.

"It must be time for the Salat al-Janazah," Jasmine says. She knocks at the door.

"Enter," the priest calls.

Jasmine enters the bedchamber. "We must take the body to the mosque grounds for prayers, Priest."

"Okay, Jasmine, are we all ready?" he asks.

"Yes, Priest," the Chikitsak says. "Men," He is talking to the three servants. "Each of you must get hold of each end of the stretchers." Two servants hold onto either end of their master's stretcher, and one the leopard's stretcher, which is longer than the one their master is on. The shaman grabs hold of the other end. The shaman and the manservant pick up their stretcher and stand at the foot of the bed, their arms are at full stretch upwards. The other two servants collect their master, carry him to the foot of the bed, and at waist height carry him under the floral tribute. They all, along with Jasmine and the Chikistak, walk through the palace; all the Sultan's servants are stretched out along the path they take. Most are crying, men and women. They leave the palace through the back door. As they pass the pyre the shaman and his helper move to one side and all stop, as they place the flower leopard on top of the pyre. The Sultan's procession carries on to the mosque, where the Sultan is placed on top of a stone stand that sits a few meters away from its entrance. The two servants move to one side with the Chikistak, and the priest and Jasmine make prayers.

It is early evening and the priest is finishing the prayer that Jasmine is reciting.

"We must bury your husband, Jasmine." He calls the man's servants. "Take your master to his grave; he needs to be placed into his place of rest."

There is a procession to Madesh's grave. All is quiet. He is on the edge of a graveyard made for all of his ancestors. Three balls of dirt lay by the simply turned-out grave that carries low markers so that no one will desecrate the grave after Madesh has been buried. Two grave diggers stand behind. The priest asks Madesh's loyal servants to place the body in the grave, making sure Madesh faces Mecca. They taking Madesh's body and lower him into the grave, placing the soil balls under him to position the body correctly, then climb out. There are no flowers or any other representation of an offering at the graveside. Jasmine is the first to take three handfuls of soil, reciting the words 'We created you from it, and return you into it, and from it we will raise you a second time.' Then the Chiktisak takes his turn and the Sultan's loyal servants next take their turns. Then the priest makes prayers for forgiveness, along with asking the Sultan Madesh to profess his faith. During this time the shaman has been dancing around the un-burnt pyre. Chanting a strange rhythm of words, for life to take on the form of Madesh when the time is right. "Faithful Madesh, Sultan of his lands, take flight into the night sky. Let nature capture his soul and carry it to me. Then we will see if I can capture his cry." The pyre is lit.

Jasmine walks towards the sounds of the crackling pyre, along a path that winds through the trees to the pyre. The Chikitsak and the men servants follow; all are quiet. The Sultan's garden opens up in front of them; there are many servants watching the effigy of the leopard start to catch fire. As Jasmine enters the garden suddenly the flower shape shoots up in flames.

The shaman shouts, "Yes, Yes." All the servants cheer and start to dance and make noise. The leopard in the surrounding jungle roars many times.

In the jungle the leopard sits in his favourite tree. He can see the light from the pyre created for the summoning of the Sultan's spirit by the shaman. The leopard stands, roars once more, turns and climbs down the tree. The shaman is dancing around the fire. Then he stops; he has a confused look upon his face. He searches for Jasmine. She is standing to the rear of the crowd with her loyal Chikitsak. The shaman grabs her hands.

"The time is right, I must go and search…"

Jasmine becomes weak. The Chikisak puts out his arms and catches her before she falls to the floor. "Ha ha ha, the time is right. I must go, I must go. Your time will come, my lady, your time is short."

The shaman runs towards the tea fields and his mountain cave.

Ojas and a handful of women take Jasmine into the palace.

The shaman walks his lonely way up the hillside of the tea fields, turning as he is still dancing as he goes, past the tree that marks the path to his cave up the mountain side, and into his cave. He takes something from a pouch around his waist and places it onto his fire. He claps his hands a few times and the embers catch fire once more;

he places a few sticks of wood upon it. Outside the cave chanting can be heard and the flicker of a fire can be seen. The leopard is on his way towards the shaman's cave, it roars once more. Laughing can be heard from inside the shaman's cave. The leopard walks along the path, around the rock, and slinks up the side of the mountain and then creeps into the shaman's cave dwelling. The shaman is sitting cross-legged behind his fire. The light from the fire dances on the cave walls as we turn behind the shaman. He has dark eyes; he looks nervously into the blackness of what is in front of him, past the light of the fire. There is a roar, then the leopard can be seen slinking like he is hunting prey towards the shaman. The leopard crouches to pounce, but before he leaps, he roars, and the fire rages a torrent of flames, sparks and smoke. The fire sucks the roar from out of the leopard. The breath of the leopard makes movement into the fire. The fire rages some more, and the shaman sucks in what he desires from the flames. The shaman's eyes light up, the fire dies down as before. The leopard is now cowering away from the fire. "I have you now. I have you now, Madesh, Sultan," the shaman says, letting a fiery roar from his mouth. The leopard turns and runs away. The shaman is laughing as the leopard jumps from the cave and into the night.

Jasmine has been helped into her bedchamber. She is being offered some elixir to calm herself before she is helped into her bed. She is shaking, all is not well. The chikitsak helps her into her bed.

Backing away through the window of the bedchamber, we turn into the baying presence of the light, the congregating mass of the full sun.

We are zooming out from the sun. We can see we are in England, Leicester, to be precise. It is a fresh new day in Blackberry Way, and, as we ride down the middle of the street, a man is walking his dog, which takes a pee, and we cross the road.

We are approaching Richie and Sherry, to come up behind them. A lone cyclist meanders down the street.

It is Saturday morning for Richie and Sherry, the Sultan who they know nothing about has died, yet the celebrations and his burial have not yet happened for those living in and around Blackberry Way. Richie and Sherry near Richie's house, they have some very important news for Richie's family; they turn into the front garden and approach the door that Richie loves so much. He opens it.

There is much activity inside the Gyndall residence. Aarzoo is cooking for Saturday night's family meal, a rich smell of butter chicken can be smelled throughout the house. Daivey is still in his pyjamas, drinking coffee, as he has been asleep after his night shift. Richie's grandpa and grandma are watching old films. Aarzoo is simply shutting the oven door, as she has just checked on her dish; she places her oven gloves to one side. She is ready to scold Richie. "Bachcha, I am in dismay." She is leaning against the kitchen worktop. Her husband moves to look who exactly has come through his front door. "We left you alone last night to speak to you this morning, yet you slipped out before any of us could plead Charu's case with you. It is not too…"

Daivey interrupts his wife, "Uh, oh. I think we have a problem." Daivey's mother-in-law is standing at the living room door, and spies who has come through it.

Richie is standing by the side of his fiancée. "Grandma, Father, Mother too. This is my fiancée, Sherry. We have fallen for each other, we…" Sherry carries on from where Richie trailed off from his first words about them inside his family home. "You forgot your granddad, Gaurav, you must remember him. He must be invited into this relationship, Richie. We have been fond friends for some time; we didn't know just how in love two people could be, until last night. We work together at the bank." Gaurav is smiling, chewing on the fruit from his fruit bowl. It is sitting on his lap. "You must be Richie's Grandmother, Kuvan. I have heard so much about you and have seen you in the park."

"Aaaahh, so this is why you didn't want my son to go to the park anymore. Mother, why didn't you stop him before when you first knew of his plans? You have broken my heart." Richie's mother stands back away from the kitchen worktop and faces her son. "You lot have done this to spite me, haven't you?" Her pita jee starts laughing at something on the TV. "Father you will curse us all with your outlook on life."

"My patnee, your maan, explained everything to us last night, and if you don't like it, then you must have something wrong with you, ladakee," Gaurav says.

Aarzoo throws her dish cloth to one side, collects her coat from the back of the kitchen door, and says, "I am going to the temple early; you, my family, have a lot to sort out and teach this boy. I will be there until I leave. As for this mayhem," she walks towards the front door and Richie and Sherry, "I suppose you think it is funny and will not join me." Sherry parts from Richie's side, as way of standing toward the side of the staircase, and Richie stands by the side of the connecting wall to his living room. Aarzoo reaches the front door and opens it; she is staring at Sherry. "I suppose you think this is funny." Aarzoo shuts the door behind her with force. She is crying as she walks up the garden path and turns towards the temple she loves so much. "Alligators are carnivorous animals, now I know so."

"So Richie, you have done it now," Daivey says.

"I knew this whole thing would upset her, but not this much." Sherry holds Richie close.

"When I say done it, bachcha, I mean you've got engaged. You are more of a man to me now than you have ever been." Daivey walks towards Richie and Sherry, Sherry lets go of Richie, slightly in shock, and Kuvan follows after her son-in-law. Daivey hugs his son, placing his head on his shoulder. "Well done, son."

Kuvan hugs Sherry. "You are beautiful, my dear, you seem like you suit each other perfectly." Her husband clears his throat, deeply and with meaning. "Oh, my stars. We don't know that truly, though, do we?" She walks backwards, staring at the two, with Sherry's outstretched hand still in hers.

"Not you too, I expect…" Richie reaches out in dismay, but is cut short.

"Ha ha, Richie, come now. You expected more from me, and more is what we shall give. What arrangements have you made? Relax, and tell Kuvan more."

"Well, well, Sherry and I have made…" Richie stutters and then is interrupted by his grandma.

"You have made none, have you, bachcha?"

"No, this is true, Grandma. We haven't even thought…"

Sherry finishes her fiancé's shocked passage of thought. "We haven't planned, sought help, or even thought of what we will do yet, Kuvan."

"Well, my dear, we will fix that up, Sherry is it. Yes, yes, all three of us must go to the temple. Richie, I suggest you go to the temple after us if you are going. But what I will need for you, Sherry, is to bring me your astrological information tomorrow, when my daughter is not in the house. She will visit the temple with Mrs. Patijna, Pat, tomorrow around ten o'clock. Bring it all then, and I will sort out when and if you will get married. It all hinges on the stars, my dear." Kuvan winks at Sherry, Richie's new love.

"I see; I can do better than that. My mother and father are into astrology and horoscopes, Kuvan. I think they have had all of my information written down and analysed a long time ago. I will bring it all, Kuvan. American astrology goes a long way back, the Native American Indians were big on it, and so are my mother's relations. It has something to do with the Voodoo religion."

"That all sounds very spooky, Sherry, ha ha," Richie confesses.

"Come on, Richie, ha ha. I was born in America. There are many values to be learnt from these things."

"Yes, bachcha, there is lots to be learnt from the many religions, not just our own, and if I get a look at Sherry's astrology charts, and dates of Sherry's time line, I can make an astrology chart showing the best thing to do for us all."

Gaurav is now standing at the living room doorway. "There are good times yet to be had, stuff my ancestors, bachcha."

"I don't know what you're implying, Grandpa, but I trust your judgment."

"They were never the lucky ones; that is one of the reasons we had to move away, bachcha."

"My father's family are from Italy, sir…" Sherry says sincerely.

"Gaurav, call me Gaurav. So with what you are telling me, that means he would have had the Roman's views on these things in his history. Ha ha, they made these lands their own, strength they have."

"Always did have, Gaurav, so astrology conforms into Hindu history; but why, Kuvan?" asks Sherry.

"Well, ha ha, that is something that I cannot answer. Though we all have taken this learning into our hearts, and especially at these times, as a way of you two coming together in holy matrimony. You both can be understood as like islands separated by something more than nature. As if you are not a true couple. This could mean that you are still not meant to be together," Kuvan explained.

Sherry questioned Kuvan's speculation, "You are Joking, Kuvan; we have come so far together."

"Yes, this may be, though my husband and I came so far, and still we weren't sure if we would be together until I placed our passages of personal histories into astrology. I trust you, Sherry, and I trust Richie. But what I do not trust is the stream of life holding you two islands together. They may not be ready to let people cross over you two yet."

"I see, now I understand, Kuvan, Thank you. Come on, let's go and speak to my mother and father, Richie. They will want to know what we have planned."

"Okay, this is all happening very fast. Sherry, my son will walk you home. As long as he gets to the temple later, everything will be fine as far as I can see by the way things are happening. Now be off with you both, and don't take too much notice of your mother, she will be fine, bachcha. I will try and talk her round." Daivey waves them away.

Richie and Sherry turn, Richie opens the door, lets Sherry leave first, then as he is shutting the door, Kuvan speaks to her son-in-law.

"Don't be too complaisant yet, son, anything can happen."

Daivey says, "It must be time to get ready for the temple. Let them walk home to Sherry's house. Wow, a Sherry soon to be in the family. This topsy-turvy world just doesn't stop giving. Come on everyone, let's go and try and talk Aarzoo round."

"I'm with you, son," says Gaurav.

Out in the street people are coming and going about their business as Richie and Sherry walk to Sherry's house.

Islands In The Stream by Kenny Rogers and Dolly Parton: please be respectful and listen. There is much context, and also content hidden within the text.

Line 1: Richie Sings. [Richie and Sherry are walking the streets towards Sherry's home. As they walk people follow]
Line 2: Richie Sings.
Line 3: Richie Sings.
Line 4: Richie Sings.

Line 5: Richie and Sherry sing.
Line 6: Richie and Sherry sing.
Line 7: Richie and Sherry sing.

Line 8: Richie and Sherry sing.

Line 9: Richie and Sherry sing.
Line 10: Richie and Sherry sing.
Line 11: Richie and Sherry sing.
Line 12: Richie and Sherry sing.
Line 13: Richie and Sherry sing.

Chorus:
Line 1: Richie and Sherry sing. [Mr. Joshi chases Jason out of his shop. Jason's friend is waiting outside; they follow]
Line 2: Richie and Sherry sing.
Line 3: Richie and Sherry sing.
Line 4: Richie and Sherry sing.
Line 5: Richie and Sherry sing.
Line 6: Richie and Sherry sing.
Line 7: Richie and Sherry sing.
Line 8: Richie and Sherry sing.

Line 14: Sherry sings.
Line 15: Sherry sings.
Line 16: Sherry sings.
Line 17: Sherry sings.

Line 18: Richie and Sherry sing.
Line 19: Richie and Sherry sing.
Line 20: Richie and Sherry sing.
Line 21: Richie and Sherry sing.

Line 22: Sherry Sings. [They reach the fountain and there are suds coming out of it; everyone jumps into the suds]
Line 23: Richie and Sherry sing.
Line 24: Richie and Sherry sing.
Line 25: Richie and Sherry sing.
Line 26: Richie and Sherry sing.
Line 27: Richie and Sherry sing.

Chorus:

Line 1: Richie and Sherry sing. [Richie and Sherry make the last length of their journey towards Sherry's house]
Line 2: Richie and Sherry sing.
Line 3: Richie and Sherry sing.
Line 4: Richie and Sherry sing.
Line 5: Richie and Sherry sing.
Line 6: Richie and Sherry sing.
Line 7: Richie and Sherry sing.
Line 8: Richie and Sherry sing.

Line 9: Richie and Sherry sing.

Line 1: Richie and Sherry sing.
Line 2: Richie and Sherry sing.
Line 3: Richie and Sherry sing.
Line 4: Richie and Sherry sing.
Line 5: Richie and Sherry sing.
Line 6: Richie and Sherry sing.
Line 7: Richie and Sherry sing.
Line 8: Richie and Sherry sing.

Line 1: Richie and Sherry sing.
Line 2: Richie and Sherry sing.
Line 3: Richie and Sherry sing.
Line 4: Richie and Sherry sing.
Line 5: Richie and Sherry sing.
Line 6: Richie and Sherry sing.
Line 7: Richie and Sherry sing.
Line 8: Richie and Sherry sing. [Richie and Sherry have reached Sherry's house]

Line 1: Richie and Sherry sing.
Line 2: Richie and Sherry sing.
Line 3: Richie and Sherry sing.

Richie and Sherry arrive at Sherry's house, and walk through the front door. Richie stands just inside the front door, while Sherry greets her mother and father, who are watching TV in their living room.

"Oh, hello, darling." Sherry's mother welcomes her.

"Hiya, you two. I have something interesting to tell you. The friend that came around this morning," Richie smiles to himself and edges towards the doorway. "Well, his name is Richie." Richie walks into Sherry's parents' living room. "Richie and I would like to get married."

Sherry's mother is the first to speak. "My goodness, that was quick."

"Yes, Sherry, you've just got rid of Jason, and now you're going to get married," her father says.

Sherry looks at her fiancé, "Yes, but he's the cutest thing you ever did lay your eyes on."

"He might be handsome, but is he the right man for you, Sherry?" Sherry's mother is sympathetic to Sherry's case, but questions her logic.

"Yes, that is a good question. Hey, let's not hang about, let's ask him," Sherry's father stands up to talk to them both.

"Dad," Sherry says.

Sherry's father is insistent, "What do you think, Richie, do you believe you are the right man for my daughter?"

"Yes, sir, I do believe I am. My family are not yet sure of our decision, but they are coming round to the idea that your daughter, Sherry, is the right person for me and my future. They know," Richie smirks. "I'm the best thing this side of the river."

"Ha ha ha, our decision, I like that, son, and, Richie, self-motivation is what drives us all, no? As long as you do things right by my daughter, Richie, I believe everything may just be alright." Sherry's father shakes Richie by the hand.

"At least you got rid of that terrible boy, Jason, Sherry," Sherry's mother says.

"Yes, he was never the right person for you," Sherry's father adds.

Sherry is in shock. "Mother, Father, I never thought you understood me until now." Her face flushes, the colour showing her understanding, "I'm so pleased."

"We are not all philistines, Sherry darling, what do you expect when you make two completely different journeys? I think Jason was just there to make us jealous of him."

"Well, I don't..." Sherry is flustered.

"Now Richie here," Sherry's father pats Richie on the shoulder, while Richie views Sherry and her mother. "He must have a fine, fine family, and strong genes, yes?"

"Well, I'm not sure my family are sure that we can get married yet, you two?" Richie says.

"Yes, that is true, Richie's family have invited us all to go around to their house and have a star chart drawn up to plot how things should be done towards the wedding. They want us there after ten tomorrow."

"Why ten o'clock?" asks Sherry's mother.

"Well, Richie's mother is not fully understanding of what we want to do yet."

"Ah, mothers are always the last to see what is right and understand what is meant for their sons."

"I'm her only son, and an only child, sir," adds Richie.

"Huh, I see, even worse, Richie."

"She'll come round; now tell us all about this star chart, you two." Sherry's mother pats the sofa next to her for her daughter to sit down. Richie heads for the armchair. "I'll make some drinks, and you two tell us exactly what is happening, and exactly how you got together."

Aarzoo is in the temple, praying for forgiveness of her son by all the deities that she has pitted against him for not marrying Charu.

The rest of her family enter.

"So, you all turned up to see my embarrassment. I do not believe this is real, it is a joke, and a joke against all the odds. How has such a loving child of the Hindu way become cursed by something so destructive?"

"Aarzoo," Daivey whispers to her. "Don't be so disrespectful. It is our ancestors that asked of us so much, and set in place rules that Richie simply couldn't abide by. Just remember Richie did not know of any rules that were set in place for him. So with respect, Aarzoo, Richie has not broken anything, he did not break any rules. He didn't even know that he needed to get married, yet he is."

"This is true, ladakee," Kuvan says while she has her head down, praying.

"Ek chhota sa, just remember that he means no harm. He is making this happen as we speak," Gaurav says.

164

"This may be true, pita jee, but the Sultan was adamant in his letter that no rules must be broken, and yet Richie has not married one of us!" Aarzoo stood, and pressed her hands together. "I don't believe, and I don't think you should either, that any good will come from this relationship that Richie has found." She walks out of the prayer room. Her family follow.

From outside the Traverso house we see figures appear inside the front door. The door opens. Richie steps down onto the threshold and Sherry shuts the door slightly behind her.
"I must go to the temple," Richie tells Sherry.
"Okay, Richie, go and see your family." Sherry gives Richie a kiss on the cheek.
Richie smiles, turns, saying his goodbyes and heads to the temple; Sherry watches him leave. Outside the temple the Gyndall family are leaving; Daivey is holding his wife's arm, his two in-laws are following after, arm in arm too.
Richie reaches the temple and walks inside. He is ducking and weaving between families to find his own. He cannot see them. So he prays:

I have thought about this one single moment for all of my life, it seems. But unlike how Charu was forced into facing unbearable uncertainty, I am now faced with the most singularly beautiful girl in all the worlds. There are many of you deities to look after us all. English religion is so confusing, one god to rule over all those people, how is he able to change what he says to so many people at the same time, he must have so many faces with mouths to talk individually to them all. All I need is good luck. He looks to all the deities in the room. *Please help me, all of you.* One of the priests walks over and stands beside him; he prays with Richie. Richie feels overwhelmed. "Thank you," he whispers. Richie is stunned when the priest winks at him; he smiles and backs away. *That is all you lot need to say, I will not ask another thing from any of you for a long time.* Richie winks at every one of the deities in turn, turns and leaves.

It is Sunday morning as we look from the top of Blackberry Way. Mrs Patijna and her friend Aarzoo walk off towards the temple. Sherry's mother and father are driving up the road towards us and pull up outside the Gyndall residence. Sherry's mother and father get out, while Sherry's mother lets Sherry out of the rear of the vehicle. Richie is walking quickly to the front door of his house; he knows exactly who it is. Sherry's mother and father, plus Sherry herself, stand at the door.

"Come in, please…" Richie says.

"Yes, come in, please; don't stand outside, the day is much brighter in here," Daivey calls.

The three members of the Traverso family walk into the Gyndall household. Kuvan comes to the living room door.

"Please, Daivey, my son, do not let your guests wait in the hallway. Bring them in."

Daivey ushers the Traverso family into his living room.

"Wow, this is great. Some fond photos of your family you have. Is this Richie?" Sherry's mother asks, looking at a photo of a small child wrapped in sheets, lying on a table.

"Yes, that is our son, Mrs. Traverso. I need to add, I cannot be any part of this wedding until my wife realises it is the best thing for her only son. I will try and help, but I feel I must take myself away from these types of events until she realises the truth."

"Do what you want to, Daivey, if I can call you Daivey. Sherry has filled us all in on all the details." Sherry's father continues, "These are hard times for us all, but love is the right way, and that's how the children are handling all of this."

"Yes, Richie has told us about you guys too. I'm sure everything will work out right in the end." Daivey leaves the room to retire upstairs. Kuvan is sitting beside her husband on the sofa; he is sitting in his normal chair.

"Sit down, you two. What are you carrying?"

"Sherry's astrology chart and special dates," Sherry's mother replies.

"Yes this is all we have had done. My husband and I had a Native American Indian map of Sherry's astrology done when Sherry was born; this was before we left America."

"Woah, I did not know Sherry was born in America. This may magnify the stakes of the procedure. To be born that far away from

Richie and to still have gotten together is a miracle." Kuvan presents Richie's information to Sherry's mother.

"Oh this is interesting, they will look good together. What do you have planned if all goes well?"

"What do you want as your daughter's place in all this? Sherry needs to come first; she is the woman of the relationship."

"Well," Sherry's mother looks at her husband. "We understand that things are not as they might be between our families at this moment, but we would like Sherry to be married in a church. That's it really. Oh, she needs to wear white too."

"If all goes well, it is done…"

As Kuvan finishes what she is saying, Daivey climbs into bed to get some rest for work, and Aarzoo and Mrs. Patijna walk into the temple together. The Gyndall, Malli, and Traverso families finalise what is to take place.

It is now Monday. At the Leicester Allegiance everyone is standing around the refreshments table inside the office.

Richie and Sherry have decided not to tell everyone that they have plans to leave. They plan to tell the Partners on Friday, only then giving in their notice, and then announce that they will wed, if all goes to plan, but things are not that simple.

Lady Rosetta walks in, via the stairwell. She walks to the boardroom door, enters, then turning, she shuts the door behind her. Sherry looks on just as she is shutting the door. Lady Rosetta seems to wink at her.

"She seems like a stuck up cow," says Geoff; there are a few laughs and shocked gasps.

We are inside the boardroom.

"Ah, Mumsy," the oldest partner says. The two other sons of Lady Rosetta are staying quiet; they seem slightly shy of their mother. Refraining from saying good morning, they ask, "To what do we owe the pleasure?"

"You three need a kick up the arse. The money I have asked for is not in my account." Lady Rosetta rebukes her sons.

"We all thought that as you gave us a month to sort out the finances of our bank, we really didn't think you would need the money until then," the oldest says.

"Can't your brothers speak for themselves? Is this true?" Lady Rosetta asks menace in her words.

"We…" the middle brother.

"We…" the youngest.

"As I thought, you three haven't got a clue, or an ounce of brains between you," Lady Rosetta says, "and if you think you are getting away with this you've all got another thing coming."

"You will have your money before you walk out of here, Mumsy. We wanted you to be here, so that you can listen to our plan of how we will get our finances in order, and to make your document seem disingenuous, and for you to fail in your plans to make us sign the bank over in your name, there and then making it null and void."

The older son looks exultant. Lady Rosetta is becoming even more angry. "Call Richie Gyndall into the boardroom." He is looking at his youngest brother.

The youngest partner walks to the boardroom door. The door opens. In the office all the staff are still standing at the water station. As the door opens, the office workers individually start to peel from the crowd they are making, and walk to their desks.

"Richie, please come into the boardroom," the youngest partner asks. Sherry grabs hold of Richie's hand, Richie looks to Sherry for strength, Sherry nods at her fiancée with fortitude and offers the strength in her looks; this is what Richie is seeking. As Richie walks away the two of them cannot seem to part company. Still holding hands, Richie says, "Come with me."

Sherry walks with him; they both have joyous smiles.

"Only you, Richie," the youngest partner tells them both.

"If you want to speak to me, then you need to see us both, sir," Richie says.

"Well, it's a bit out of the ordinary, but come, come in, the pair of you." The youngest partner is unsure, but he feels unsure about what he was being asked to do already.

The youngest partner walks through to the boardroom, waiting for Richie and Sherry to follow. Richie enters first, his arm outstretched. Sherry follows; all those within the office are calm and joyous.

"Ah, Richie." Richie stands side by side with Sherry. Sherry is on the right, he himself is on the left. "To what do we owe the pleasure of young Sherry here?" the oldest partner asks.

168

"We will trouble you with our situation once you tell us what you now have planned for me. It is you three who have called me into your office. I'm not sure we've met, ma'am. I do not mean to be unruly, it's just your friends here seem always to have other plans for me." Richie talks to the oldest partner, and then introduces himself to the woman standing by the boardroom table. She sits, and crosses her legs. "My name is Richie Gyndall, ma'am."

"Why, thank you for introducing yourself. I, I am, so I seem to be today, your current bosses' mother, Lady Rosetta. Richie Gyndall, and so, may I ask, who is this? I see you are well known to each other."

"I am Sherry Traverso. Soon to be wed to Richie Gyndall, ma'am," Sherry tells her.

"W, w, what are you two suggesting, I thought…" The oldest brother looks to the others. Lady Rosetta is staring at her oldest son; he blushes with embarrassment and rage. "Looks must be deceiving, I thought, we thought, you were to Marry Charu Patijna, Richie, for you to then collect the inheritance of your estranged family in…"

"Cutchy, please don't get flustered. Sherry has already explained," Lady Rosetta says.

"We're slightly confused, Richie," the oldest partner says.

"Yes, confused, we thought…" The middle son of Lady Rosetta says.

"I knew we shouldn't have trusted you brother," The youngest son says.

Richie butts in, "I have no idea who or what you are talking about. All I know is what was planned for me is no more. Now Sherry and I are in love and are going to get married, with our families' permission, that is. And as soon as possible. You three, sorry Lady Rosetta, have now got to change your ideas over what you want from me. I can tell. So whatever you had planned for me is now over. And Sherry and I have had a change of heart. We are going to set up our own business as financial advisers. You three, and the whole workforce, have never listened to a thing I have suggested. We could have made one hundred percent more profits, or more so, if you had only just listened to my advice at the start of the financial year," Richie tells them all.

"You have changed our plans once too often. Richie. I, we, wish not to see your face around here from now on. You are both sacked, get out of our sight," the oldest partner tells them.

"On what grounds do you have to get rid of these two. It sounds like they have one up on you three, Cutchy." Lady Rosetta is shocked, but is laughing at the end of her assessment.

"You can't sack us, sir, we quit, don't we, Sherry?" Richie says.

"Yes, Richie, good idea, we quit."

"Get out of our sight, our boardroom, and our bank, Gyndall, and take this hussy with you," the older partner tells the couple.

"It would be our pleasure, sir, and I hope you get your comeuppance." Richie pulls Sherry to the door of the boardroom and opens it. "I hope you regret ever having to rely on something that was never true. Trust is the key in this world, and Lady Rosetta, I hope you take your sons to the cleaners, because their accounts need tidying up somewhat." Richie walks from the boardroom into the office, still holding Sherry by the hand. Slow clapping comes from the boardroom; it is Lady Rosetta. As Richie and Sherry slowly walk through the office space, everyone is looking at them, and they start to clap too. Richie pulls Sherry from the office and down the staircase into the bank, through the security door, past Sid, who is in shock, and into the open air of the street.

"I don't know what they had planned, but they will stop at nothing to try and stop me doing what I want, Sherry. I'm glad we left today."

"Well Richie, we are out of a job, but tomorrow sure is a different day; you were my hero up there. Come on, let's go and see if we can finish what you've started." Richie and Sherry walk down the street holding hands.

Aarzoo is in the back garden of her family home. She picks some vegetables from one of her lengthy turned patches of earth. The whole garden has been divided into portions for home growing and for saving the family income. She has tended this crop from seed, like she does with every crop she grows. It is challenging at this time of year, storing what she can to stretch out the lifetime of her crops. Her basket is half full. She is so proud of her accomplishments, putting her hand up to block the sun shining in her eyes. She is taking in the fresh air. Turning, she heads back into the house.

Richie and Sherry, all their troubles behind them, enter Blackberry Way and head towards Richie's house.

"You look troubled, Richie," Sherry says.

"Ha ha, time is money, and money is time, Sherry. We need to be earning. I do have an idea though, let's see if we can start our business from home."

The closer the couple come to Richie's house the more Sherry wants to charge her fiancée with vacillating with his suggestions. She titters and jokes, "But I thought you wanted to write books for a living?"

"Yes, but that was when I was single. At this moment in time we need more to use our business attributes to make a living. That's just a hobby at the moment, and it's not even a full time hobby, yet. Maybe I could do that in the future."

Sherry suddenly runs off, joyously holding hands with Richie, pulling him into a trot into his front garden and down the front path.

Richie: "Hello Aarzoo!" (the door of Richie's home opens inwards).

He is looking for the recognition he feels he deserves, as he is this close to his wedding day. He is resigning himself to the fact that he may not be able to marry Sherry yet, if he does not get his business plans together, that is; he is not in full-time employment yet. Oh, and the star chart, that needs to be all in order. What will he tell his grandma, his parents, and how will the star chart affect his life? So Richie is in wonder as he leans in to listen through the open space of the hallway. Drawn towards opening the door, Richie now opens it fully.

Aarzoo: "I am your maji, Richie, and who can take that away from me? Only you, it seems." Richie's mother turns from putting the vegetables on the kitchen work surface, washes her hands, and starts peeling potatoes from the pile at the sink. "I suppose you have wasted all your savings on this sham already."

Sherry (heard from afar): "But Aarzoo, it was only a comment."

Richie and Sherry enter the kitchen, to try and lay down some form of comfort. Richie's father walks out of the living room.

Father: "Yes, but a selfish one! So don't go there again."
Aarzoo: "Thank you, Daivey, you are a good man to me, your wife."
Richie: "Now look, Mother,"
Aarzoo: "Maji, bachcha, I am your maji."
Richie: "Yes, there is no-"
Daivey: "-doubting that, son! Now come, let us all calm down. At least Sherry's family has stepped in and brought this all up to speed. I do not think we all could live like this for many more days."
Aarzoo: "That is not true, I live my life like I should, unlike someone other than I, so it seems, and you all should understand this. You still have enough money to pay your way within this household, bachcha, don't you? You haven't even managed to get another job yet, and yet you've embarrassed me in front of the whole street. I have slaved for you a long time. I also help Maan look after grandpa. I grow my own vegetables to help with the finances; we are on the breadline, you know. I haven't grown peas for years because they take up so much room, and frozen peas are cheaper, and last a lot bloody longer in the freezer. It's all so very depressing. We haven't had fish for months. Can you solve our problems with your wisdom, Bachcha?"
Richie: "Ah, Maan, more problems. Yes, I have some more to say about this," Richie looks to Sherry, Sherry smiles at him, and so he relaxes. "We have just given in our notice at the bank, but we made sure that we quit on those old misers before they did a proper job on us. Sherry and I will hopefully set up our own business with some of your help. If we can all pool our resources together, then we have a chance at making a new business opportunity that can slowly grow into something much greater than what we had, I am sure, oh, and Sherry's family can help, of course."
Aarzoo: "You let me think all was well, so you didn't need a second job, by coming here with her. And now, oh my goodness, and now what will all the nosey ones think, that we'll be destitute soon! You've actually given up your jobs, and you need money from us. We should be the ones receiving money to recuperate what we have spent over the

years on you, Richie. Never mind what we should give to your bride."

Richie: "Sherry's family are in the same boat, and yes, maan, I have what I owe you, but look, it won't be long and everything will be better. I have a few things lined up outside of my hobbies, like thinking of ideas like this one."

Aarzoo: "Yes, but it is not just about the money. It is about the …"

Daivey: "Look, Aarzoo. Those fuddy-duddy partners would never have taught Richie any more than he was doing for them. He was in a dead-end street, and anyway we couldn't go on living like this, and money would never have come into it." Richie's Father is secretly smiling from within himself. He is not sure that the letter was ever that real. Daivey knows for sure, though, that he would never have been this lucky. "Money is not a problem for what we have to provide, but I hear you, Aarzoo! You are right to question reality for all of us. Magical money is never an option."

Sherry: "Magical money?"

Aarzoo: "Yes Magical money. Richie always thought he was special!"

Richie: "Maan, you can't tell me this sort of thing when you've all hinted that my name is something that it is not over the years, meaning it is something more than it is. I mean why mention that I've always been your source of money? Tell me Maan, why Richie in the first place?"

Daivey: "Are we all not heading off in a different direction to where this conversation was going?"

Richie: "You must wait, Father, for my maan to answer. I need to know."

Aarzoo is biting her lip, still peeling potatoes. Daivey, having stood back to listen to Richie's argument, has now stepped forwards to take on exactly what Richie wants to know.

Daivey: "Richie, it means brave ruler, that's all. Ever since we knew you were going to be our son, we thought you would be our shining light. We knew the name meant something to urge you on, Richie."

Aarzoo: "Yes, we never believed it ever would ridicule you, Richie, rather you would become something we could not. As it is, it is the diminutive name of one of our country's Kings. Richard the Lionheart!"

Daivey: "What more could we ask for from our country than giving us, your mother and I, something wild and free, and it all stemming from our homeland. Huh, what do you think now, Richie?"

Richie: "So I am supposed to think different now as I am secretly named after a king?"

Aarzoo: "Yes, well, just think of this. You could have been so much more, Richie, if you had just..."

Daivey: "Yes, and here we go again. Aarzoo's Magical Money. Aarzoo believes that she has a money tree. Isn't this true?"

Richie: "It is not magical for any other reason than it comes from our extended family. Who I am yet to hear about?"

Aarzoo: "No! Don't be silly, and don't listen when I say, 'good riddance'; if that was ever true it is now not binding, or even blinding us any longer, but that is not the point. What do you think we are talking about here?" She stops peeling and turns. She is holding a potato in one hand and the peeler in the other. "We are talking about reality, and in reality Richie hasn't even had a star chart drawn up to tell him when, or if to get married. Yet this is all happening far too fast."

Richie: "Ah."

Richie's grandma walks out of the living room. "Ah, aha." She resonates with the ending diminuendo of her grandson's fall in speech. "That is where you are wrong. Isn't that true, Sherry?"

Sherry: "Well, it is, I suppose. That's if you would like to clarify that we have traversed those parts of the wedding tradition. Sorry, Aarzoo, but we were finding it hard to communicate. So me and your maji, Cu-hum, made this our own, didn't we, Kuvan?"

As Sherry pronounces her soon to be in-law name, Kuvan closes the folder that she is holding. "I have found out that Richie and Sherry match all thirty-six of their Gunas in the Kundali. With their business ideas, together with their fondness for business, and their close association in business, they need to stand on their own two feet. To become stronger together within the community of business. So you see. All up to scratch." She turns to re-enter the living room to see her husband, her beloved.

Richie: "Oh, I see. This is already done."

Sherry: "Well, what did you think? We should be having a party as soon as possible to celebrate."

Aarzoo: "Not a Sangeet! This soon, oh my."

Kuvan: Shouting from the Living room, "The chart says that the marriage should be as soon as possible too, Priy!"

Sherry: "So yes, a Sangeet, this weekend. Wow, I will work on the invitations with my parents." Sherry gathers herself together to ask her soon to be mother-in-law to please come to the sangeet. "Aarzoo, we are not doing this just because of my family; Aarzoo, please, we really want you to be there. There will be a grand table at the edge of the dance floor for all the older family members to sit."

Aarzoo: "I wouldn't be seen dead at this childish charade before you make fakes of yourselves to disgrace this family in front of our gods."

Richie: "Mother… maji, how could you?"

Aarzoo: "You all mean nothing to me." Aarzoo turns, splashing the potato that she is holding in her left hand into the bowl in the sink. She bows her head and raises her right hand towards her forehead.

Daivey: "Come now. We must give her time."

As the conversation finishes, Richie and Sherry walk back towards the front door, with the arbitrator, Richie's father, following. Aarzoo is left peeling potatoes, and you can tell she is smiling, but not from looking at her face.

She looks down, away from her reflection in the kitchen window, to see what is in the bowl. She hears what she has been waiting for; Richie calling to her. "We would love to see you at our Sangeet, Mother." He is standing by the front door.

"Not on your Nelly. See You Later, Alligator." She plunges the knife she is peeling the potatoes with back into the water as Richie's father shuts the door behind his only, and so favourite, bachcha.

175

In the street Richie is hugging Sherry. Slowly we back away and turn the corner of the road. Everybody is going about their daily business.

It is the night of the Sangeet, and everyone who is everyone is dancing or standing to chat. All this to the sounds of the local band that is playing on the stage. All the family members are sitting, or picking at the food, from the tables provided. The group is waiting for Richie and Sherry to arrive.

Kuvan is sitting next to her husband. Sherry's mother and father are sitting two spaces away from them. These empty spaces are left for the love and respect that the two families have for Richie's mother and father. Who should be seated within them?

Richie's cousins are the first to alert the party-goers that the two main arrivals are about to appear.

"Quickly, everyone: they are coming, they are coming!"

Someone whistles with their fingers from the back of the room. The lead singer from the band asks someone whether they should stop or not. As Richie's youngest cousin looks back from where she is now situated, meters from the door, everybody crowds around. The band, after the conversation, carries on playing.

Sherry's mother leans past her husband to speak to Kuvan. "This is exciting, it really is."

Kuvan's reply is, "Don't worry, woman. This has all been done before. It is one in a long line of family traditions." She looks to her husband, who looks around the room to fulfil the comfort of his non-party going antics. Gaurav is eating a chicken drumstick. "Isn't that right, husband of mine?"

Richie's Grandpa looks up lovingly from hovering over his plate of food. He is looking towards his wife with bated breath. He is bowing his head while making a rasping noise deep within his throat.

"Yes, I know all about your family history. Sherry has told us that you visit the temple every Saturday," Sherry's father interjects as the lights go down, and the music keeps playing. His wife echoes his sentiments by saying, "Yes!" She knew, and, "Sherry has brought the most magnificent dress we have ever seen. We are besotted by the whole occasion."

Sherry's father adds, "Well, I bought it. I'd do anything for my girl."

"Oh, honey, look."

At this, Richie and Sherry walk into the beginnings of the theatre of their dreams. They look shocked after walking into the hall. The crowd all cheer as the lights come back on simultaneously. They are aware that Richie and Sherry would not have looked so significant unless they put their arms into the air and then bowed, and the crowd's arms are raised at their arrival.

The crowd of party-goers then begin to chant, "Richie, Sherry..." and so on. Richie and Sherry are hugging each other at the crowd's response in the doorway. The band finishes what they were playing and start another song. Everyone turns at once towards the lead singer, who announces, "And so the sideshow begins." They begin a different song.

Richie and Sherry walk over to their joint venture of soon to be joined family members.

"Hello, everyone, I'm sure you've all seen me before," He is wearing a dark green striped suit with thin yellow pinstripes and a purple shirt that extends beyond his suit's sleeves with a yellow gold tie and yellow gold brogues. "But have you met this startling young woman!"

Richie's Grandpa, after wiping his mouth with a serviette, jokingly strikes a chord to Richie. "But Richie, we all do. Though, well, no. I do not personally know who exactly you have with you."

Everyone, including Richie, at arm's length to Sherry, is now staring at her. Her hair is up for the first time. She is taking off her shiny white coat, with a peppermint belt. Underneath she is wearing a tight-fitting dress, cut in steps to three different lengths. It reverberates around the back in a diagonal. She adds to its effect with a light, see-through wrap that covers her shoulder, and then waist. It falls to the rear, but does not drag on the floor. The dress is made of purple silk and has pink flowers upon it, with Sherry's neck fitting obscured by the collar. The see-through wrap is mauve. She is wearing slightly higher than flat pink slip-on shoes.

Everyone is in shock. Richie is in his element, flattered by the woman that he now holds on his arm.

Richie and Sherry walk towards the two empty chairs. The rest of the family walk around behind them, filling the space that was there. Everyone is cheering again, and the band announce that the group is called "By the way". The drummer is now beating the drum to his right. The singer carries on, "We are so glad you could make it!

177

We're proud to be here." They are ready to sing words to the beat that they have been playing since the couple walked inside.

Richie pulls Sherry around the tables, and onto the dance floor to dance the night away.

Time seems to go nowhere fast for Richie and Sherry. All night it seems. Intimately. There appears to be a camera filming them at their most intimate times as each one of them, and their family members have their separate thoughts taken out from the centres of their loving circle of emotions. Their feelings and their motions are cared for by every other person in the room. The party are all magnified in an instant with the couple dancing on the dance floor while the hired photographer takes snaps at every given opportunity. In the room, everyone's attention is fixed. All the party-goers' experiences are elevated to different areas of the room, but instead of being visible on isolated screens, the moments are stored as saved actions of the night's perfection. All this is done as everyone watches Richie and Sherry engage in their celebration.

To mark these moments, for all time, people ask Richie and Sherry to look at photos that individual party-goers have taken before they all left. They will see everything.

Richie and Sherry are spinning as one. The lovely music of the band surrounds them. They are making more thoughts drift to different areas as they muse over the conversations they have had. Plus, the one-off encounters they experienced.

The band is seemingly playing their song for all to hear. There is a platform of love, constructed by both families so that everyone's emotions come together for the loving couple to sing their experiences. Their memories are bound through the next day and the rest of their lives. They stop skipping around in a circle, arm in arm, and Richie pulls Sherry towards him.

"You couldn't break my heart if you tried, do not think about my maan and pita jee not turning up at the sangeet a disaster. Think of things as more of a coming together. My father has stuck by me and his wife, do you see? He holds the greatest respect for us all. My maji will come round in the end." Richie is nervous behind the imaginary mask he is wearing.

"Oh, Richie, whatever will happen, it, these things, will never change how much I love you." Sherry hugs Richie.

Richie and Sherry stand at the table set aside for family members behind the dance floor. This time, there is just them and their families, and no crowd to inhibit their awareness. They were drinking, eating, and dancing.

Richie says, "I'm sorry, people; we must be off. We have loads to do before the wedding day."

Sherry's father replies, "I know, son, but that is going to be the same your whole life through and from now on!"

"Yes, but at least then we can have a rest," says Sherry, looking at her in-laws to be. "Sorry, I didn't mean that with any malice. Maji, your grandson's mother is struggling with her feelings towards me. I feel we will have to try more."

Kuvan, after her husband whispers in her ear, replies, "Something will happen, or me and your grandpa, Richie, will not appear at the wedding. Now, this is our wish." Looking back at her husband, Kuvan says, "We cannot go back now. So what can be put right? Firstly: it is that you two must come with me out into the car park, so that I can realise your wishes. We must do this before anything else can go wrong, Come, come!"

She gets up as she speaks and heads to the doorway that leads outside.

Outside in the car park she gathers the two of them around her. Kuvan speaks fluently, as if she does not want anybody to interrupt her teachings.

"Richie and Sherry!" She points around herself and towards the night sky. They stand in the darkest parts of the car park outside of the Sangeet. The lights of the car park highlight them where they stand. Kuvan's romantic interlude begins, and Richie and Sherry follow her eyes. She speaks to them. "Now listen! We are all lights like the stars, my children. I am going to upset you now, I know, but each one of these is individual and separate, and this is where I feel for you. As they shine together they become one, they speak as one. This whole universe is silent without them, so your moments are reflections of this. For that is what you will become; a shared light. To be admired by all those that look upon you, while they are reliving their own ecstasy, their own self-deliverance, through your coming together. Now remember, babies, these moments are made only by what you give, not the light that you shine."

Sherry "Oh, Kuvan!"
Richie: "Thank you, Grandma!"
Sherry: "Yes, thank you, Kuvan, I know that this has been hard for you, but we, us two, we mean no harm."
Richie: "Yes, that is true." He looks at Sherry. "We just want to get on, and get along with all those that live beside us."

Sherry, kissing Kuvan, smiles at her soon to be Grandma.
Richie and Sherry walk away from Kuvan away into the night, towards the car waiting for them.
Kuvan follows. "I know, children, but don't let your love spill into other people's cups, like your own light. Their love is kept only at a certain level for a reason. So don't make their cups overflow. Or your grandpa and me, we won't have enough love left to fix this."
As Richie and Sherry get into the car Kuvan says one more thing. "Now you know who I am talking about, bachcha, do your best to fix things, won't you?"
As all drift away into the night, the beat from the band is heard playing deep into the next day's trials.

The morning of the wedding has arrived, with the beat from the band still playing in Richie's head. Nervous tension is welling up inside them both. Like no other time of their lives, the last few days have been full of intoxication. Time has ticked by, though, and with the days passing, how they kept themselves sane is understood only by them.
Richie is standing in his kitchen; his maan is upstairs, his grandpa in the living room, Kuvan is in front of him. Richie is on the phone:

Richie: "Hello Sherry, have you got your haldi ready?"
Sherry is in her kitchen too; her family have requested that they don't see each other, though they have agreed that Richie can talk to her to ward of the evil spirits before the ceremony.
Sherry: "He he he, yes, Richie, I'm putting it on my hands and rubbing it up my forearms."
Richie: "Ha ha he," His grandma holds his phone while he pours haldi into his hands too. He rubs it up his forearms and around his neck. "Don't forget to get it behind your ears or

180

else you won't hear me when I whisper into your ear later on."

Sherry rubs some behind her ears.

Sherry: "No evil spirit is going to stop me from hearing anything you say today, Richie."

Richie rubs some Haldi up his legs.

Richie: "Ha ha ha."

Sherry's mother takes the phone, and speaks.

Sherry's Mother: "Right, that's enough you two. Sherry needs to get into her wedding dress."

Kuvan takes Richie's phone.

Kuvan: "Okay, okay, enough is enough. Richie too must get cleaned up. We are all looking forward to seeing you later."

Sherry's Mother: "I hope so, Kuvan, I hope so. See you later."

Kuvan: "I hope so too, goodbye." She puts the phone on the work surface.

Richie: "Oh, that was so much fun. I must go and get showered and changed."

Richie runs upstairs, while Kuvan cleans up the mess.

As Richie walks into the bathroom and shuts the door, his maan walks out of her bedroom dressed in a large puffed jacket, down the stairs, and quietly goes out through the front door. Kuvan hears the door click. Turns and can see nothing visible. She walks into the living room. Her pati is looking out of the window. "She's gone, meree pyaaree patnee, she just walked out through the door and headed towards the temple."

"Let her go, Gaurav, she is carrying a heart full of chaos; at least Richie doesn't know. He is having so much fun. Our daughter may need to pray to let her temper subside."

Richie is getting changed in his room, still with some of the colour yellow on his neck and hands. The door is closed to all. Then, Richie shouts from his bedroom. The sound glides down the staircase and into the hallway.

"Kuvan! Kuvan!" he opens the door a little wider. "My mother, where is she?"

At that moment, the bedroom door opens, and Richie runs out and down the stairs to find his grandma. She is coming out of the living room, and he nearly bumps into her.

Kuvan says, "You know where she is, bachcha."

Richie's grandpa walks to the door. "No, Kuvan. You told him she was still here when he called Sherry; it was me who made the mistake of telling him she just popped out this second. That was when he was in the shower."

Kuvan reorganised herself. "Okay, pati, I will tell him. She's gone to offer prayers, bachcha! It is no good. I tried to make her stop. Look, your father will be back soon. He will do his best to come. You know what is written in your heart. Hopefully, he will bring his loving wife. No questions asked."

Richie's grandpa speaks again. "Hopefully, that is as true as it gets, Richie, but boy, you do look handsome."

"It is getting late. You lot are all dressed?"

"Yes, our car arrives after yours, but you must be at the church doors to welcome everyone in." At that, the door opens.

"Oh my gosh, have I missed something?" Richie and his father start to laugh together.

"I didn't think you'd have time to make it. Let alone mother. Where have you been?"

"Richie, son, you know I wouldn't have missed this for the world, but we still have to earn money. We are not on the breadline for no reason at all. We all have to do things that we don't like, and look, all this talking, and you haven't caught on that the car is already outside. They are waiting for you. Now I have no doubt that the car for me and your grandparents will be here before I get washed and changed, but they are paid to do their job, and their job is what they will do. Now go out there and get to the church, Richie."

Richie walks past his father. His grandma sees him out of the door. His father comes to the closing door.

Before it shuts, he says, "Don't be despondent, Richie. But I don't think your mother will make it. She's gone to the temple to pray."

Richie, halfway down the front garden dressed in a blue wedding day suit jacket and white trousers turns back to talk. "I am not despondent, Pita jee. I knew she wouldn't turn up!" He got into the taxi to leave for his wedding day.

From a distance, we see Richie's car pull up in front of the church. He gets out of the vehicle, brushes himself down while looking down at his jacket, and then, picking his head up, walks towards the church. We are already situated further away from the paved walkway into the church, so now we come to sit on the borders of its land, walking in time with Richie as he walks into the church's open front door.

We are now situated directly outside the church. Richie, having just walked back outside, is standing by the doors. He is looking at his mobile phone, searching for messages left upon it. He is hoping for good luck messages. He is at odds with himself; the high-intensity feelings that everything will go all right, or that Sherry will not turn up at all.

"Sherry, the cars are here!" Sherry's mother calls from the open front door.

"Come on, honey. We've been waiting for this for a long time." Sherry's father calls from outside.

He walks back into his home.

Sherry, dressed in her wedding dress, the colour yellow still upon her, walks out of the house. The head bridesmaid stands at the doorway; though she is holding her flowers, she cannot outshine Sherry's.

"My word, you are a sight for all to see," Sherry's father says proudly.

"Yes, but not Richie yet. Now come on, let us get you into the car." Sherry's mother hustles her out to the car.

Kuvan's pati is looking out window of their living room.

Kuvan is shouting up the stairs to her son-in-law.

"Daivey."

Daivey is swathed with towels, in the bathroom, and rubbing his hair with another.

"Oh, no, it's not here already."

"What, Daivey, you sounded like you were on a loudspeaker system and not a very good one."

"What!" Daivey now, removing the towel from his head, repeats. He looks towards where the voice of his mother-in-law is coming from. Looking down, past the towel in his hands, with care not to get too annoyed, he shouts, "It's not here already!"

Kuvan says, "Oh. N-"

Just as Kuvan is about to say no, her husband enters the conversation. He speaks to her from the hallway. "It's here, Kuvan!"

"Err. Sorry, Daivey, yes, it is here."

Daivey shouts, "Look," and opens the bathroom door. "This isn't working. We've got too much to sort out. If he comes to the door, I'll deal with him. If not? I'll deal with him anyway."

Kuvan looks at her husband.

At the church, Richie is standing outside; we see him from afar.

Up close, Richie is warm, even in the autumn weather that has arrived in the last few days. He does feel, though, that he should be cold and keeps rubbing his hands together. As the churchgoers arrive, Richie physically has to restrain his hands by his sides to stop himself looking foolish. He is shaking whoever's hand is offered.

Sherry says, "Dad. Is mum still in tow? We don't want to lose them and turn up at different times."

Sherry's mother looks petrified. She is sitting in the car at the rear of Sherry's procession.

Sherry's dad looks behind, turns frontwards and tells Sherry, "Yes, honey. She's still there. You'd never get rid of her at this stage of your journey."

Kuvan is standing in the living room of the house. She is holding her husband's hands while trying to look past him.

Outside, Richie's father has left the car taking his family to the church, and the car drives away. He makes his way back to the house.

From behind Kuvan's husband we can hear her son-in-law speak to her.

"It is no good, Kuvan. We cannot go without Aarzoo." Daivey is standing and cursing himself. "No one would forgive us, and Aarzoo would be ostracised."

Daivey can be seen and then heard to shut the front door. He is warm in his dressing gown.

It seems to have taken an age to get to this place, thinks the person sitting in the back of the limousine. It is taking the last turn before entering Blackberry Way.

Having returned to the living room, to Kuvan and her Pati, Daivey speaks. "That's it. I've sent the car away. We cannot go without Aarzoo!"

His father-in-law says, "But Daivey! How are we going to pick Aarzoo up without a car?"

Daivey says, "Damn you. Not you, but damn all the same. How stupid have I been."

"How stupid we can all get. Come on. Let us make our way to the temple. Aarzoo is sure to be hiding there. Like she always does."

"Well, let me put my suit on, and we will go!"

The man riding in the back of the Bentley limousine, coming to a standstill, is guided out from its luxurious gold painted frame and into the front garden of Richie's house. When the man finally gets to the Gyndall front door, he knocks with the educated correctness of a man that has knocked on many closed doors in his lifetime.

Richie's dad approaches the door and opens it. Kuvan and her pati following his actions from the living space doorway.

Seen from outside, Richie's father is a little shocked but feels, as his two in-laws walk up behind him, that he has too much on his mind to deal with the man at his door.

Tying his tie around his neck, and with no shoes on, and his shirt not quite tucked in, he speaks after opening the door. "I'm sorry, but we haven't got time. We must get to the temple."

The man at the door speaks, "Ah, I have come a long way to be here."

"Yes, well, that maybe, but your long way, it is not as long as it has taken me to notice that I am just as bad as my wife, Aarzoo. Now. I'm sorry, but-"

"Ah, Aarzoo, so I am at the right abode. You must be Daivey."

"Yes, I am, though sorry, as we really must get going. There is a wedding we must get to."

Kuvan passes Daivey his shoes, and he starts to put them on.

"A wedding? Today? But you must get to it. Who is getting married, may I ask?"

"It's my son's wedding, and my wife has run away from it; it's part of her abnormal temperament. And I just sent our car away. Now, if you please, we must walk as quickly so we can to get to the temple, and then find my wife."

We see the owner of the voice for the first time. We see that it is the Sultan's servant, the chikitsak.

"Well, let me not get in your way, but instead offer you all a lift to this festival of life." The chikitsak leads the way, gesturing with his left arm, and we can see the gold limousine. "Come now. Your means of transport is sorted. I will explain who I am on the way!"

Daivey obeys, in utter silence, with his two in-laws following. Grandpa is carrying Daivey's Jacket.

As they arrived at the limousine, Charu is standing nearby, with her mother to one side and the boy from the temple. He is standing further back.

"We saw the car, Daivey. So I brought Charu to see you," Mrs. Patijna says.

Charu is looking at the ground. Her black hair is falling in line with gravity.

"What have you to do with the situation?" Daivey asks.

"Well, if it's all true, then perhaps we can give it one more go. Like a shot in the dark!" Mrs. Patijna moves towards him.

Charu's boyfriend walks a few paces forward and puts his arms around Charu's shoulders. His hands meet on the other side. Charu takes, what she feels, is one last longing look towards him.

"Nice try, but our family does not need any more tricks! It is my boy's wedding day. He needs our love."

As the chauffeur opens the door, Richie's Grandpa shouts, "Come on, let's get going!" They all enter the car.

On the way to the temple, the limousine is the quietest car Richie's family has ever been in, but there is no time to talk about it. Daivey gathers his thoughts and speaks to the man who knocked on his door. "So, who are you?"

"Well. You must have received a letter from my master. The Sultan Madesh?"

"Well, yes, we did. That is what has created a rift our family. But who are you?"

"Ah, well, I am the virtuous Sultan Madesh's chikitsak. I am sorry to hear what you say. If this is so, what you are telling me, I can come to your aid. We must do everything we can to keep your family together."

"Why, thank you for your concern, but I feel that this letter business was only make-believe. A made-up story, by someone trying to put a curse upon our family."

"No, that is not true. In reality, the curse was upon your relatives, back in India. It is your father-in-law who, seemingly, broke the spell, by moving away from India."

Looking out of the car, we are at the temple.

"Come now. Is this where your wife may be?"

In a rush, the chikitsak opens the door for Richie's father to get out. "Come now, be quick." Richie's father exits the car.

Richie is standing outside the church, close to the porch. He looks at his watch and then looks out at the rest of the world. Richie is hoping that there is something written, maybe, in his future, maybe outside his reach, to pull his family affairs back together. He turns and walks back into the church.

Richie's father is running back from inside the temple.

Through the open window of the limousine Aarzoo's father can be heard shouting 'where is Aarzoo' in Hindu. His son-in-law shouts back that she has not been there this morning. The door of the limousine opens, and Daivey gets inside without even stopping. Chikitsak says, "Wife or no wife, we cannot miss the wedding of another. To the church!" In great haste the limousine pulls away from the curb.

Sherry's wedding car has pulled into the street where the church is situated. As it nears the church, Sherry looks out from the right-hand side rear window.

"You know you're soon to be the father of the bride, but some things cannot be counted on."

"What do you mean, darling?"

The wedding car pulls up to the curb.

"You're not pulling out before you even get married?" Sherry shakes her head, and leaves the wedding car alone. The bridesmaids, nonplussed, sit in the car behind.

"No, but there is something urgent that I must do." Sherry breaks into a trot. She is carrying her train bunched in front of her.

She is half walking, half running, towards the church's fence.

Now slowing as she moves closer to the furthest corner of the fence, and a turn in the path, Sherry calls out, "Aarzoo. I know you're there."

No one can be seen from the corner of the church property. Then from somewhere down the other end of the fence, we see movement. Someone is looking in Sherry's direction. As Sherry moves around the corner, she shouts again. "Come on, Aarzoo, don't be silly." Aarzoo comes out from behind one of the vehicles parked further down the street.

"Oh, Aarzoo, I'm glad you could make it."

As Aarzoo approaches, she is ready to make things right again.

"Oh, Sherry, you look so magnificent, yet I fear I have spoilt your day. It looks like the rest of our family are not going to be with us. It is all my fault."

They share a hug. Sherry's father arrives.

Inside the church, Richie is standing at the altar, having walked past all of the guests who are dotted around the inside of the church. The organ is playing, but there are a few off beats as the organist is not the best in the world. Richie looks towards the organ player and asks him to play a better tune. The inside of the church is simply decorated with flowers. There is a choir to help the congregation sing.

Outside the church Sherry's family and bridesmaids are gathering. Sherry's mother has organised the bridesmaids, and, after looking lovingly at her husband, walks into the church.

As she enters, all the people talking go silent, and the majority of the people turn. Richie looks at the clergyman. He is about to set eyes on his future wife for the first time today.

Sherry's father looks at his daughter, outside the church. He goes to speak. "You know, you are-" He falls silent when a gold limousine pulls up behind the wedding procession.

Aarzoo looks and can see her family. She is wearing a red dress with a coat over the top. Her relatives get out of the limousine.

Aarzoo cries out for sympathy, "Cripes! Hide me; it's Daivey. He mustn't see me like this. Yes, I have dressed for the occasion, but still I only wanted to hide and pay my respects." She pulls the coat around her to cover her actual wedding day dress some more. Sherry and her father move to obscure Aarzoo.

Sherry's father calls out, "Aarzoo, take Sherry to the door!"

As she links hands with Sherry, Aarzoo presses a thumb of turmeric onto her forehead to make a Tilak, then her father says, "What's going on, Daivey?"

188

Daivey attempts an explanation.

"There is far too much to talk about. All I'm glad of is that we are all here."

Daivey sees Aarzoo and Sherry at the front of the church.

"She's even wearing her wedding day dress. Oh my gosh! What a day I'm having."

Sherry's father Says, "Come on, Daivey. All of you get inside quickly. It is starting to get cold out here."

Daivey speaks to the chikitsak, "Come now, it is time to honour our children's love for one another. You must come inside."

"That is what I am here to administer." The chikitsak leads Kuvan and her pati into the church.

Sherry's father meets up with Aarzoo and his daughter. Taking Aarzoo's coat, he hangs it on a hook in the entrance.

Sherry's father says, "Today you will seal your love for eternity. This will be the best day of your lives. Aarzoo, take one side, and I will take the other, and we will both walk Sherry to the altar."

"Thank you," Aarzoo says, and relaxes into her new role.

Inside the church the organist plays the Wedding March. Richie looks proud as his family file into their seats.

Sherry, Sherry's father, and Aarzoo walk into the church. Sherry is resplendent in her wedding dress. The sunlight through the stained glass windows makes it seem whiter than mere white.

Aarzoo leaves Sherry and her father to continue the walk up the aisle and sits with her family. The priest brings the couple together, and they hold hands.

The choir is smiling.

Richie's wide grin lights up the church as he looks at the congregation.

> Priest: "Dearly beloved, we are gathered here today to unite Richie and Sherry as one.

Lady Rosetta is standing at the door of her sons' house, on the edge of Leicester. She knocks on the door yet again, impatiently. The door immediately opens; her middle son is standing at the door.

"I thought it advisable to wake you three up," Lady Rosetta says. Her other two sons are standing at the door as the youngest brother opens it fully. "I've been looking at the data that Richie Gyndall left on file. All his time was spent trying to make you more money than you realised; he was right when he told you no one would listen, and they were all wrong. I have found out it is his wedding day today, with that lovely girl Sherry. We are going there now to offer him his job back." "We are not that bothered anymore, Mumsy. You have taken control of what was most rightfully yours in the eyes of the law. And we all abide by that decision," the oldest says.

"So you are going to give up on me now? You gave up on your family ancestry and home, and now you are giving up on what was made by you and is mostly yours. If you ever clubbed together – but I know you are all so selfish, you never would. So, rather than getting down in the dumps, you chumsy-wumsies," Lady Rosetta loses her temper. "You will come with me right now and see the side of life you are missing." She walks to the car that is waiting for her, opens the front door and back door, and gets in the driver's seat on the opposite side. "In!" she shouts.

The three partners of the Leicester Allegiance bank walk towards the vehicle and enter.

Back at the church.

> Priest: Richie, do you take Sherry to be your loving bride?"
> Richie: "I do!"
> Priest: "And Sherry, do you take Richie to be your loving husband?"
> Sherry: "I do!"
> Priest: "Then I now pronounce you man and wife. You may kiss the bride."
> Richie and Sherry kiss for the first time as a married couple. As the organist plays, we move to the back of the church along the aisle.

I'm So Excited by The Pointer Sisters: please be respectful and listen. There is much context, and also content hidden within the text.

Verse 1:
Line 1: [Sherry breaks from her kiss] Richie sings. [Choir at all times sings]
Line 2: Richie sings.

Line 3: the congregation sing.
Line 4: all sing together.

Verse 2:
Line 1: all sing. [There is plenty of dancing]
Line 2: all sing.
Line 3: all sing.
Line 4: all sing.
Line 5: all sing.

Chorus:
Line 1: Sherry sings alone.
Line 2: Sherry sings alone.
Line 3: Sherry sings alone.
Line 4: Sherry sings alone.

Verse 3:
Line 1: Sherry and Richie take turns singing.
Line 2: Sherry and Richie take turns singing.
Line 3: Sherry and Richie take turns singing.
Line 4: Sherry and Richie take turns singing.

Chorus:
Line 1: Sherry and mother sing.
Line 2: Sherry and mother sing.
Line 3: Sherry and mother sing.
Line 4: Sherry and mother sing.

Verse 4:
Line 1: Richie's mother and father sing.
Line 2: Richie's mother and father sing.
Line 3: Richie's mother and father sing.
Line 4: Richie's mother and father sing.

Chorus:
Line 1: Sherry sings.
Line 2: Sherry sings.
Line 3: Sherry sings.
Line 4: Sherry sings.

Line 5: Sherry sings.

Chorus:
Line 1: Sherry and mother sing. [Sherry's Father and the Gyndall family harmonise]
Line 2: Sherry and mother sing.
Line 3: Sherry and mother sing.
Line 4: Sherry and mother sing.

Line 1: Sherry's father and the Gyndall family sing. [Sherry and mother harmonise]
Line 2: Sherry's father and the Gyndall family sing.

Richie and Sherry kiss once more. They pool their honesty in a clasp of emotions and move to the doors of the church, and hold each other in their arms, as the choir and the wedding guests bring the song to an end.

Act Six: Is This Really The End?

Inside Lady Rosetta's car there is no talking as the vehicle pulls up behind the gold coloured limousine outside the church, then, "What the hell," the oldest partner says.
Getting out of the car all four walk towards the church; Lady Rosetta takes the lead, but isn't surprised that her three sons stop to inspect the limousine.
Outside, on the church parade, everyone is talking and congratulating the married couple. The family members stand around them. The Sultan's loyal Chikitsak moves in to speak.
"Richie Gyndall, it is my pleasure." The Chikitsak grabs Richie by the hand. "And you, my dear," he says to Sherry.
"Sherry."
"Ah, Sherry Gyndall. It is now my pleasure also. I am here,"
"Who is this?" asks Aarzoo as the Chikitsak looks on.
"It is your family's servant from India. Would you believe it?"
Daivey grabs Aarzoo to give her a face to face hug and whispers in her ear. Aarzoo pulls away, and Daivey Gyndall can see the smile that first adorned his wife's features on the day of their marriage.

"Aha. I am here to take you on a long and fruitful honeymoon, but I fear we must leave as soon as possible as my master has left us, and soon his loving wife, Jasmine, may be taken from this world, and I need to be by her side."

"Then, we must go!" Richie replies.

"Yes. At once," Sherry adds.

Lady Rosetta approaches the couple. "Firstly, I am sorry to interrupt, and congratulations. But there is business afoot. You, Richie Gyndall, are a miracle; all your interpretations of the stock market were on the nose, my boy. I am sorry to lose you. Perhaps you can stay, as a part of the bank. I hope you appreciate what I am offering to you." Her sons arrive behind her.

"But, Mumsy," the oldest.

"Yes, where, does…" the middle.

"That leave us?" the youngest son.

"Where you should be; picking up the pieces of your family's fortunes." Lady Rosetta clears up her sons rebukes.

"Give me time, I'm just finding out what the partners tried not to tell me, about our family ancestry. If Sherry and I can invest in something manageable, then we can fulfil what you are asking of us. I will, if we have the right legal advice, get people onto it straight away." Richie smiles.

"I feel a partnership coming on," Lady Rosetta says; her sons all cringe.

"Come then, even as we speak about enlarging my master's fortunes, time is running out for Jasmine. There is no time to waste." The Chikitsak bows, and the three of them move quickly toward the waiting limousine.

"What do we do now?" Aarzoo asks.

Rahil Joshi is the first to reply. "Why, buy some tickets from me to travel after them."

"But we do not have enough money to do such a thing while looking after what little we own," Aarzoo cries.

Kuvan is the first to step into the kindred conversation, "Now, don't be silly, Ladakee, Richie now has more than is required to look after everyone. That will be great, Rahil, thank you all for making this the greatest ending to our family's day ever."

The door of the limousine is held open by the Chikitsak's chauffeur. They all proceed to climb in.

The Chikitsak puts down the window to the rear, for Richie and Sherry to look out through. As they pull away from the church, all the people are waving, the six married family members of the Gyndall, Malli, and Traverso families are all holding hands. Richie's grandma is also waving from the end of the line.

The Chikitsak whispers some orders through the interior window of the limousine. The driver speeds towards the next clothes shop he can find on the map.

"Here's my credit card." The Chikitsak orders Richie to take his card. "Run in, and buy some suitable clothing to relax in during our journey." The newly married couple runs out of the limousine, still with their wedding clothes on.

After buying clothes for the journey, Richie is the last to leave the shop. He holds the boxes of the wedding clothes.

Richie and Sherry run out of the shop. They are dressed in sensible clothing that will suffice for the trip ahead.

The limousine pulls away as the door shuts.

The rest of the journey was quickly over and seems to take less time than the trip in and out of the shop for new clothes. The newly dressed couple, and the Chikitsak, arrive in a hangar at a nearby airport. The Chikitsak puts his arm on Richie's shoulder.

"This is all yours now, Richie." He shows him the jet.

From the corner of the hangar, we see Sherry, Richie, and the Chikitsak walk away from the limousine and onwards towards the twin jetted business plane. It is gold, just like the limousine, and carries the emblem of Richie's family empire in India.

All three get onto the plane.

The plane takes off.

Inside the plane, all is calm.

"So, Richie! What do you know about your family empire?" the chikitsak asks.

Richie and Sherry are served drinks by a manservant who is preparing dinner at the back of the plane. Richie replies to the Chikitsak. "Not much at all. In fact, nothing. My grandpa explained some of it as we left the church. I had no idea that this all existed. Why am I so important?"

Chikitsak, "Well, Richie. A curse was made upon your family, a long time ago, by Alexander the Great. He was shot by one of your family, in a battle a long time ago. All those who have taken the

194

responsibilities of your family have now been taken. Your grandpa somehow, it seems, broke the curse by moving to England a long time ago. So you seem to be the last in line of the existing members of the Sultan's family. My employers."

"My word. This is unbelievable!" Richie looks at the table in front of him. "What may that be, chikitsak? It has my name upon it; not another invitation?"

"This is the letter my master Madesh left you. Read it at your leisure."

The chikitsak is smiling a broad smile, and the smile completes the picture Richie was waiting for; the chikitsak raises his glass of champagne towards the married couple. Sherry leans in on Richie, as he too takes a sip of his champagne. Sherry relaxes back into her chair, and takes her glass from the table. Richie looks at her. Sherry looks at him again. They raise their glasses in response.

Jungle, and more magnificent jungle, can be seen from the plane; the canopies, Richie feels, are the many pathways to the undergrowth that he cannot see. He turns to the chikitsak. "Where are we now?" He looks puzzled. He glances back out of the window, then towards Sherry, and says, "Pardon my rudeness. I haven't even asked you what your name is."

"It is Ojas, sir, and you are now flying over your domain."

"Ojas, this is unbelievable. I suppose we must get to your palace as soon as we can, but that must be many miles away from any airport around here."

"That is where you are wrong, Richie. There is a strip of land near here. For us to all land safely on, under the safety of the trees of your new lands."

 Somewhere deep within the jungle in India we see the shape of an airfield. A Range Rover is waiting for them. The inhabitants watch the gold jet circle, and then come in to land.

As Richie and Sherry move down the aisle, the jet finally comes to a standstill. The chikitsak leans outside of the plane and says, "Ah, our homeland." He waits for Richie and Sherry to leave first.

Richie, Sherry, and then the Chikitsak walk down the jet plane stairs. Sitting in the Range Rover, we hear the Chikitsak shouting towards the men inside, he is the last to leave the steps. "How is Jasmine?"

"Not good, Ojas. We must get there quickly," says a voice from the open door of the waiting vehicle.

The Range Rover speeds along a dirt track through the jungle. Inside, all are shaken from the bouncing of the vehicle on the uneven track.

The Range Rover pulls into the courtyard of Richie's family's palace, in front of the fountain. Servants are standing on the front doorsteps, which leads to the palace. Peacocks scatter as the Chikitsak jumps from the Range Rover. He runs into the palace. His embroidered black, red, and yellow short-armed jacket flows in the rhythm of his footsteps, as all the others get out from the vehicle. Jasmine is lying under a throw on the Sultan's bed. A cup of tea is on the table by her side.

The door opens, and the Chikitsak walks in. Jasmine opens her eyes, looks towards the Chikitsak, and stretches her arm towards him. Suddenly outside, about the silence of the palace courtyard, murmuring can be heard. Everyone turns to see where the murmuring is coming from. A shaman walks in through the palace gates. He is smoking his pipe. He dances forwards to stand in front of the fountain, takes a draw on his pipe, and then puffs out a stream of smoke. There is more murmuring. He draws again, then exhales another puff. The two strings of smoke join together in a spiral in front of him. He gets to his knees, and draws again. The last puff of smoke is drawn out in a long outburst of energy by the shaman with the painted face. The wind picks up, grasping the three tendrils of smoke, descending it as it turns to the floor, turning into an eddy, which starts to form on the sandy ground by the foot of the fountain. Gravel is disturbed around its base; as the wind picks up, it slowly blows worse and worse. People standing in the courtyard put their hands to their faces and stand back. There is now a twister starting to climb. Interweaved with two, now three primary sandy eddies, altering at the differing altitudes of its bends, vortexes all around it. It circles the fountain.

Inside the Sultan's bedchamber, the chikitsak is kneeling at the side of the bed. His hands make a prayer in front of his face.

Jasmine still has her arm outstretched towards him. The hollow voice of the Sultan can be heard saying the name 'Jasmine', again, and again. Her children can be heard laughing too as the breeze picks up inside the bedchamber itself.

Jasmine speaks and holds her hands outwards towards the window. "Madesh," she says. "Madesh, is that you!"

The Chikitsak moves towards the window, to close the shutters. Chikitsak has his hand upon the screen itself. Hearing Jasmine gasp, he turns and looks back to her. With his hands held out in support, he tries one last obsecration. He feels haunted by his loving master, and his two loving boy children.

"Jasmine, please stay. One more moment and this may all be a dream."

Jasmine looks at Ojas. She still has her arms outstretched towards the window. "Ojas, it was not your fault. It was not your fault." Her hands transmute into multi-coloured sand. This transmutation leaves only her long sleeves showing. The sand is blowing all around the room.

Nothing can be done as Jasmine's face, from the tip of the nose, starts to disintegrate and disappear into dust. The parts are pulled away towards the window, in the direction of the Sultan's voice calling Jasmine's name. Through the midst of the breeze, and the deafening noise of the vortex. The rest of the dust, the remains of Jasmine, ever-increasingly turning into dust, is pulled continuously, out through the window, and then out into the tornado that has formed.

As the dust-storm slowly dwindles, the bedsheets, and Jasmine's clothes, drop onto the bed. The Chikitsak is on his knees. He looks like he is screaming. The last of the dust circles him.

Jasmine's hands reform for a brief moment around the Chikitsak's face. Then they relinquish their grip.

Suddenly, the last of the dusty sand, pulled through the window, enters into the tottering vortex.

The Chikitsak runs out of the bedchamber.

In the courtyard, the tornado twists outside of window of the palace. It is bending and contorting under its pressure. The Chikitsak enters the yard through the entrance to the palace, as the tornado totters on its base. The Sultan is hugging Jasmine within it as their children embrace them both. Then the dust storm is dragged into the sky and is gone. A few surrounding clouds are partially pulled up with it as it leaves.

The shaman is gone. All that is left is his pipe, rocking gently on the side of the fountain. Richie walks forwards and picks it up. He is not quite sure, but thinks that, as he did so, he heard laughter coming from within the pipe itself. He holds it to his ear, but nothing can now be heard.

Days have passed since Richie arrived in India; it is now the rest of his family's turn to fly. The Gyndall family, the Malli family, and the family Traverso, are in the airport departure terminal.

Sherry's father is at the drinks dispenser; he puts the money into the machine and presses the button. The machine does its dutiful work and dispenses a can from its heart directly into the holder below. He takes it out and walks towards his wife and his in-laws. They are sitting on a row of chairs; someone has taken his seat. He stands in front of them with his back to the departure gate.

Sherry's mother says, "Why have you gone to all the trouble of getting a drink now? It won't be long and we will be on the plane."

"I'm not paying those prices on the plane; besides, we will have to be in full flight before the stewardesses come along with the refreshments. I remember the last time."

Aarzoo perks up, "I hate flying, even though I have never been on a plane!"

"Ladakee, don't worry. This is the first flight your father and I have been on since coming into the country." Kuvan tries to settle her daughter's first time nerves. "If it will help, it might be good to get whatever is on your chest out in the open, if you can do that here?"

"Okay! I know your secret, maji," she says.

"What secret? I do not keep secrets."

"So, I prayed to invoke Ganesh before the wedding, and saw that father and you were not married when stepping from off the plane on your arrival in England." Aarzoo recollects the invocation ritual she performed before the wedding day events.

Daivey is at work at the crisp factory, and Aarzoo's parents are in bed, fast asleep. Aarzoo is crying and looks at all the pictures of the deity around her bedroom. All she can hear is her father snoring. Getting out of bed, she walks to her bedroom door, down the stairs, and into her living room. She listens to see if she can still hear her father snoring, and she sure can. In front of the curtains at the far end of the room is a small wooden table with a statue of Ganesh. Aarzoo gets to her knees, squeezing in between the TV and her father's chair. She starts to pray.

"Please give my son the best future for his coming together with Sherry, Ganesha; you are our wisdom. Which brings me to ask why, oh why, did the letter come from our ancestors? Without cause I trusted your wisdom and my faith, but nothing but heartache came from this. Unless you have something up your sleeve. So, if you can tell me, Ganesha, what other wisdom should I receive? It is breaking my heart that Richie cannot fulfil his full potential; perhaps there is something else I should know. My family's ancestry roams from afar, does it not, yet I wait for your sign."

At the very moment Aarzoo finishes her invocation, her father snores loudly and the picture of her mother and father getting off of the plane when they first arrived in England turns lopsided on the wall. Aarzoo jumps, gasps, and looks at the disturbed picture. Getting up, she walks over and takes the photo frame from off of the wall. Turning it, she grabs the cord that holds it up lengthways. She can see a note on the back of the photo; it is peeling at the edges. Turning, she moves to the light switch, shuts the door momentarily, and only then turns the light on. There on the back of the photo is some typed writing:

Gaurav Malli and Kuvan Acharya, Heathrow, 1961

"Oh, Lord Ganesha, why do you break my heart so!" Aarzoo comes out of her dream.

"No wonder you always placed that photo on the wall yourself," Aarzoo says.

"There are no secrets between us, or Lord Ganesha, Aarzoo. Perhaps he was simply telling you something was on its way. Like a new letter from the Sultan. You didn't have to go and look at what was on the back of it, unless you wanted to upset yourself some more. That photo is the closest thing I have to reminding me of the old days. What do you expect, Ladakee? Our love, your father's and mine, is different to yours. Our love stretches from our homelands all the way to England, and when we finally arrive back there, all the way back."

"My love too, I thought, so it carried with yours, maan. But not now; how can I feel love for a place that does not receive my full family name and honour? What makes you think that I could find out about you two not being married when you first came together and still feel the same?" Aarzoo felt sad.

"Aarzoo, we were not married before we left America; we married in England too, didn't we, hubby?" Sherry's mother said. "You should still be proud that your parents made it this far. It's so romantic to think we too travelled so far to marry in a place we were to settle in."

"Oh, yes, and that means we had Sherry out of wedlock." Sherry's father blushed.

Aarzoo grumbled, "Well, I find this whole scenario very strange."

"Yes, that may be, but you didn't want your son to marry our daughter, though you knew it was the right thing to do in the end," Sherry's mother replied.

Daivey called for calm. "Listen, Aarzoo, we all travel far in our relationships, be it with love in our hearts, or expectation. You tell me what you feel at this moment in time?"

"Expectation."

Kuvan replied, "Well, I can tell you, both your father and I have love in our hearts, all because you and Daivey are travelling with us so we can arrive home for the first time together as a married couple. Just remember your siblings are there already as a married couple, what more could you ask for?"

Daivey says, "You're just nervous, Aarzoo."

Over the Tannoy the flight the two families are to catch is called to depart. People start to get up and move to the departure gate and to queue to get on their flight.

"I know; let us all just get on the plane, even though the cause of all my worries may now be over. I just need to confess to my parents exactly what was the problem with me letting Richie marry someone who is not Hindu. Maan, I thought my parents were always supposed to be together." Aarzoo owned up to her confusion.

"Aarzoo, you do have a lot to learn, and you are not harbouring expectation, you are experiencing nerves before getting on the plane," her mother replied.

Getting up, Daivey says, "Come on, perhaps we should be getting in the queue?"

"You sit right here until I have finished, my girl." Aarzoo had tried to get up with her husband, but her mother pulls her back down to a sitting position. "You have never been outside of your own country, and, I know, you thought our family's history stretched all the way to your father's and my own homeland, but India is more special to us as we were rather than the people we are now; that is why England will always be our home. Don't you see?"

Gaurav gets up to stand in the queue. "Don't be nervous, Aarzoo. Everything will be fine."

"Yes, Aarzoo, we all have Richie, our son," Daivey says.

"Yes, our son-in-law," Sherry's father shouts from the queue. Daivey adds, "And Sherry's love of married life is carrying us over the seas and foreign lands, and will see us to the land of our Gods, and the lands Richie and Sherry now own."

"Now I see what Lord Ganesha was telling me," Aarzoo answered.

"Yes, I think we all do, so can I add, let's all get on the plane," Sherry's mother says. "All this moaning about us being beaten by our future means nothing if we don't get on the bloody plane."

"Yes, come on," Gaurav agreed. "You lot get in the queue, or we will miss all the fun."

The gate starts to let people on the plane. It their passage to the lands of their siblings in India. The journey takes on a feel-good vibe, with everyone having fun. They take in the images of putting their carry-on bags in the overhead compartment. Sitting in their seats, some with neck pillows. Looking out through the plane windows and looking over the wing while raising a glass. They all, in turn, have a visit inside the cockpit with the flight crew, care of Mr. Joshi, and when night falls there are more images of each of them falling asleep, and getting nervous again as they come in to land.

It is early morning and it is still dark outside. Then there are more moments of them reaching for their baggage and walking down the aisles to get on the transport to get to the terminal of the Gandhi International Airport in Delhi.

Sherry has travelled a long way to get to the airport. She climbs out of the first Range Rover in the convoy of two vehicles. She is impeccably dressed in modern Indian clothes; she makes a phone call while standing on the curb. The climate is humid, even though the sky is filled with darkness.

When they get through the departure lounge, a man is waiting for the families. He walks towards them, talking on the phone. He says goodbye to the person on the other end of the line and introduces himself to the two families. The flight crew and all the stewardesses are behind the families and join in the conversation.

"Hello, welcome to the Gandhi International Airport. I am the curator of this place. Your friend Rahil Joshi has some very influential friends, and it will be my pleasure to walk you all through my special place of work."

The flight crew applaud the two families, and they all walk onwards to get to another part of the airport.

"I am to show you all the importance of coming through our beautiful building. Come with me, follow and I will show you how magnificent our building is."

The Gyndall, Malli, and Traverso families follow the curator, followed by the flight crew, until they reach the marvellous strengths of the airport's sculptures.

Modern Girl by Meatloaf: please be respectful and listen. There is much context and also content hidden within the text.

Line 1: Sherry's father sings. [Richie and Sherry's family follow the flight crew and airport Curator
around the sights of the Gandhi Airport]
Line 2: Sherry's mother sings
Line 3: both Sherry's Father and Mother sing.

Chorus:
Line 1: all harmonise with Sherry's Father
Line 2: all harmonise with Sherry's Father
Line 3: all harmonise with Sherry's Father

Line 4: both Sherry's Father and Mother sing
Line 5: Sherry's father sings.
Line 6: Richie's Father sings.
Line 7: Richie's Mother sings.
Line 8: Richie's Grandpa and Grandma sing.

Line 9: all harmonise.
Line 10: all harmonise.
Line 11: all harmonise.
Line 12: Richie's mother and Father sing.

Line 13: Sherry's Father and Mother sing.

Line 14: Richie's Father, and Sherry's Father sing.
Line 15: Richie's Grandad sings.
Line 16: Richie's Grandma and Mother, and also Sherry's Mother sing.

Line 17: the flight crew sing
Line 18: the flight crew sing
Line 19: the flight crew sing

Line 20: the curator sings.
Line 21: the curator sings.
Line 22: the curator sings.

Chorus:
Line 1: all harmonise. [Sherry is waiting outside the airport; the group, including Sherry's family, and in-laws, walk towards the exit to meet her]
Line 2: all harmonise.
Line 3: all harmonise.
Line 4: all harmonise.
Line 5: all harmonise.

Line 23: all harmonise. [Cases are brought to the two families, and they leave the airport to meet and greet Sherry]
Line 24: all harmonise.
Line 25: all harmonise.
Line 26: all harmonise.

Chorus sings out till the end of the song.

The new arrivals take in the morning air of Delhi. Sherry runs forwards for a group hug. The whole group congratulate her for coming to pick them up.
"It's okay, it was the least I could do; maybe we need to get going, or maybe you are hungry?" She turns and speaks to the driver of the first vehicle through the side door window. "Maybe we can get something to eat?"

"Yes madam," the driver says.

"Oh. You have a driver. It seems a bit strange that you need to rely on someone to pick us up; couldn't you have arranged a cab? At least they would be earning their own money." Sherry's mother is curious.

"He gets paid too, mother, like all of our employees."

"I see, you have others?" Sherry's mother seems interested, but is also masking her disappointment.

"Ha ha, yes, we have one for every job in the palace. It really is beyond my imagination," Sherry tells her. "Come on, let's all get in the vehicles and go and get something to eat."

Sherry's mother gives her a cuddle around the waist as they move to the vehicles, "It sounds lovely, but you're obviously overstating things, honey; come, let's get going." Sherry's mother is keeping a close eye on her daughter. Even though she made her feel she was relaxed with the whole idea, she is slightly worried just what her daughter's ethics are about servants.

The vehicles pull up to one side of a road in the heart of Delhi. The driver radios the other vehicle via a walkie-talkie. Sherry explains to the occupants of vehicle she is sitting in, her mother and father.

"Aksata, here, will go and get some food for you two now, if that is okay? What do you fancy? I tell you what; I will tell him that you want to be surprised." Sherry's mother frowns. Sherry turns to her driver and says, "Ha ha, did you hear that, can you get them something from the food stalls, Aksata? Thank you."

Aksata leaves the vehicle, meets up with the other driver and walks off into the distance. There is a wave from the back of the vehicle in front. It is Kuvan.

Sherry is joyous once more.

"Oh, mother, it is so nice to see you again."

"I am worried about you, girl, you are not sympathising enough with your servants," Sherry's mother says.

"Aw, mother, I am just trying to relax with you all and then you bring up my attitude."

"It is your attitude with your servants that makes you the person that you are, Sherry. I am watching you closely, my girl."

"It's okay to relax, darling, isn't it? Come on, honey, let Sherry alone." Sherry's father tries to ease the mood.

"By not sympathising with your servants you fall into the train of thought that you yourself are creating some kind of slavery. Especially with the prospects of all this new wealth, Sherry. Listen to me when I say, you are becoming a slave of the creators of the world of slavery and the word 'slave', and accidental or not, becoming one with the world of slavery."

"Mum, I was relaxing."

"You're not listening to me, Sherry, this is important. You know what I've told you and taught you all your life long. You were never like this before."

"Yes, I know; the fact is that the word 'slave' comes from the deprivation of the Slavonic people, and also the Latin word 'scalva', which means Slavonic captive. So it says the English dictionary, mum."

"Don't mum me, Sherry." Sherry's father grabs his darling wife by the thigh in the back of the vehicle. "Like I have always said, whoever thought they could derive a word like slave from esclave really put a downer on your English language."

"Yes, mother. So just remember that America does not even have an official language."

"That is what I am talking about, Sherry, exactly. It is very easy to overwrite what happens. Just be very careful. What I propose is that you and Richie look at what else you can do for your new employees. Like helping them with healthcare insurance. If there is none, provide your own. Look into how far they have to come to travel to your palace. If it is a great distance put in place some kind of transport. Also, you can look into what services their family homes have, or don't have. Even though Madesh and Jasmine were good people, they were under so much stress at the end of their days, things might have been overlooked."

"Yes, Mum, like pensions."

"Yes, and Sherry," Sherry turns towards her mother. "Don't relax, it's unbecoming of a princess, girl."

"Ha ha ha, yes, mother."

"Okay, at least that is over with, until I think it's time to bring it up again."

Sherry's father pats Sherry's mother on the thigh.

"Where's our food. Ha, does this mean we're having an Indian takeaway in India?"

"Yes, mother. Aksata won't be long. I'm just going to see Aarzoo, and Daivey." Sherry leaves the Range Rover.

"Okay, Honey."

Sherry leaves the Range Rover and approaches the other vehicle. It is parked in front of the one she rides in.

Back at the palace the chikitsak is speaking with Richie.

"Master, the men have fitted the new satellite dish you required for use of your telephone."

"Oh, great, Ojas. We'll have some fun; I will use it immediately."

Richie walks out into his gardens pressing dial on his phone.

In Lady Rosetta's manor house there are many men busy renovating the property. Lady Rosetta is with her architect. Her phone starts to ring. She leaves her architect to answer the phone. Answering the phone she realises it is her sons' ex-employee. "Hello."

"Hello, is that Lady Rosetta's property?"

"Oh, Richie, Richie Gyndall, you are lucky, we're working round the clock to get this place back up to scratch. It's a little after twelve here. You received the text I asked Malcolm to send you with my number."

"Yes, Lady Rosetta. How are things your end?"

"Fine Richie, just fine; to what do I owe the pleasure?"

"Well, ma'am, I would like to use your bank to keep my money safe when my family move back from India. They will need to have funds, and of course I myself will need to have a reliable bank to use when visiting. So I will be sending you a large sum of money over."

"Dispense with being so formal, Richie, ha, it's Lady Rosetta to you, Sultan Gyndall."

"Oh, my, that sounds so official. I like it though, Lady Rosetta."

"Listen, Richie," Lady Rosetta is being hailed by the architect as two other men look at his plans. "Two moments, Chris," she half says, half whispers; then she carries on the conversation with Richie. "I am glad of the equity, Richie, but I do need you to look at what I need to be getting my three sons to invest in, to keep them and things ticking over at the bank."

"Ha ha, okay, Lady Rosetta. Call me when the funds arrive at the branch."

"Okay, you Sultan rogue you, speak to you soon, darling." Lady Rosetta places the phone back on the receiver and walks back to the huddle around her plans for rebuilding her home.

The side windows of the Range Rover that Sherry is approaching are both open, reducing the claustrophobia inside the vehicle. Aarzoo is sitting beside the curb, turns, and is happy to alert the rest of her family that Sherry is here.

"Hello, everyone. Are you all ready for the long journey to our palace home?"

"Oh, Sherry, we are so excited. This is all so unbelievable."

"Aarzoo, Aarzoo." Kuvan is trying to get her daughter's attentions.

"How long will it take us, Sherry?" Aarzoo asks.

"Oh, we will get to the palace by mid-afternoon. It is quite a way; there are many miles between here and the mountain."

"Tell us, how is Richie?" Aarzoo asks.

"Richie! Richie is fine, mother."

"Call me –" Aarzoo is cut short.

"That's what I've been trying to say. We've all been so regimental," says Kuvan, changing the conversation.

"Maji, Sherry, call me Maji." Aarzoo leans into the vehicle to talk to her mother. "Now what are you on about, regimental? Regimental about what?"

"Let her speak, Aarzoo." Daivey apologises to his mother-in-law. He is sitting between his wife and his father-in-law.

"What I am trying to say is that we've all have been caught up so much in the romance of this whole episode and we still do not know what Sherry's mother and father are even called."

"Ha ha, you mean Mr. and Mrs. Traverso, Kuvan. Ha ha ha." Sherry giggles.

"Hmmf." Gaurav lets out a burst of air from his nose.

"No, no, no, you mustn't," Kuvan cries.

"Oh, my, I can't believe how inept we have all been," Aarzoo realises.

"Oh my, well, that really is a disaster. We must look so silly." Daivey is looking from one person of his family to another in the back of the vehicle. "We all need to go to the cleaners and have our brains de-flossed from all the fluff that has stopped them from working. We are such impolite people."

"Daivey, you were one of those people too. So don't come the big kahuna with me, or my family." Aarzoo kicks back at her husband. She turns to Sherry. "We were all so caught up with Richie and your situation, and with things happening so fast. We all must have just forgotten to ask. Sherry, you are so at home with your parents, it seemed impolite."

"Yes, yes, yes," Kuvan replies.

"Hmmf." Gaurav.

Daivey leans towards the open window. "Now that is the good way, that is, if I can just think how we all see it, Sherry. Tell, us, as we are all not so informed, how we can make this up to you and your parents, please. I do not think we can take any more irrational stupidity from our single-minded family antics. All agreed?" All the occupants of the Range Rover agree, either nodding their heads, or signalling with their voices.

"Ha he, Daivey, don't worry. All of you, maji even, I have enjoyed all of your great intentions. Your attention has meant a lot to me ever since Richie and I decided to marry. It is fitting we will be in our new home when all of you, my new family, get together and we can learn something more about ourselves. Just wait until we have dinner tonight. Richie and I have arranged a large meal for us all at the palace. We can discuss everything that has happened and will happen. Then, there is always the new calendar day." Sherry is overgenerous; she is looking forwards to the meal tonight more than she wants the family to know, her pride with her new family is more important to her than tomorrow, or any other day.

"Okay, okay, we will leave things as they are until tonight." Aarzoo spies her driver coming back with the food they have asked for, over Sherry's shoulder. "Right, time to eat."

Sherry turns sharply to see her driver approaching her vehicle. "Too right, Aarzoo, and time to depart. See you all at our new home."

Both the drivers open the doors onto the side walk and issue the food, dividing it between whoever is asking. Sherry takes hers, takes a bite, and then smiles at Aksata, saying "Thank you" to him, and gets into the vehicle at the same time as him.

Inside the Range Rover, Sherry's mother is more pleased with her daughter. "Now that's better, darling. Don't ever let him hold the door for you."

Sherry is enjoying her food, and laughs as the driver of her vehicle pulls away behind the motor in front. "Now that's what I've got Richie for, Mother!"

Everyone is pleased. The convoy of cars drives away from the curb; the streets have gotten busier and some people watch as they move into the distance.

Two black Range Rovers pull into the palace grounds.

Richie is standing at the double doors to the sandy-coloured palace. There are turrets and many windows framed in white. There are also white sculptures set into the stonework on half-moon plinths made of white marble, either side of the entrance, and one higher, above the front doors.

Richie runs to greet his grandma, who is nearest to him. Then he turns and welcomes the rest of his family.

"It must have been a long journey for you all." He is full of happiness, "More for you, honey, as you've travelled both ways," he tells Sherry.

"Hey, don't forget the drivers; they dealt with the tough terrain and the jungle roads."

"Yes, we just put our backsides into action," Richie's mother-in-law says.

"Ha ha, well, let us not stand here too long. The lads will bring your luggage in, and then go for refreshments. You lot will all come inside. I have prepared ice tea for you all; then you can go up to your rooms and enjoy the palace after you all get cleaned up." Richie is enthusiastic. "Then its dinner; we're having Wild Boar from the jungle."

"Wow, that all sounds great, son." Daivey congratulates his son with a large hug.

Sherry's mother is trying to take the cases from Aksata; he relents and she gives her husband the nod to take his case from the back of the vehicle. Mr. Traverso walks around the back of the Range Rover. Aksata is saying "Are you sure, sir?" Mr. Traverso nods his head.

"It's fine, son, Everything's fine. Go get your iced tea." Aksata gives Mrs. Traverso her case, then gets into the driver's seat and drives around the back of the palace. Everyone moves to the nearside of the drive to let him pass by. Richie, Sherry, and the rest of their family enter the palace. The Gyndall and Malli family have their driver leave their baggage inside the doorway, and inside the great hall. The chikitsak, Ojas, greets them.

"Oh, my goodness, Richie. What have you done to deserve all this? I never thought there would be so much lavishness arrayed around and upon my family until the end of our dying days," Aarzoo says.

"I know, maji. It's fantastic,"

"Isn't it just beautiful, Maji?" says Sherry.

Ojas says, "Well, I am sure you all need to rest after your long journey. I will retire and let your family come together as one for the rest of your stay in Richie's lovely palace, and its grounds." Ojas turns and moves away from the arrival party.

"That's a good idea; I don't know about you all, but I need to freshen up." Kuvan says.

"Yes, it would be nice to get changed," says Gaurav.

"Okay, I have arranged the rooms for you all." Richie says, "There's a surprise in your room, grandpa, for you to look at. Perhaps one day you will be able to play with it back in the park, when you get back home."

"No surprises for me, I hope, Richie," Richie's mother-in-law says.

"No, mum, none." Richie turns to his maids; they are all waiting to help his family up to their rooms. "Just let the ladies help you to your rooms; they will show you the way." Sherry's mother pulls her case past Sherry. She gives her a stern, but also appreciative, look. Her husband follows. "And, so, we all will meet when the bell is sounded." Everyone moves up the staircase while Richie turns to Sherry and hugs her.

Inside Sherry's mother and father's room, the maid shuts the door behind her, and tries to take her case. "No, it's okay, honey. I can..." The maid cuts her off.

"Master Richie has asked me to cater for your every need. I am at your beck and call. I wish to pack your clothes away into their correct places. Then you can get changed later."

"It's okay. I can do all that. Go and get yourself something to eat. You look like you need a good meal, girl. Give her a well-deserved tip, Frank, and don't hold back, either. Do you have a family?" Sherry's mother asks.

"My family live in the village, I have two brothers and two sisters, ma'am."

"Give her a couple of those red ones, honey. She has more than herself to look after." Francesco peels off two notes from the stack in his hand, and passes them to the maid.

"Thank you, sir. That is very nice. But I'm afraid to leave you. Master Richie said…"

"I'm not going to take no for an answer, honey. Now go and get something to eat. I will deal with Master Richie." Sherry's mother opens the bedchamber door and beckons the maid to leave. She places her hands together and exits backwards. "By Christ, what have we walked into, Frank?"

"This is unbelievable, this all just so unbelievable."

"Just what Aarzoo said, honey, it's too much. Too much for one couple, surely."

"They'll adapt, Durah. They'll have to; just make sure you keep teaching them the way. Sherry is like a bouncing cotton ball in the breeze. She doesn't believe this is all happening, any more than we do. She won't forget what you've taught her over the years. But she may regret forgetting her principles in these first few days if she is the daughter that I know and love so much."

"She shouldn't be forgetting her principles, Frank. I've taught her better than that."

"I know, honey, but after the first few days she's probably readjusted a little. It's not a hard life, honey, and having all this lavished on her twenty-four seven, it must all become so routine."

"Like I said, I've taught her better than that. We will see what happens later. And, honey,"

Durah Traverso starts to unpack her case. "If I get my way, the servants will have the night off."

In Daivey and Aarzoo's room Daivey is hugging Aarzoo by the bed. In the other room Gaurav is inspecting the large sailing boat that sits on the table, while Kuvan folds and packs her clothes with the aid of her maid.

It is now night time, and all is calm in the grounds of the palace. The people inside are either relaxing to the band playing their music or doing their night-time chores. A peacock runs away as we enter the palace through the opening door. As we enter the grand hallway, the band is playing, while servants move around their workplace. One servant walks up the staircase, walks to the side dressers, and picks up a silver tray laden with drinks the maid stationed there. The

211

servant turns and then knocks on Gaurav and Kuvan's door. Kuvan answers.

"Oh, hello, what is this?"

"It is fresh tea from our gardens on the mountainside, madam."

"Gaurav, would you like a fresh cup of tea, pati?"

Gaurav walks to the door, standing behind her.

"Yes that would be great. Let us take the tea and go downstairs, priy."

They take the cups and saucers from the tray. Kuvan is astonished. She places her cup back onto the tray. She stoops, looking at the tray with great interest. "Wow," she says as she retakes her drink from the tray. She looks at her husband as the servant walks towards the next room. Walking out onto the landing she is smiling from ear to ear. The servant knocks on the next bedroom door. Daivey answers, but Aarzoo walks out of the open door.

"Tea, fresh tea, would you like some?" the servant asks.

"Why," Aarzoo starts to thank the girl, but the conversation is interrupted.

"Aarzoo," Kuvan takes two steps towards her daughter. "Look at the tray, priy."

"I would rather have a cup," Aarzoo is bending and taking a better look at the silver tray. She stands once more. "of tea from this lovely tray." The door opens further down the landing.

"What's all the commotion, guys?" Francesco asks.

Durah pokes her head out the door.

Aarzoo answers, so as not to be rude. "It's this tray. We have the exact same one at home. They are identical to one another."

Kuvan is her normal witty self. "Now that is correct, meree khoobasoorat putree. Your father and I brought ours over when we came to England. This has blown me away."

"I always wondered where that old tray came from, ladakee, hu ha," Gaurav says, taking a sip of tea.

"Well, I am gobsmacked," says Aarzoo, taking a cup and passing it to Daivey. She takes a cup for herself.

"Ha ha, surprises never cease," Durah replies.

Suddenly the dinner gong is struck downstairs. All the couples shut their doors and walk to the top of the stairs. The landing is curved either side of the staircase with banisters running around the leading edge of the landing and running either side of the staircase. The three couples are hailed from bellow. It is Richie.

"By now you have noticed the delightful tray that they use to serve from in this place."

Durah is the first to shout down the stairs. "It is your home, Richie, now don't forget that. Even if it is a palace. He he, I can tell you it's easy to forget that you own such magnificence, coming from another country and moving to England myself. If you just remember that," Sherry arrives at Richie's side. "You will never forget where you came from, Richie."

"Now that is right, baby, you never will forget your heritage. So now, Richie, if that is what goes to your head the most," Sherry's mother is being followed down the stairs as she talks by her husband. Gaurav and Kuvan stand away from the foot of the stairwell, and Aarzoo and Daivey are arriving at the bottom of the stairs. "Then those things that you own will not cloud your judgment or your understanding and knowledge of what once you did not own or have."

"Leaving you with an understanding of where you came from, and not forgoing the knowledge that you started with nothing," Sherry added.

Francesco finished. "Making you more of a man for understanding where you first came from, Richie. And not belittling the person you first was, my man." Sherry's father slaps Richie on the arm, Sherry cuddles both of them.

"You are beginning to understand my family and their values, Richie. I am telling you, you have never met anyone like them in your life."

Richie is thinking about himself and the way his family and people he meets have been to him in the past. "No, maybe not, but everyone must know. I have always listened."

Everyone laughs; a servant walks out from the dining room. "Dinner is about to be served, ladies and gentlemen. Please come and be seated."

All are seated and wine is being carried around the table by a servant holding another silver tray. He offers Richie his drink last, and Richie stands to make a toast.

"It is my pleasure that I can welcome you all to this side, sorry, my side,"

"And mine, Richie," Sherry adds, and everyone smiles.

"Of, ha ha, happiness." Everyone says cheers and takes a sip of wine.

The food enters the room after everyone has taken a sip of wine. The servants, in regimental fashion, move around the table and place their items upon it. The room is lavishly equipped with differing furnishings. Silver arms for the double wall lights come out from the wall and fill the room with blushing light. There are smaller paintings in this room, unlike the rest of the palace which has large canvases on the walls. Around the table the family fills only some of the seats, as it is so large there are empty chairs between each seated person.

Mrs. Traverso gets up from her seat and starts to follow the servants from the room. "Please, excuse me for a second. Hubby, please dish me up some of that delicious food. I won't be long."

"It's down through the great hall and to the right, mother."

"Okay, Richie. But that is not what I want," Sherry's mother shouts as she leaves the room.

Sherry takes a bite of what she has been dished up from one of the maids waiting on them in the room.

Richie asks for gravy; Sherry interrupts him from telling the maid where to put the gravy. "I wouldn't bother eating that just yet," she says. "I know my mother, she has something more on her mind than simply surprising us with something from the airport."

The Gyndall and Malli family have dished up their food and are tucking into it. Daivey turns to Sherry's father. "You not eating. Oh, Aarzoo we don't,"

"Don't what, Daivey?"

"We don't even know… Well, oh my, simply put maji, we haven't even asked," Daivey tries to finish, but is prevented from doing so by Durah walking in from the Great Hall.

"Sorry Daivey, and sorry everyone. Everyone must get up and follow me. Please come with me, come, please." Francesco climbs out of his chair holding both his and his wife's plates in his hand. Sherry leaves her seat holding her plate too. The Gyndall and Malli family are in differing phases of eating. Daivey's meat is dripping from his fork as he tries to dip his head to put the food in his mouth. "Please, come on, come, come." Everyone else climbs out of their seats holding their plates. Sherry's father passes his wife her plate, and a procession of people walk out from the dining room across the great hall and follow Durah to where she is going. Outside a door leading from the great hall toward the kitchen area there is a group of staff. Sherry's mother sends them to the dining room. "Go and eat, all of you, please, there is lots to fill your bellies. Right," she says, "follow me. We will be eating where the servants eat tonight, and they will be taking up residency in the dining room. The two groups of people leave in opposite directions. The kitchen door opens and Francesco walks into the kitchen first. There is a large open fireplace in the massive wall. There are embers, and a boar rests, half carved, on the spit within it. "Oh, good, a table." Sherry's father sits at it. It is large, like the one in the dining room. But rustic. Richie's family all sit at the table. "Now this is what I call living, ladies and gentlemen. Let the eating commence." There is laughter and happiness all around the table.

Inside the dining room, one of the manservants takes Richie's chair, sits at the table and invites all the arriving staff and those that are already there to sit. Other servants start to fill the other seats. He takes a plate from the stack in the middle of the table and starts to dish himself up some food. He is smiling and talking to himself in Hindi.

Back in the kitchen, Richie's new family, and some old, are in a talkative mood. Daivey is trying to remind them and himself what he was talking about when Durah left the dining room table.

"So, what was I saying, come on, ohh, Ganesh give me wisdom." Daivey awakes Richie's memories of before the wedding.

"Oh, grandma, did you invoke Ganesh before the wedding day? Like you said you were going to, as I know you must have?"

Kuvan, "Actually, no, Richie, but it is funny you should say this. As your mother," she looks at Aarzoo, "and I talked about this before we left the airport and England."

Aarzoo pipes up, "Yes, so I knew no one would do such a thing, so I took it upon myself to wake him before your special day."

"Ha, actually, maji, grandma and I thought she would be doing this. But if you wanted to do this final deed, then thank you very much. Then I wouldn't have been so distressed into thinking that you would never turn up."

Aarzoo is embarrassed. "What do you mean? Maan never said she would perform the task, you all seemed to be not following the rules,

215

and I thought that as I opened the letter from the Sultan, then it should be I that preformed the invocation."

"We didn't think you were interested, Aarzoo, but it is funny, when you are awake hearing your husband snore, and you hear your ladekee walk down the stairs to perform her duties, you fill with pride at these times." Kuvan tells the table about the secret she was holding back from her daughter.

"So it wasn't a secret? Oh, so that makes me look lame." Aarzoo frowns.

"Sherry, that reminds me." Richie turns to Sherry, and then turns back to talk to the table. "I have received another letter from the Sultan. I must read that later,"

"That just proves what a good job I did, bachcha," says Aarzoo.

"Ha, that is true, now father, you look like you have given up on your story. Tell us what you have to say."

Daivey is propping his head up on his left palm, while his elbow rests on the table the family are dining at. He straightens up. "So, after all this excitement, we, the Gyndall, and Malli families, have not asked what Sherry's mother and father's names are yet." Kuvan agrees by poking her knife towards her son-in-law.

"Why, Daivey, don't be stupid, Mr. & Mrs. Traverso," Sherry's says, laughing.

Sherry's father adds, "You all know that."

"Yes, but what I think he means, is that they have all been too busy to ask you for your first names, dad," Richie joked.

"Oh, my, this is all so very true," Aarzoo coos.

"Ha ha ha, okay you lot, we were joking too, I'm Durah," Durah says.

"And Francesco."

"Francesco, Durah, you must forgive us. We all have been very rude." Gaurav apologised for his family.

Durah started an all new and different conversation. "I was relating to Sherry, earlier, about how close Richie and her could be to creating some kind of slavery within their hordes of staff, if things got out of hand."

Aarzoo looked puzzled. "Is it because the staff originate from their homelands?"

"Aarzoo, you can be a slave to your own back yard, yes, but a slave can be anyone," Durah says.

"Richie could never be racist or a slave trader, he used to have me cleaning up after him for so long. He doesn't know the meaning of the words, thank you, let alone anything else." The table laughed at Aarzoo's comments.

"It's funny you should bring this topic up though, Aarzoo," Durah says.

"The sultan Madesh and princess Jasmine were in no way being racist, or making me a slave to this empire, when they passed on their fortune to me. Come on, everyone settle down."

"No, Richie, but I did have a bad feeling about the way I thought about that as we are in India, it would be better to use Indian staff, Durah." Aarzoo looks puzzled.

"Yes, but modern times bring modern methods of slavery. Anyone of Richie's employees could be forced to work for slave gangs. It's true, you hear it every day."

"So slavery isn't racism?" Kuvan asked.

"Ha ha. No, Kuvan, it is not, but racism is very similar to slavery in a way," Francesco says. "If you think about it, racism is a form of ownership and power the owner, the abuser, holds against the abused. As such, they try and beat the person with abuse. Turning them into something that works for the abuser, but not the abused."

"Making the abused feel like they should accept being oppressed by the abuser," Durah adds.

"I have felt like that at times, but thought it was just a situation I managed to get myself into. Sherry and I will have to be careful with our staff. Ha ha, as I'm not exactly totally Indian myself, I'm an English Indian, does that mean I'm racist?" Richie asks.

"No, Richie, you could never be racist in my book," Sherry says.

"The facts of the matter, and the realities of this racism thing, are that the arts of family life can be the most racist things of all," Durah explains. "Take Sherry for instance, she must be in a constant state of flux with the ideals that Francesco and I have inculcated in her."

"Love helps mother,"

"And brains never fail us," Francesco adds.

"Ha ha, yes father, you do make things hard for me sometimes, but life is a test, no."

"Right, that's it," Kuvan yawned. "Is that coffee on the stove? Perhaps we can have coffee poured and then head up to bed. I'm pooped."

"True," Richie added. "I need to get back to the bedchamber and finish up what I was doing. Are we all satisfied with the results of our dinner, and the company we had tonight?"

"You were a great host, Richie," Gaurav says.

"Right, well you all know where your beds are for the night, me and Sherry are going to bed." Sherry leant in on Richie and whispered something in his ear, "Oh, by the way, we have some more important news for you all."

"I'm pregnant!" Sherry announces.

Everyone stops what they were doing. Kuvan at the stove, Aarzoo collecting cups for the coffee, all else at the table, everyone together looks at Sherry and then congratulates her and Richie.

Richie gets up and Kuvan pours him a cup of coffee, Sherry says good night as she too leaves the table. All reply kindly, and with kind regards. Richie and Sherry leave the kitchen. Kuvan pours more coffee and hands out the cups. Daivey has something more to add to the conversation now his son has retired with his new wife.

"I totally get racism, but I cannot see how it is the same as slavery. And when I see Sherry, I see nothing of racism. I see a calm human being who loves all those that she meets. There is more to these things than you believe. Slavery can come from the same people and religion of those that enslave, or put people up for slavery. Racism can come from a deep regret that the holder owns over his or her fears of the unknown. We are all animals in a way, and our emotions can just simply get out of hand and rule our bodies. In this world we do our best to get along, but we do not get on with everyone we meet. It is not called racism when two people of the same colour and creed do not like each other."

"So what do you suggest we do to stop this kind of thing happening, Daivey?" Francesco asked.

"We are constantly at odds as a race; we encourage equality, but put down communism. Peace is hard to find, Durah, even more so when we do not find peace inside ourselves, or maybe we have been disrespectful before. I believe we all need to look at the qualities that will bring out the best in ourselves, and if this is wrong then I have lost faith myself."

"Ha ha, you will have to look for your faith time and time again, Daivey, especially in this world. And especially if I understand all the wrongs that happen in this world." Durah spreads her arms and smiles.

"At least we're one family now, Daivey." Gaurav is pleased.

"Yes, but with different surnames, ha ha, I get what you say, Durah, and Francesco knows it."

Francesco says, "It is a hard life, but maybe not for Richie and his family from now on." All smile and relax in the warmth the food and the meal time conversation has brought them.

All the staff around the dining room table are sitting back full, burping, playing with their cutlery, or still dabbing their mouths with serviettes.

Outside the palace the lights in the windows look warm and make the palace walls look red in the night air. The Chikitsak is sitting inside Richie and Sherry's bedchamber listening to the insects through the open window.

A maid stands at the top of the stairs. She has a pot of tea constantly warming on a side table. She passes Sherry a tray with two cups and a pot, at the top of the stairs; she walks towards the bedchamber where Richie is heading. He sits and opens a large reading book on the table, and he looks through it.

A door opens to one of the bedchambers on the landing. The maid stationed there asks, "Would you like refreshments, madam?" It is Durah.

"No, it's okay, hun, I just wanted to catch my daughter."

"The Lady of the house has just retired, madam. Would you like me to fetch her for you?" the maid replies.

Sherry's mother walks out of her room, shuts the door, and approaches her daughter's bedchamber. "No, it's okay, hun, I will see her myself." She knocks on the door.

Richie is still reading the book; Sherry says, "Come in." There comes another knock at the door.

Sherry stops pouring her drink, and answers the door.

"Oh, hello, mum."

"Keep it down, Sherry, I want to talk to you on the quiet."

Sherry is confused and walks out through the doorway, carefully shutting the door behind her. "What's the problem, Mother?"

"It's just, I heard from Aarzoo about the curse attached to her family, and now that it is your family I felt you might need some kind of memento to keep the evil spirits away, honey."

"You're just being silly, mother, the curse is not related to our side of the family in any way. Come on, don't worry yourself." Sherry tries to calm her mother down as a voice behind Sherry announces itself; it is the Chikitsak.

"Is everything alright, Sherry?" he asks.

Sherry leans back into the bedchamber. "Yes, everything is fine, Ojas. It is just my mother."

"Okay, as long as all is well."

"Yes, Ojas, I just need time to put my mother at rest with her imagination." Ojas walks back to be seated.

"Listen mother, we did see things happening when we arrived; the spirits took Jasmine. I know, spirits come in all shapes and sizes. And yes, they seemed to be controlled by a shaman. But he has since disappeared, and all has gone back to normal." Sherry laughs. "Ha ha, nothing more has happened, and Ojas assures us the whole ordeal is over."

"So if this is true you don't want what I have for you?"

"What have you got, mother?" Durah is holding something behind her.

"You know what I got." Durah produces an indigo coloured doll from behind her. "This is to keep you on side with the spirit world in this new world you live in, Sherry. Take it." She passes it to her daughter. "The voodoo religion is very powerful; you know this started in our homeland when we arrived years ago."

"Yes, supposedly the Mississippi Valley,"

"Right."

"Study the concepts of the doll when I'm gone. It may come in handy. Their religion is much like the Hindu religion. Especially the animism parts."

"What are you on about, mother?"

"Animism, the theory that creatures, places, and objects all have a spirit, in essence. Listen, Jasmine was Hindu by birth, but she practised being a Muslim. There is such a thing as religious syncretism, you know; who knows what she has given openings to, she could have opened up many doors without anyone's knowledge, so who knows what has derived from her house." Durah holds the hand of her daughter that is clasping the doll. "All I want you to be is safe, Sherry."

"Are you done worrying now, mother?" Sherry is exhausted with her mother's ideas.

"Yes, now be good, and take the doll."

Sherry opens the door. Richie looks up from his book. "Everything okay, Sherry?"

"Yes, Richie, my mother was just leaving." Durah waves and turns to leave them. Sherry shuts the door. "Goodbye, mother," she says just before shutting the door. She walks to the refreshments and props the doll on the side by the tea tray.

Richie places his book to one side. There are all types of writing equipment on the table, and then Richie spies the letter from Madesh. The Chikitsak is standing behind Richie as Sherry walks to Richie, bringing him a cup of tea. They are all dressed in regal clothing, Richie wearing jewels, Sherry wearing white gold. Richie, having spied the letter, takes it from the table. A golden turban sits on the table beside it encrusted with jewels. He opens the letter with a knife. He takes the letter out and reads it. Sherry puts her hand on his shoulder.

> *Dear Richie,*
>
> *It has been my displeasure to try and make you do things you may not wish to have to do. The invitation to my lands should always have been for you to take up without any form of contract. I married the person that I thought I was meant for, and that is Jasmine. Now I know this is true, I can wish no more than for you to marry the person you are most truly meant for, with no forced convictions from anyone else along the way.*
>
> *By now you know the vastness of my lands; look after them well, Richie, and they will look after you. Though first you must find out the name of these lands. Just ask and someone will show you the way. As with everything that exists, it is meant to be, Richie,*
>
> *Madesh.*

Richie: "It says here in this letter that there is a secret family name for this place."

Chikitsak: "Yes. It is only ever known by the masters of the property."

Sherry: "So what is the name, Ojas?"

Chikitsak: "I cannot tell you. Simply, I do not know. It is secretly written on the pages of that book you are reading, Richie."

Richie: "But I've looked all through it, Ojas, and can see nothing!"

Chikitsak: "Open the book from the end, and the wrong way up, and flick through the pages. While you are doing so I shall leave!"

Ojas rises from his seat, walks to the door of the palace bedchamber, walks through the door and shuts it behind him. Richie closes the book, turns it over on the table, opening it from the rear. Then he flicks through the pages.

Ojas paces across the landing talking to himself; he is holding Jasmine's pin, which held her head scarf in place. "Just what have you started?" He says, and walks onwards towards his room.

Back in the bedchamber Richie flicks though the book one more time. Strangely, the book comes to life and spells 'Xanadu'. It is written in golden letters which seem illuminated to Richie, as if they are magically spelled out with the sparkle of life.

A little while before he read the letter, and the Chikitsak told him how to find the secret name of his kingdom, Richie had noticed a firefly in the air around him. He had followed its meandering flight, distracted from his reading by its apparently purposeful movements. As he looks at the illuminated letters spelling out the name, he realises that the firefly was spelling out the name 'Xanadu' in the air around him, a secret message he can only now understand.

Sherry watches the firefly fly to the open window, towards a family of fireflies hovering at a level with the window itself. Richie looks at Sherry, as the fireflies descend out of sight, and Sherry smiles.

A sparkling residue is left in their wake as the firefly family twists their way away.

"Sorry, Sherry. It's known as Xanadu, Sherry, Wow!"

Sherry smiles again.

"Xanadu," says Sherry. "Why, that is simply hypnotic!"

Xanadu by Olivia Newton-John: please be respectful and listen. There is much context and also content hidden within the text.

Line: Sherry sings. [Sherry sings. Richie, sitting at the desk, harmonises]
Line: Sherry sings. [All Xanadu staff dance in the great hall]
Line: Sherry sings.
Line: Sherry sings.
Line: Sherry sings. [Sherry looks down from the bedroom window and spies a bush with fireflies gathering around it]
Line: Sherry sings. [One firefly peels off from the rest and climbs into the air leaving a trail of sparkling dust behind it]
Line: Sherry sings.
Line: Sherry sings.
Line: Sherry sings.
Line: Sherry sings.
Line: Sherry sings.
Line: Sherry sings.
Line: Sherry sings.
Line: Sherry sings.
Line: Sherry sings.
Line: Sherry sings [The escaped firefly flies into Sherry's hand]
Line: Sherry sings.
Line: Sherry sings.
Line: Sherry sings.
Line: Sherry sings.
Line: Sherry sings.
Line: Sherry sings.
Line: Sherry sings. [Sherry looks into the night sky and spies a twinkling star. The firefly escapes her glowing hand]

Richie, sitting back at the table, pushes the book to one side and places some writing paper in front of him. He notes the lengthy pipe that is sitting at the top of the table. He hadn't fully appreciated what it was when he first looked at it. He realises he placed it there earlier with the letter from the Sultan. He thinks he can hear something, a giggle, coming from within the pipe itself. Richie picks up the pipe and places it to his ear. Then a cool breeze blows through the window, and one of the shutters bangs against the wall a little, creaking as it does so. Placing the pipe back on the table, he now takes up a quill, and starts to write.

Richie's voice is heard as a voiceover narrative as he starts to scratch at the paper with the quill he is holding.

My name is Richie, Richie Gyndall. I used to live in England and am a Hindu of Indian origin. I used to lead a simple life, living in Leicester. I share an end of terrace house – in the middle of Blackberry Way. Why would I become rich, like my name suggests? Or how, even, did I grow to end up with any understanding of this?

As we see Richie and Sherry enjoying the soft lighting within the bedchamber we move out through the window of the palace. Out into the jungle, away from the palace grounds, and we hover over the treetops of the surrounding forest. As we move away, a single star can be plainly seen. It is more striking than any other around. Then, from below, a firefly moves into our view. It is circling the bright star in the night sky with its luminescent golden trail.

So, the truth of the matter, this is something different. Even if we are with someone we are missing something, that being the someone we are not, or the something missing from our existence. It is the something that hasn't been gained, to then be added to that of our knowledge. Ha ha ha, the something to make us knowledgeable.

Back in Blackberry way it is daytime, and all the children are playing on the street.

In the middle of the street we see every member of Richie's household, Sherry's mother and father, the Patijna family, Geoff, Jacky, Lady Rosetta, and the three Partners from the bank; Sherry and Richie, dressed in their resplendent new clothes, and the Chikitsak. Sid and Bob are there too. The band from the palace is in the middle of them all, and all are talking. The band begins to play.

We've Only Just begun by The Carpenters [End title song]: please be respectful and listen.

Verse 1: all sing. [The band plays]

Verse 2: all sing. [The band plays]

Verse 3: all sing. [The band plays]

Sherry and Richie are standing by the open bedroom window of the palace looking into the night sky. A star is seen.
We are rising now towards the star. It becomes larger and larger in front of us. Breaking through the atmosphere, we see the star transformed; it is now a bubble of life for Madesh, Jasmine, and their two children.
It is gathering light from the sun, this bubble situated in the extremities of outer space. The bubble slowly gains a hard crust as it moves towards Earth. The bubble turns into a comet and enters the Earth's atmosphere.
Sherry and Richie are still standing by the window. They watch in silence as a star changes its form and becomes a shooting star. It streaks through the night sky. As we turn, the disintegrating star can be seen in the distance as Richie and Sherry hug and kiss each other. Now as we are moving away, Sherry and Richie look out into the night sky; they hold each other. Smiling, they do not see the two giant and two smaller fireflies that spring from out of the darkness as a sparkle of life below them lights by magic and the shaman's laugh can be heard. The fireflies join the huddle of other fireflies, congregating around the bush in the palace grounds.

It is a fresh new day outside the Leicester Allegiance Bank. Moving through the building everything is running like clockwork. The only thing out of place is in the office, as Jacky is not at her desk. She is in the toilet. The door is locked. She has a pen in her hand, and places the pen to her mouth. Pulling the pen away from her mouth she says, "Jacky is a…" Scribbling at the door we see her write the letters W and O above what Geoff had written all those months ago. It now reads 'Jacky is a woman eater,' Jacky turns her head and roars to let off steam.

Printed in Great Britain
by Amazon

10759663R00129